THE INSATIABLES

BRITTANY TERWILLIGER

Amberjack Publishing
New York | Idaho

Amberjack Publishing
1472 E. Iron Eagle Dr.
Eagle, ID 83616
http://amberjackpublishing.com

Publisher's Cataloging-in-Publication data
Names: Terwilliger, Brittany, 1983- author.
Title: The insatiables / by Brittany Terwilliger.
Description: New York : Amberjack Publishing, 2018.
Identifiers: LCCN 2018005088 (print) | LCCN 2018009749 (ebook) | ISBN 9781944995607 (eBook) | ISBN 9781944995591 (pbk. : alk. paper)
Subjects: LCSH: Businesswomen--Fiction. | Business ethics--Fiction. | Corporate culture--Fiction. | Work environment--Fiction.
Classification: LCC PS3620.E7736 (ebook) | LCC PS3620.E7736 I57 2018 (print) | DDC 813/.6--dc23
LC record available at https://lccn.loc.gov/2018005088

Cover Design: Jaclyn Reyes

For Jason

PART ONE

1

THE DAY I got my big break was just like any other day. The wings of Findlay Global Manufacturing, Inc., spread across the suburban office park like fingers beckoning. From Lot E, where I deposited my beater car every morning in the dark, I could see the glow of Dayton in the distance. I tucked Phil Collins's bowl under my arm and jogged inside, speed-walking past the same desks brimming with #1 Dad paperweights, sticky note pads shaped like lips, a dim gallery of motivational mountains and sunsets and hang gliders. Ours was identical to Findlay's other divisions—a nest of cubicles fenced by an outer ring of executive suites—except we had a push-button cappuccino machine that sat outside the Vice President's office like a monument. His name was Gus Hanley, and he wasn't just Vice President, he was Chief Executive Senior Vice President, Director of Sales, and Acting President of Findlay's Devices Division. A Level 7. He encouraged everyone to use his cappuccino machine, but everyone generally understood that it was, in fact, off limits.

I reached my chair just in time to see Darren across the aisle, folding a gray fleece blanket into a square. He dropped it in a drawer and looked up.

"Hey," I sighed, setting Phil Collins's bowl on the desk. "You beat me again." It was a sort of unspoken contest to see which of us would be the first to arrive and the last to leave the office every day.

Darren's skin glowed the color of cave fish. "Nah," he said, "I never left."

"Where'd you sleep?" His cubicle contained nothing but a desk and a black mesh swivel chair.

"Floor," he said.

"Resourceful."

He smiled at the compliment.

I shrugged out of my coat and signed in to my computer as the fluorescents blinked on. Phil Collins swam out of his little castle and scanned the cubicle with buggy goldfish eyes. I sprinkled a few flakes of food into his bowl.

"Celeste still not back?" Darren said.

"Should be back today." I lowered my voice. "One of her attendees got alcohol poisoning and had to go to the emergency room."

"Who was it?" Darren asked.

I looked over at him. "I'll give you a hint. Nashville Marriott biohazard."

Darren mouthed an ah-ha. "One of these days that guy is going to get himself killed."

The office began to stretch and wake as others arrived. Doors opened and closed. The clatter of keys on desktops heralded the symphony of a hundred Microsoft Windows start-up jingles. Cups were filled with cafeteria coffee, and soon the smell of it—both the coffee and the coffee breath—filled the air above us. I tore into a granola bar—

the crunchy kind that crumbles as soon as you bite into it—
and started updating a flight departures manifest, absentmindedly brushing crumbs into the wastepaper basket next
to my feet.

Celeste walked in and dropped her purse on the floor.
"You're never going to believe what happened," she said,
brushing a long strand of hair from her forehead.

A small smile crossed my mouth. When she was there,
our cubicle was always a more interesting place. Celeste
had been born and raised in Dayton, just like me, but she
had the aura of someone from someplace else. She even
looked a bit exotic, with her tall, voluptuous frame and her
jet-black hair. She capitalized on this innate mystique by
making everything about herself a bit unusual. She wore
men's tuxedo jackets and plaid trousers, vintage shirtdresses
and Chuck Taylors, sequined tank tops and knee socks, and
it all looked exquisite and right somehow. Her soul had
already left boring, conventional old Dayton, it was just her
body that was still here.

"Stuart Nadeau got himself killed?" I said.

She rolled her eyes. "No, he's fine."

I told her about Darren's death prophecy.

"We got out of the ER around two a.m.," she said, "and
I put him on a plane back to Toronto before he had another
chance to ruin my day. But you're not going to believe what
happened to my suitcase."

I cringed in anticipation. The previous week, Celeste
had been so excited about her new pristine white Tumi, an
early Christmas present she'd bought for herself, that she'd
actually brought it to the office to show me. It was a big
splurge for a Level 1. She'd eaten nothing but off-brand
frozen vegetables and rice for months to save up for it.
We snapped up every opportunity to symbolically distance

ourselves from mediocrity.

"When it came off the conveyor belt at baggage claim," she said, peeling off her coat, "motherfucker had a big black tire mark across the middle. Like it fell off the luggage cart and got run over by a truck."

"Oh my god," I said.

She tossed her coat over our gray cubicle wall and sat down across from me.

"Don't you think, if you were a luggage handler, you'd say to yourself, 'Gee, this one's white, maybe we should put it on top where it won't get *run over*'?" She glared incredulously at Phil Collins as if he might have the answer. He swam in a circle and then disappeared into his castle. "I mean, I figured it'd get dirty, but I didn't think it would get *tire marked*. Now I'm wondering how often normal black luggage gets run over."

I continued to watch her, in case this was just the preamble to a longer discussion, but she stopped talking and turned to her computer.

"I got us a new box of granola bars," I said, motioning.

"Sweet. You're the best."

She reached for the box that marked the separation between my neat and tidy side of the cubicle and Celeste's side, which was always a mess. If we'd hung a *Seventeen Magazine* mosaic of circa 1996 Leonardo DiCaprio clippings, the whole thing would have been the spitting image of the fort we'd built in the woods in sixth grade. Celeste and I hadn't imagined back then that a decade later we'd be sharing a cubicle at Findlay. Back then, we'd measured our lives in magazines and movie stars. Celeste had wanted to be a cruise ship captain, or maybe a photographer for National Geographic. I wanted to marry a royal. We knew we were destined for something special, bound to embody the elegant, magical future we saw inside our heads. It wasn't until later that we realized Findlay was our ticket to that magical future. And now here we were, working for Gus Hanley, high on daily whiffs of boardroom prestige and the promise of eventual greatness.

All the Level 1s had a similar story. We were all eager to rise, all of us infected with the same no-holds-barred drive to master our domain. In our case, that domain was consumer devices, and we were the Service Staff. We all dreamed of reaching Level 2, Support Staff. At Level 2, you could really be somebody. We weren't after Level 5 or Level 6; that would be absurd. Just Level 2. I'd been especially dreamy lately because Marcie Harrington had just made the jump. One day she was an ordinary Level 1 service staffer like us, and the next day she was an inductee into that mysterious and wonderful club of 2. As she prepared to move to the adjacent wing, we watched her gather her cubicle ephemera with newfound actuality, disposing of photos and postcards that had once meant something to her Level 1 self as if they were tainted with rot. I watched her and imagined, with envy so visceral it made my eyes water, she was me . . .

"One of the sales reps killed an American bald eagle," Celeste said without turning around.

"What?" I looked back at her, but she was typing something. "How?"

"It was injured or sick or something," she said. "The guy caught it near our hotel, and the other reps started passing it around for selfies, and it died."

"Jeez," I mumbled.

"He didn't want to get in trouble, so he asked the concierge for a trash bag and threw it in a dumpster out back."

I imagined it for a second, tucked into a shroud of rotting pizza boxes and potato chip bags, used condoms and wads of miscellaneous blackening sludge. The acrid smell of garbage juice, the dark, hot plastic closing in. The awful extinguishment it all amounted to. In the neighboring cubicle, Molly opened one of the Mounds bars she kept hidden in her desk, and the rustle of its sleeve echoed off our fake wood walls. Then my phone rang, clearing my head.

"Miss Faust," the voice said, "Gus would like to see you in his office."

I gave Phil Collins's bowl an affectionate tap and grabbed my notepad.

The walls inside our building had been designed to float—so they could be moved easily as the organization grew—and as I passed the lacquered sliding doors of the executive offices, I could hear muffled snippets of conference calls and performance reviews. Presentations, one-on-ones, and lone whistlers, tapping computer keys. Connie from Administrative Services and Stan from IT huddled in a corner gossiping about one of the new technicians. "He took a two-hour lunch last week, Connie. Two. Hours." Mail deliverers dropped manila envelopes next to lipstick-marked Starbucks cups. Hidden space heaters—which were forbidden—blew pockets of warm air from underneath skinny women's desks. Every couple of months, these women would arrive in the morning to find their heaters sitting on the seats of their mesh swivel chairs, power cords wrapped up, Post-its affixed to the top scrawled with the word "NO." Sufficiently reprimanded, they'd take the heaters home. But after several days spent blue-fingered and shivering at their desks, they'd bring the heaters back in again, silently vowing to hide them better and only to use them for a few minutes at a time. Thus would begin the slow slide back to full heaterdom.

I reached Gus's secretary—Charlene, a Level 1—with her vertical files and matching baskets of candy. A Yankee candle burned a wide perimeter of Macintosh Apple scent that had come to define this part of the building. Charlene, or, as everyone referred to her now, "Poor Charlene," looked a little more rumpled than usual; word around the office was she was going through a divorce. She was the third person in our division in the last three months to be getting divorced, and people joked that it might be contagious. Poor Charlene asked me to wait in the hall where I had the privilege of staring at the off-limits cappuccino machine—a shiny black box with a digital screen and the word "Jura" in silver script across the front. From the conference room next door, the voices of brand managers—Level 3s— debated the ROI of a new direct-to-consumer sales scheme.

"It's not our target audience, Baldwin."

"But look, Chad, this is a chance to really disrupt the market."

After a few minutes, the door marked Gus Hanley slid a few inches to the right, and Darren slipped out. He smiled at me and took off down the hall.

"Gus will see you now, Halley," Poor Charlene announced.

I advanced quietly into the office and lowered into a big blue wingback chair next to floor-to-ceiling windows that overlooked the parking lot. The sun filled the room with an enchanting dust-moted glimmer. Gus typed on his computer with his back to me. "Give me just a second," he said.

Gus Hanley was a striking figure. The centimeter of gray clinging to his head made his dyed black pillow of hair look like it was floating untethered just above him, and his eyes sunk deeply into his skull, permanently ringed dark purple. He had the leathery, wrinkled skin of a decrepit rock star, and a gap between his two front teeth he could stick his tongue through, which held a certain Brigitte Bardot-ish eroticism if you didn't look too closely. His hedonism was well known throughout the company, along with his increasing paranoia, in recent years, that people were going to steal his stuff.

Gus picked up the phone and pressed a button. "Charlene, could you page Darren?"

He lowered the phone again and turned in my direction. "Poor Charlene," he said. "You know, I'm getting divorced too. Thank god for prenups."

Before I could respond, Darren appeared at the door, nostrils flaring like he had ants in his pants. Among his many responsibilities, Darren worked as Gus's "carrier," the person in charge of The Backpack that held all of the important documents that Gus refused to keep on the company server. He didn't want those "thugs" Tim Cook and Jeff Bezos using their internet sorcery to nab his trade secrets. Therefore, anytime Gus needed a document, day or night, Darren came running. Darren had missed family dinners and important meetings, had run out of theaters in the middle of movies, because he knew that these were all chances to prove himself.

"I need the Railer document," Gus said.

Darren unshouldered The Backpack, unzipped it, flipped through its contents and produced a packet of papers, then left quietly. Gus stared at the document for a few seconds, typed a few more words on his computer, then turned to face me.

"Halley. I called you in here to talk about something

very important."

He shifted his weight in his chair.

"We're doing a test launch of a new device in Europe next year, before we bring it to the States. It's called the Tantalus—you've probably heard people whispering about it. No? Well, it's really something special, the Tantalus is like nothing the market has ever seen before. This device is going to put us on the map. I can't tell you too much— proprietary information, you know. But it's going to revolutionize consumerism. Anyway, I'm taking a group of Americans on expat assignment for a year to plan and execute the launch. This is going to be the biggest rollout in Findlay's history, and we have to make sure the Europeans don't botch it."

I studied him without taking a breath. He continued. "We need a Support Staffer for the team, a Level 2 position. Are you up for it?"

I mentally collapsed to the floor like a beggar. Sweet Jesus, Mary mother of God, please please please give it to me. Please please please please please. Of course, all Gus saw of this was me leaning forward in the blue wingback chair, nodding a vigorous reply.

Gus clapped his hands together. "Great," he said. "Well, we can only take one person, and there are several interested. So I think the best way forward is to analyze your performance over the next couple months. You're working on the San Francisco meeting that's coming up, right? We'll see how that goes. Then whoever does the best job will go with us to Europe. Sound fair?"

"Who else are you considering?" I said.

"Well, Celeste, for one. And a couple others."

Celeste. My heart sank. For one of us to win, the other would have to lose. I couldn't do that to my best friend.

Gus's eyes turned poetic. "This is an incredible opportunity for you," he said. "A product launch is a sort of rebirth. It's a chance for the company to remake itself, to show what we're made of. You'll be making history. Chances like this come along once in a lifetime."

He paused for effect.

"It's going to be a hell of a party too," he added with an evil grin.

"Where in Europe . . ." I started.

"Where will we live? France, I'm told. It's the easiest place for us to get visas right now. But don't worry about that just yet. Let's wait and see who we end up hiring, then we'll go over all the details. Tax issues, salary, insurance, relocation. Lots to consider."

I opened my mouth to speak again.

"Oh," Gus said, "and we're looking for someone to manage future launches. So this could become a longer-term position—a Level 3—if all goes well."

Jesus, a Level 3? I couldn't even imagine it.

His phone rang. "Any other questions?" he asked.

I stared at his tooth gap in thought.

"Okay, great," he said and picked up the phone. "Gus Hanley."

I rose and rambled toward the door, intoxicated. The dim heaviness of Findlay's interior couldn't diminish the exhilaration of the secret knowledge that lives were about to change, and if by some miracle Celeste wasn't interested, one of them could be mine.

"So . . . this product launch," Celeste said. "Are you thinking about going for it?" She'd been called down to Gus's office right after me.

I took a sip of the lukewarm cafeteria coffee I'd neglected all morning. "I don't know, what about you?" I said, making my voice sound as casual as possible.

She paused to eyeball me. There were complex rituals to be observed. I could tell she was desperate for the job, and she knew I was desperate for it too, and the perennial symbiosis of our friendship restricted all possible forward motion to one narrow, conciliatory path.

"I'm sure Gus will end up giving it to you," I said.

She smiled, a burst of excitement making her shoulders shudder, and didn't say another word.

Bitch.

2

I was a Level 1 at home too, and this new potential advancement—to be *someone* not just at work, but in life—began to dominate my thoughts. I became aware all too quickly of the strange escalation of desire that occurs as you get closer to the things you want. Something that was ungraspable yesterday, and therefore stored in the "pipe dream" section of your mind, suddenly becomes distantly attainable, and then it's all you can think about. What if? What would it feel like? Who would I be then?

The box of Slim Jims had been wrapped in chintzy green paper with big gold circles on it. My mom had pulled the plastic ribbon into loopy curls with her kitchen scissors so that it was camouflaged among the normal presents. Loretta Lynn's "Country Christmas" echoed from the kitchen stereo as my family sat under the sparkly-white glow of our artificial Balsam spruce, watching me unearth a year's supply of mechanically separated meat sticks. Courtesy of Sam's Club.

"Thanks, Dad," I said.

"Need some meat on your bones," my dad replied matter-of-factly. "Thought you could pack them in your lunches for work."

"You know, your aunt Eileen got diabetes as soon as she stopped eating meat," my mother said. "I'm telling you, Halley, this veganism is not healthy."

"I'm not a vegan; I'm a vegetarian," I said. "Or maybe it's pescatarian since I still eat fish sometimes."

"Wasn't Hitler a vegetarian?" my brother said. Grandpa's eyebrows went up.

"Hippie fad diet, that's all it is," my mom said, looking away. "Like that Atkins craze. Of course, you won't listen to us. Gotta be different."

It was true, I suppose. I *was* different—you might even say I was the black sheep of the family—although I wouldn't have said I wanted to be. At work I wanted to stand out, move up. At home there was no possibility of moving up, so I tried to keep a low profile.

My mom looked at her watch again, and then looked at me as if I was holding things up. "We should probably get a move on," she said.

My parents' beagle Guthrie lay at the foot of the coffee table, gnawing a new rawhide in the shape of a pretzel, as my mom opened a "Beagle Puppies" wall calendar from my sister. We went around the room from youngest to oldest, taking turns unwrapping while Grandpa snapped photos with his old Kodak. He and Granny always spent Christmas morning with us because, of the four of their children, my mother was their favorite. This wasn't something anyone ever said out loud, of course. But it had always been that way, always giving us this inkling that we were supposed to be exceptional.

Soon there were hugs and chatter and Coca-Cola-

glazed ham, counters filled with pull-apart rolls and casse-
roles covered in gravy. Guthrie released a deep, protective howl whenever the door opened. Aunts, uncles, and
cousins streamed through while the nine-year-old neighbor
girl stood outside smoking a cigarette, traces of her smoke
wafting into my parents' living room with every cold burst
of air.

"I've said it before, and I'll say it again: I feel sorry for
that girl," my dad said, peering around the corner. "Those
people haven't cleaned their gutters in years."

It wasn't dirty gutters that made him feel sorry for the
girl, though. It was her lack of spirit that bothered him. The
same lack of spirit that my mother lauded.

"That kid has the good sense not to expect much," my
mother said as she pulled another tray of rolls out of the
oven. "She probably didn't get anything good for Christmas.
But do you see her crying about it? Nope."

I looked back at the girl again. She cupped her smoking
hand in a weird sort of way, cigarette tucked between
her middle fingers like a Vulcan salute. Maybe she'd seen
someone else cup it that way—a boy down the street,
perhaps, or some lead singer from a band—and taken that
as her model. It occurred to me as I watched her that I
could have been her, if a few basic things had been different.
If my brand of aspirationalism had been rockabilly instead
of pop, I could be out there practicing my cigarette grip
and daydreaming about whether to get an anchor tattooed
on my shoulder or my inner thigh. We were all aiming for
something.

The Disney parade, and then the football game, blared
from the TV while my weird uncle Levi, burned out from
doing too many drugs in the seventies, stared from the
corner in his googly-eyed way, falling in and out of sleep.

My cousin Jade—known to everyone as the one who used to steal money from my dad's wallet—apologized for being late; she'd lost her three-year-old and spent twenty frantic minutes searching for her, only to find her standing naked on the bathroom sink in front of the mirror because "she wanted to see if her butt looked like Barbie's." I sat at the counter eating a bowl of Granny's marshmallow-topped fruit salad and was startled out of my mental hideout by the last few words of a conversation my mother was having with my Aunt.

". . . like the time Halley sodomized that poor billy goat," my mother said.

"What?" Granny shouted at full volume. She couldn't hear very well, but she refused to get a hearing aid.

"Can we not go a single Christmas without bringing that up?" I said. "I was just petting it!"

They all laughed as if they hadn't heard this story every year for the last twenty years.

"For god's sake, I was four years old," I said. My exasperation felt real but also rehearsed, as if I was playing myself on a stage. This was the fixed identity from which I would never escape as long as I stayed in Dayton, in this family. The girl who sodomized a billy goat.

"Language, Halley," my mother said.

I frowned.

Soon my sister came home from her boyfriend's parents' house, all smiles, flashing a trendy pavé diamond ring, and all attention was refocused. In the Faust family, this was the very definition of "exceptional." This was the way you lived a good life—by replicating the lives of those who came before you. The kitchen was hot and noisy, and my mom cried, even though she'd gotten advance notice of the engagement when Justin asked my dad's permission.

"Lindsay will make such a beautiful bride," Granny shouted.

"Seems like just yesterday I was the one getting married," my mom said, wiping away tears with a red poinsettia-print paper napkin. "Now my girls are all grown up."

"Halley's not," my brother Luke chimed in from behind the refrigerator door, the stench of his Axe body spray surrounding him like a protective shield. "She doesn't even have a boyfriend."

"I thought you did," Aunt Lois said. She took another bite of pecan pie. "What was his name? Mike?"

"We broke up last fall." I shrugged an apology. Such high hopes I'd had of my first serious boyfriend, and in the end, I'd spent the first half of the relationship wishing he'd show up and the other half wishing he'd leave. I didn't know how to explain to people, without sounding arrogant and pretentious, that the ordinariness of it all had been suffocating. All my life I'd dreamed of fairy tales, but what I'd gotten with Mike had been a distant, basketball-obsessed fart machine who assumed that fidelity, half-priced appetizers at Applebee's, and the occasional red rose was the same thing as love. I could never quite put my finger on what was so dissatisfying about all of that, just like I could never quite put my finger on what made me feel like an outsider in my own family. So when I finally broke it off, they took his side over mine and prodded me about it every chance they got.

Aunt Lois paused to lick a crumb off the tip of her finger. "You'd better get a move on, Halley. Before you know it, you'll be my age."

"Halley says she doesn't want to get married," my mom said, side-eyeing me. "I don't think it's true though, I think she says it just to torment me."

"Why wouldn't you want to get married?" Aunt Lois said. She half-smiled like you would if you were asking a little kid why he doesn't want to wear pants, knowing he'll say something cute in response.

"I don't know," I said.

"Every woman wants to get married," Aunt Lois said. She looked over at my sister, who was picking a piece of lint from one of the prongs of her ring. "Right, Lindsay? Or else who's going to take care of you when you're my age?"

"What?" Granny shouted.

"She said every woman wants to get married, Mother!" my mom yelled.

Granny nodded.

"I might be moving," I blurted.

My dad looked up from his conversation with Uncle Larry. "Oh yeah?" he said. "Where to?"

"France," I said.

They all turned in my direction.

"Like France, the country?" my brother said.

My mom opened her mouth, closed it, then opened it again. "Why?" she said, preemptively annoyed, as if this might have been a tiresome joke.

"Well nothing is decided yet," I said quickly. "A few of us are up for the position; they're telling us after the San Francisco meeting, I think. So I probably won't even get the offer. But they're sending a team of people to Europe for a year to work on a product launch." The words "product" and "launch" seemed to echo through the room like a gunshot. It was a loaded phrase, not only because it was the fodder for my strange announcement, but because I knew what a product launch was, and they didn't.

My mom started to speak but my sister interrupted her. "What does that mean?"

"You know, when they release a product for sale, they have to tell customers about it before it comes out so people want to actually buy it."

"It's too bad they're going to France," my dad said. "Germany would've been better. At least they have Oktoberfest in Germany. Why France?"

"I'll never know how you got to be like this," my mom said.

"Like what?"

"Like this," she said in a world-weary voice. "Never satisfied. Nothing is ever good enough."

I went to the sink to wash my bowl and spoon in the gray dishwater. Our conversations always ended the same way. With me hungry for something I couldn't get from them, the futility of returning again and again to suckle at a teat that couldn't bear milk. This had never seemed to apply to my siblings; it was only me who'd been born under strange stars, full of some foreign energy that couldn't be used. It was in these moments that I clung most desperately to the belief that somehow, somewhere, life must be better than this.

3

AFTER CHRISTMAS, I wanted more than ever to explode out of my life, to flood out and experience everything there was to experience in the world all at once. That's when I started to notice the little betrayals. I began to measure our friendship by them. Celeste, describing the perfect French Riviera bikini she wanted to buy. Me, daydreaming about French cheese. Celeste, smiling surreptitiously at Gus in the hallway. Me, working extra hard on my portion of the San Francisco meeting. Celeste, talking about how ready she was to move up. She probably thought she deserved it more than I did. Okay, she was better at organizing meetings than I was, better at navigating the corporate world, but only because she'd had more practice.

While I was in college, Celeste had gone to technical school. Her degree had only taken two years while mine had taken four, giving her a two-year head start. Except she didn't think of it as a "head start"; she referred to it as "doing her time." When I finished college, she helped me get hired at Findlay too.

But I started at the same level as Celeste, a Level 1, even though I'd studied for two extra years. Not to mention, she'd started at Findlay with almost no debt, while I started with $60,000 in student loans. I sure as hell wasn't buying any Tumi luggage. And regardless of all this, I'd been prepared to concede to her anyway, until I found out she wasn't going to even pretend she'd do the same for me.

The frizzy head of Molly Barnes—another Level 1—prairie-dogged over the top of our cubicle wall. "Halley, can I talk to you about these agenda booklets for the San Francisco meeting?" she sang. Her lopsided grin gave you the feeling that if you got too close she might pull a knife on you.

I stopped typing and walked around the partition that separated my desk from hers. Hers was dominated by an unironic display of squirrel memorabilia—squirrel finger puppets, porcelain squirrel figurines, and a big stuffed squirrel holding an acorn embroidered with the words "I'm nuts about you." She pulled one of the finger puppets off its pencil home and attached it to the end of her finger before she spoke, one of Sun Tzu's lesser-known *Art of War* tactics.

"Fire away," I said.

"Well," she began in her best squirrel voice, shaking the big-eyed puppet at me, "we aren't going to be able to create the agenda booklets. There just isn't enough time!"

"Time?" My eyes darted between Molly and the squirrel, unsure where to look. "You've had the work order since October."

She grinned at my implication. "You know, believe it or not there are other things going on around here besides the sales meeting."

I bit the inside of my lip. "But if I don't have the agenda books, everyone at the meeting will be all lost and confused.

Can I make them myself?"

"You're so funny, Halley," she said, conjuring a little squirrel laugh. "You know you're not allowed to do it yourself. We can't have *just anyone* making print pieces, they won't be on brand!"

"But . . . they're just meeting agendas," I said. "They're for our own people . . . Surely nobody is going to care what the font looks like."

She smiled. "Sorry," the squirrel said. So we were playing hard-ball then. She must be gunning for the France position too. Molly was a Level 1 like the rest of us, but she had a slight advantage as the coordinator for our division's graphic designer. Our success was, to a large extent, dependent upon her good will—she had the power to delay, reroute, "lose," and otherwise botch our projects if she so chose. It was a delicate balancing act; she couldn't screw things up so badly that it would make *her* look incompetent, but within those bounds were hundreds of ways she could make *us* look incompetent, so we had to be careful to stay on her good side. Which was difficult, because she was an evil goddamned demon, and only those of us who worked directly with her on projects—other Level 1s—actually knew it. To everyone else, she was just sweet little Molly with her weird squirrel fixation. I tried telling Gus once that Molly was evil, and he stopped speaking to me for a whole month. How could anyone who loved squirrels so much be evil?

"Okay." I rubbed my hands together. "Are you still going to be able to send my box?"

"Box? What box?" she said.

I sighed a little too loudly, and she smirked, and we both knew she was getting to me.

"The box. The box of materials we talked about that has

to be sent to San Francisco. You said the welcome packets won't be done until the last minute, and I'll already be en route to the meeting by then, so you were going to box them up and send them."

Molly cleared her throat. "Oh yes, *that* box. If I told you I'd do it, then I'll do it."

"Okay, but it's really important. It's the most important box of the whole meeting. Name badges, instructional materials from Gus, presentation booklets. It will make *all of us* look bad if I don't get that box."

This was the only way to get Molly to comply—to convince her that it was in her own best interest.

She deployed the squirrel finger puppet a final time. "Of course I'll send your box, Halley!" the squirrel sang.

"Thank you." I backed away, turned the corner, and collapsed into my swivel chair. Phil Collins swam to the side of his bowl, looked up into my tired eyes, and blew me a "hang in there, buddy" bubble, before retiring to his castle.

Later that day, Jamie Aaronson—Level 3—invaded our cubicle.

"I hope you can manage it this time, Celeste," she said. "Tell them it comes directly from the president if you need to. The company is not going to foot the bill for all these canceled activities just because people are too hungover to show up."

At Findlay, Jamie was known for three things: her disciplined approach to scheduling, "The Rachel" haircut she'd maintained since the mid-90s, and the glamour shots of herself in a cowgirl outfit that she kept on her desk. The very fact that these were the things she was known for, that she was rendered so small in her daily life so as to have an email signature that only took up four lines, made her all the more determined to insert herself into every situation simply to put her thumbprint on it, a constant battle with the brand of insignificance that administrative staff were supposed to accept as a given. The only real power she wielded was in her proximity to the president as his executive administrative assistant, and she stretched it as far as it would go.

Celeste looked her right in the eye. "For all the activities, or just for golf?"

"All of them."

"Got it." Celeste scribbled a note to herself, although she didn't need to. She remembered everything.

"Repeat it back to me."

"If anyone cancels an activity during the San Francisco meeting," Celeste recited, "they pay for it out of pocket."

Jamie tapped a red fingernail on the top of our cubicle wall and stared at something outside our range of vision. We weren't sure if we should continue looking at her or mind our own business, so we shuffled papers around and alternated looking at our desks and looking back up to see if she was looking at us.

"You guys need to be nicer to Molly," she finally said. In fact, she almost shouted it, as if to make sure everyone around us could hear her. The sudden increase in volume caught me off guard.

"What?" I said.

"Molly," Jamie repeated. "You need to be nicer to her."

"Why do you think we aren't being nice to her?" Celeste said.

"She told me Halley has been giving her a hard time about agenda booklets for the San Francisco meeting," Jamie said, still at full volume. "You know, it's not the end of the world if we don't have agenda booklets."

My face reddened as she walked away.

Celeste looked bewildered. She peeked into Molly's cubicle to make sure she wasn't there, then returned. "You gave Molly a hard time?" she said.

"Are you kidding? Come on. She gave *me* a hard time!"

Celeste laughed, then whispered, "Did you hear they're thinking about making Jamie a Vice President?"

"Vice President of what, secretaries?" I felt the air change, and I knew immediately that I shouldn't have said it out loud.

Half a second later, Jamie reappeared around the corner of our cubicle. I fought the urge to punch myself in the face. Even Phil Collins looked disappointed in me.

"Celeste, one more thing," Jamie said, not looking at me.

"Sure," Celeste said, turning.

"Anthony wants the company plane to depart San Francisco airport at 7:30 a.m. I made all the arrangements with the FBO, but I need you to manage the limo."

"Okay."

"Repeat it back to me."

Celeste smiled with teeth. "Set the limo for six people plus luggage March eighth to arrive to the FBO at 7:30 a.m."

"Thanks," Jamie said, then left again.

After counting to ten and standing up to check the hallway, I whispered, "Do you think she heard what I said—about secretaries?"

"Yep," Celeste said.

I raked my fingers through my hair.

"Don't worry about it. I don't think she liked you before."

"What?" I blinked. "Really? I mean I know we're not

exactly friends, but you think she actually dislikes me?"

Celeste rolled her eyes and turned back to her computer as I stewed in my thoughts. Another tiny betrayal to add to our growing list.

4

A couple days of slow but persistent rain transformed once-snowy yards into messes of muddy slush. I sat in my beater car outside my parents' house listening to the end of a song I liked on the radio before traipsing in for dinner. There was peace in suburban Ohio's winter shadows, the low muffled rumbling of the car engine, gusts of wind creaking through plastic siding. My winter boots squished through the small patch of grass that led up to the white wood stairway I'd helped my dad refinish the previous summer. The front door squealed to announce my arrival. Guthrie howled a quick greeting and licked the tips of my fingers.

I shrugged out of the warm shell of my coat and threw it on the bed in the room I used to share with my sister, the one with the big stain on the carpet from the time I threw up blueberry pie when I was seven, and framed needlepoint pictures of princesses and ballerinas hanging on either side of the pink lace-curtained window. My sister's bed was still there, but mine was eight miles away in my apartment. The living room was still littered with Santa Claus figurines, snow globes, and fake holly candle holders, which we would soon wrap in paper towels and place back in musty boxes to be stacked in my grandparents' storage shed.

My mom's oven-mitted hands pulled a bubbling Pyrex dish of potato casserole from the oven and set it on top of the stove, dribbling two drops of gravy onto the yellow linoleum below. She always forgot I hated gravy. "Forgot" was the generous interpretation; it was more likely she thought if she fed it to me enough, I'd change and start liking it. Anyway, I always scraped it off.

Rusty steak knife in hand, my mom sawed through the casserole's gummy layers, a look of concentrated determination on her face. This was the mode in which she operated most of the time. But there was always something else lingering there, just under the surface. You'd catch brief glimpses of it, and then it would flicker away. Stitches of something resembling melancholy, maybe even a bit of resentment, the origins of which I never knew.

"Is there anything I can do?" I asked.

"No, it's done," she said. "Dinner!" she called to the others.

The rest of the family emerged from in front of the television to crowd around our little dining room table. We passed the thin metal spatula from person to person, scraping the sides of the casserole dish as we scooped big slices into our bowls. Then we all spooned hunks of casserole down our gullets in silence. We weren't the kind of people who savored and celebrated food, nor did we view food as simply fuel. We didn't commune over our food either, unless it was a holiday. No, our relationship with food was more of a quiet animal voraciousness. The hot globs when they hit our mouths triggered some primordial comfort mechanism, and we shoveled more in, hoping to really feel something. Dinner was always a sort of silent pursuit. Eventually we had our fill, and that was something too.

After we'd carried our dishes to the sink and my mom had wrapped the leftover casserole in aluminum foil and wedged it into the refrigerator, we all retired back to the television once more.

"Oh, Gene Crandel died," my dad said over the top of the obits section. His right hand stirred a cup of coffee, into which he alternately piled spoonfuls of sugar and milk. He kept stirring it and stirring it, but he never drank it, and it eventually got cold.

"About time," my mom said, looking up. "Poor guy— how long has he had emphysema?"

"N!" my brother shouted at the television.

"Six years?" my mom continued. "I hardly remember seeing him without that oxygen tank."

"His granddaughter just got married," my dad said. "What was her name?"

"Holly," my sister chimed in, eyes still glued to the tube.

"Shotgun wedding, from what I heard," said Mom.

"Yep," my sister said. "She always was kind of a slut."

"Damn it, just buy the vowel!" my brother said.

"Language, Luke," said Mom.

I shifted in the chair so my sister could pass through to the kitchen for a new bottle of artificially flavored peach tea. Her eyes held a vacant, unconcerned expression, and I wondered how much of it was natural and how much was contrived.

"Did you hear Nancy Carson's daughter is having a baby?" my mom said.

"Boy or girl?" Lindsay asked, settling back into her spot

on the floor.

"They don't know yet; they just found out. She's been having all sorts of infertility problems, so it's a miracle she's even pregnant."

"It's 'strawberry,' you idiot," my brother said.

My dad clucked suddenly and looked over at my mom. "Before I forget, Linda, we need to go to Sam's tomorrow and pick up that mattress."

"I have to go to the post office in the morning. Can we go after that?"

"Wait a minute," I said, "didn't you just buy a new mattress a couple weeks ago?"

"Yep," my dad said. "It's too soft."

For as long as I could remember, my dad, the retail menace of Dayton, Ohio, had had this funny habit of buying things, deciding he didn't like them, and returning them or exchanging them for something else. He would exchange multiple things in succession until the store manager would finally tell him they couldn't take back any more of his purchases. He'd thusly narrowed his valuable patronage mostly to Sam's Club, because "they'll take anything back."

"I thought this one was a keeper," I said.

"Well, it seemed okay in the store, but my back is still killing me, and I know it's because it's too soft."

He continued reading the paper, the table lamp casting a yellow haze over his shoulder.

"See that?" my dad said to the TV. A teaser for the nine o'clock news described two fatal Cincinnati shootings as the day's top stories. "I swear, the world's going to hell in a handbasket. Halley, you really ought to come with us to the shooting range next time. Your sister came, and she liked it."

"Dad got me a pink gun," Lindsay said. She pulled a

wood-handled hair brush dozens of times through her hair, and then began meticulously clipping it back in barrettes.

"I don't care if I ever go to Cincinnati again," my mom mumbled fearfully.

My dad pointed at the TV as if the perpetrators themselves were standing in front of us. "You kids are growing up in a different world. When I was your age, this kind of stuff didn't happen. My mother let us play outside until it was dark, and she never worried. Everything was better back then."

That was probably true—the part about my grandmother not worrying—as my dad grew up on a family farm with no television, where he and his siblings entertained themselves by throwing live chickens at each other. His father, my grandfather, had been a well-respected grower of non-alfalfa hay. They'd had a modest but high-quality operation that supplied small, green bales to horse breeders. Every year at baling time, my dad and his younger brother and older sister were dragged out of bed at three o'clock in the morning when the moisture was just right. They rubbed their adolescent eyes, pulled on their work boots, and dreamed of a day when they wouldn't have to do this shit anymore. Then, to everyone's horror, that day arrived.

The year my dad turned seventeen, Dayton was hit by a storm that perforated the roof of the hay barn, allowing water to seep onto the new bales, unbeknownst to my grandfather. The excessive moisture caused bacteria to grow, generating heat inside the bales, which spontaneously combusted one night while everyone was sleeping. The barn "went up like a tinderbox," as my grandfather used to say. They lost everything: the barn, the house, the hay, the equipment, and what was left of the field. They got out just in time to salvage their own lives and the lives of their two

Australian shepherd mutts, Corky and Sparky, whose terrified barks had saved them all.

The insurance money was enough to rebuild the house
and to allow my grandparents to semi-retire, but they never
did revive the farm. For extra money my grandmother took
a part-time librarian job and my grandfather worked as a
handyman. But their children, who had always taken their
futures for granted—the inevitability that the farm would
be passed down to them and to their children and their
children's children—never quite recovered. They had to
reimagine their lives, their places in the world. My father, at
the age of forty-eight, was still trying to reimagine his.

After high school, he'd taken a job in the packing
department of the peanut butter factory. This was meant
to be a short-term thing, to buy him some time to decide
what to do with himself. But then he met my mother, the
former Pork Festival Queen of Montgomery County—
and a real catch, according to my dad—and soon they
were having a baby—me—and all grand plans were put on
hold. Put on hold, but not put out of mind. For as long as I
could remember, my dad came home smelling like roasted
peanuts, talking about his plans. Businesses he wanted to
start, investments he wanted to make, houses he wanted to
build, adventures he wanted to have. He didn't talk about
them in a pitiful, helpless sort of way. He always spoke as
a person whose whole life was still ahead of him, full of
opportunities ripe for the picking. He read stories of the
rich and famous and imagined himself as them. America
was a smörgåsbord of dishes, and all he had to do was
choose one, reach out and grab it. He loved that about this
country.

But years passed, and he didn't choose a dish. He
didn't start a business or make those investments or build

a house or have the adventures. He settled into the hectic rhythms of a low-income paterfamilias. And as time went by, the chasm between the grand world of his imagination, all wholesomeness and opportunity and Norman Rockwell paintings, and the world he lived in, with its meth-heads and murders and thwarted social mobility, became bigger and bigger and bigger. The chasm didn't disillusion him, it made him angry. These people, these criminals and terrorists running amok, were ruining his promised land.

And as we settled in to watch the final round of *Wheel of Fortune*, Lindsay with her fresh bottle of tea, my dad having moved on to the sports section, my mom clipping coupons, and Luke trash-talking Pat Sajak, I realized that herein lay my biggest fear, which I could never say out loud: if I did nothing I might wind up just like this, living my whole life and dying in front of the television in Dayton, Ohio.

5

FAST FORWARD THROUGH many more hours of family time in front of the TV. Hundreds of bullet-pointed emails. Thinly-veiled threats from Molly. Lectures from Jamie. Hallway nods from Gus. Hotel contracts. Catering orders. Motor coach schedules. Activity registrations. March was there in a flash. And somewhere between San Francisco's juice bars and funky shoe stores, there I was, heaving and cramping, bargaining with a disinterested god.

I crawled on my hands and knees to the mini bar for a cold bottle of water. The liquid felt hard and foreign in my stomach, like gravel. Phil Collins watched from his travel aquarium with sympathetic eyes as I thrashed, annoyed with my body's unwillingness to cooperate. That familiar hotel smell hung in the air, particle board and carpet cleaner and high-end french fries. Outside on the street there was shouting, muffled car horns. The heavy moaning of two people next door. The world passing by, unaware.

The ring of my cell phone woke me up. Celeste.

"Hey," she said. "You sound like you're sleeping."

"I have the California death flu."

"Oh," she chuckled, "that sucks."

"Are you *laughing* at me?" I said. Traitor.

"No. Well, not at you being sick. It's just that you're not going to like what I called to tell you."

"Oh no, what is it?" It was more of an accusation than a question.

"My flight just got canceled," she said. "There's a snow-storm in Chicago. I can't get there 'til tomorrow."

"Fuck."

Celeste laughed again. "It cracks me up when you drop the f-bomb."

It wasn't funny though. The alarm of all the pre-meeting tasks I needed to complete—packets to stuff and banquet staff to meet and miscellaneous errands to run—rang loudly through my throbbing skull. I pushed the bed pillow onto the floor so I could rest my face on the flat, cool mattress.

"Tell me what to do," I said. "Clive gets in this after-noon. I can't get out of bed without barfing."

"Drink some tea—that'll perk you up a little. Then get to a pharmacy. They can probably give you something for nausea."

I would need to lie around for a couple more hours to psych myself up for that.

That afternoon, I left Phil Collins to hold down the fort while I went out in search of medicine. The sun shone brightly, and I dug to the bottom of my bag for a pair of aviator sunglasses that would cover half my face from the piercing light. A reassuring breeze blew across the hotel lobby entrance. I'd done the thing where I wore pajamas in public, but no one could tell because I had a trench coat over them. At least I convinced myself no one could tell. They probably could. This was California, after all.

When I got to my rental car—a red Fiat 500 I'd deposited in a nearby parking lot in my haste to find a bathroom the day before—there was a parking ticket under the driver's side windshield wiper.

"God damn it," I mumbled as I calmly threw it on the passenger seat.

I started the engine, pressed the clutch, and tried moving the gearshift to R, but it wouldn't quite lock into place. I tried a little more forcefully. My dad's old car had been a manual, so I wasn't a total novice at this. When I'd arrived at the rental car check-in desk, a hostess with black-framed glasses had said there was a big auctioneers convention in the city and their branch was almost out of cars, so she offered me this stick-shift Fiat instead of the automatic the travel agent had booked. I was glad to have a car at all. Lucky for me, the commute from the airport to the hotel had required forward motion only.

I fiddled with the shifter for at least ten minutes, trying to make it work. No dice. But I realized I'd parked on enough of an incline that I could idle backward out of the space in neutral. Victory! I imagined Gus congratulating me on my infinite resourcefulness. I was definitely Level 2 material.

San Francisco vibrated with bohemian coffee shops and foggy morning bicycle rides, but I didn't care about that now. I prowled the streets in work mode, only processing utilitarian details like a computer programmer who sees the world in zeros and ones. Soon I spotted my target: a red-awninged pharmacy. I briefly considered leaving the car in the middle of the street while I went inside, opting to play the dumb tourist card if I had to, but then I noticed an underground garage on the next block. Swallowing back nausea and sweating with fever, I spiraled down the garage's narrow labyrinth of turns and parked in a place that looked to have a sufficient incline I could idle backwards out of.

I walked through the pharmacy door and was blasted with the smells of gauze and disinfectant. The woman behind the counter, whose gorgeous bronze skin stood in sharp contrast to her white lab coat, looked less like a pharmacist than an actress playing a pharmacist in a movie. I was immediately sheepish about the sweatpants I was wearing.

"I need something for nausea," I said.

"Aisle five," she replied, barely looking up.

I fetched the drugs, paid, and returned to the parking garage, relieved to make it back to the judgment-free safety zone of the rental car. Until I realized that I could not, in fact, idle backward out of my parking space. I uttered a string of expletives that would've driven my mother to drink. The engine ran quietly as I sat thinking, staring at concrete walls. I considered taking a short nap. I tried to shake the car backward by throwing myself against the seat. I mentally pleaded to the rental car gods to miraculously illuminate my dim mind to the ways of the manual reverse gear. The attempts were futile, and I started to fear I would actually break the shifter off. The only thing I could think to do was Flintstone my way out. I began to think the pathetic, self-pitying thoughts of the ill Western traveler. *Will I ever be well again? Will I ever make it out of this godforsaken place? Maybe I'll just sit here and die.* Door open, I pushed my feet against the parking garage floor. At first the weight of the car held it stubbornly glued to the spot, but it gradually, inch-by-inch, began to roll backward, all my weight pushing against it, narrowly missing a neighboring Mercedes. Noxious exhaust fumes filled my nostrils. Moisture saturated my temples, and I rested for a few seconds, fighting back the black spots that danced in front of my eyes. I put the car in gear and swirled up the garage's serpentine twists, finally emerging into the sunlight again. And as I cruised down the street back to my temporary bed, I felt as if I had escaped something really terrible.

Phil Collins picked up pebbles with his mouth, one by one, and spit them back out again, a game he played whenever he was bored. "I know, buddy," I said. "I haven't been paying enough attention to you." I put the punctured pill packet and bottle of water next to my phone on the bedside table and rolled over to stare at the plain white ceiling, running through to-do lists in my head. Strand by strand, the cords of my fever began to loosen and dissolve. My stomach still clenched, but at least it was empty. I got up to take a shower.

Findlay European Chief Sales Manager, Managing Director, and Territory Officer Clive Villalobos—Level 6—arrived at the hotel as the sun began to fall behind the neighboring building, casting thick orange beams on the lobby floor where I waited to greet him. In a cream-colored suit, orange pointy-toed shoes, and Wayfarer sunglasses he looked like a 1950s Puerto Rican gigolo, or maybe an actor in one of those commercials for boxed wine.

"Hi—" I began as he emerged from the revolving door.

He proceeded to spit out a long string of gibberish. "Halley, Iyamdete fodeaconfiedancecall canjewchakmeentomydoomendabdingmedekey?"

"What?" I asked.

I'd only met Clive once before at a meeting in New

York, but I suspected he might die soon of a cranial aneurysm. He talked so quickly and interrupted so frequently that you were lucky if you could finish a sentence in his presence. His heavy Spanish accent made almost everything he said unintelligible, a fact of which he seemed to be completely unaware. But the most unnerving thing about him was that he said my name a lot, which gave me the sense that I was always in trouble.

He repeated himself.

"Okay," I replied to his back as he walked away. I fetched his room key and set it gingerly next to his gesticulating hand on the lobby table he'd chosen from which to conduct his conference call.

I sat in a vacant lobby armchair for a moment in hopes of checking my email, but before I could pull my phone from my bag, a bellman approached.

"Miss," he said, "we have your packages."

Hotel staff had stored them in an empty meeting room because there were so many: three pallets in all, from three different countries. There were pamphlets from Findlay's Atlanta office, product samples from our Heidelberg warehouse, and demo kits from our Shanghai factory. They were all stacked in big cubes and wrapped in sheets of plastic. I borrowed a utility knife from the bellman and began unwrapping, the plastic wrap squeaking as it collected in a big ball on the floor. Eventually I found everything there. Everything, that is, except my box from Ohio. The box Molly had promised to send.

I knew it! Shitshitshitshitshitshitshitshitshit.

My only option was to get everything reprinted at a local copy shop. I had the digital files on my laptop in case of an emergency. But that was going to take hours.

I opened the web browser on my phone and started

searching for copy shops and frantically dialing. The first one was closed. The second went straight to voicemail. After the third failed attempt, I sat on the floor of the package room and had myself a good cry. Sure it was unprofessional, but I had been sick for twelve hours, gotten a parking ticket, lost my most important box of stuff, and worn pajamas in public. Level 2 was shrinking out of view by the minute. Of course this was the moment Clive Villalobos chose to enter the room.

"Halley, whateeslongweethjew?" he asked.

"What?" I said.

He managed to be intimidating while not being very tall, and every time I saw him I was surprised by how short he was. In that moment he looked a little scared.

"Sorry," I said, wiping snot on my arm. "I have the flu."

He tried not to notice this gross feminine display with the same visible disgust as if I'd just pulled a box of tampons out of my pocket and set it down in front of him. "Halley, eefjewareseekjewshouldbeeenbed. Govac tujor broomineye wheel sinnadoct oar."

"What?" I said.

"Govac tujor broomineye wheel sinnadoct oar," he repeated.

"Go back to my room? I can't, there's too much to do." I tried explaining about the lost box of stuff, but he cut me off.

"Halley, goatabedbefoorjewmekevaeryoneseek."

"What?" I said.

Clive stared at me.

"Okay," I sighed. "Celeste should be here soon."

Of course, if it had been Celeste managing this stuff instead of me, the package would have been delivered three days early by Brad Pitt covered in chocolate buttons.

Perfect Celeste . . . now she would get the Level 2 job, and I would be stuck in Dayton forever. I started to tear up again.

I handed Clive the utility knife, and he watched me slink off to the elevator. And for the rest of the afternoon, instead of holding pre-conference meetings with banquet managers and bellmen and audiovisual technicians and hotel managers, signing food and beverage orders, stuffing welcome packets, alphabetizing name badges, posting event signage, setting up the hospitality desk, monitoring the setup of staging and screens, greeting company managers as they arrived and attending to all the last-minute changes they wanted to make, Phil Collins and I sat in bed watching Telemundo while I called every copy shop in San Francisco. After a while, a local physician knocked on my hotel room door. He'd been sent by Clive, which could have been a nice gesture or could have been a hint that he didn't want to run the meeting himself so I'd better get off my ass. The doctor quickly established that I had some kind of stomach virus. For the nausea he prescribed an injection, which he administered by smacking me swiftly and inexplicably on the behind and plunging the needle in. That day would go down in history as the day I got my first company-sponsored spanking.

6

I WAS WELL enough to manage the welcome dinner. The first catastrophe was Gus's big entrance. Gus's entrance was a major consideration for every sales meeting, as each year he tried to outdo the last. Unfortunately, during setup that afternoon, the glider he was supposed to fly in on got hit by a catering truck. On short notice we were able to find a donkey for him to ride in on instead, but he sulked about it for most of the evening. A donkey was not nearly as cool as a glider, despite the auspicious Jesus Christ reference.

Then there was the heater incident.

Our venue was a huge stucco chateau with an open courtyard in the center, sitting on a sixty-acre vineyard outside the city. The place had seventeen bedrooms, two kitchens, assorted sitting rooms, and a large banquet hall with a fireplace big enough to fit an average-sized man standing inside it, but there were over 400 people in my group, so the only space large enough to put them had been the courtyard. We'd strung a canopy of big white bulbs overhead to make it look festive. Flickering black lanterns hung from the sienna plaster walls, casting an ochre glow on the cobblestones. In the center, a huge blue and white ceramic-tiled fountain lined with glowing luminarias gurgled quietly. It would have been perfect except for the weather. It was cold. So we hired some propane heaters.

We'd just taken our seats for dinner when I looked to my left and saw a drunk American sales rep with one of the heaters tilted sideways. The guy, whose name I couldn't remember but I knew started with an S, rolled the heater slowly, almost dropping it, getting in the way of servers walking through to fill wine glasses and deliver starters. I put my napkin down, pushed my chair back, and walked over.

"Hey there," I said. "Would you mind not doing that?"

"I'm cold," he said.

I put on my most sympathetic face. "Sorry, it's just that you've already got a heater, and if you move this other one, then those people over there won't get any heat, and it'll block the servers."

He side-eyed his table and chuckled. "Have a cow, why don't you?" he muttered, then reluctantly took his seat again.

Gus glanced over at me nonchalantly, tonguing his tooth gap, and I briefly wondered how he was planning to judge me against Celeste. Would he pick the nicer one? The more accommodating one? Or would he choose the one who was most in control?

In my peripheral vision I saw a different guy get up to move the same heater as before. I waited a few seconds to see if he would really go for it. He did. I stood back up.

"Hey, can you not do that?" I said. The guy was Max Bateman—a Level 3—one of our division's up-and-coming marketing managers, known to everyone there as the guy who could get almost anything through a company expense report. Rumor had it he'd once expensed his best friend's bachelor party at the Palomino Club in Las Vegas. He was in his late twenties with thick-lashed green eyes, and I felt his gravitational pull working on me, the allure of one of those ungraspable things I always found so irresistible. If I had met him in a bar, I probably would have made out with him.

"Halley," he slurred. "I've got it all under control." He stopped and put a drunken arm over my shoulders.

"Could you just do me a favor and leave it, Max? Please?"

"I could," he said, "but that wouldn't be any fun." He grinned.

I wondered if they would ever respect me. This was the paradox of Level 1. As Service Staff, you were supposed to keep events like this running smoothly. But you had no authority to do it. Who were you to tell a Level 3 what to do? And yet, the only way to get promoted was to keep events like this running smoothly. When he tilted the big steel pole to the side, I could hear the propane inside sloshing around, imagined it spraying someone and the whole place burning down and people screaming and jumping from balconies. The headline in next month's company newsletter would read "Service Staffer Kills Group in Heater-Related Fire." I definitely wouldn't be moving to France in that case.

Max could see Gus looking over at him. He glanced sideways, made a face at one of his tablemates, and went back to his seat. Yep, he was definitely the type I would've made out with. He had a smirk that never quite left his mouth. He probably smirked in his sleep. I could picture him sitting in his college dorm room in a popped-collar polo, reading *Atlas Shrugged,* and congratulating himself for being awesome. Spending hours practicing the perfect firmness of handshake.

I sat back down again. Table chatter buzzed away, a cacophony of intersecting monologues.

"Oh yeah?" I heard a guy at the next table say. "What's the weather like in Ireland this time of year?"

The guy next to him, who was Irish, replied, "Did you see that game last night?"

They had the shifty look of feral cats whose brains were encased behind a steel wall of distraction, waiting for their turn to talk in a game where the main objective was to fill every conversational pause with sound.

"I've always wanted to go to Ireland," the first guy said. "My mother's side of the family are all from there. Dad's side are mostly Welsh."

"Oh, is that right? That game was really something."

Soon the guy whose name started with S decided to try the heater-snatch again. I moved to intervene, merely out of principle. If I backed down now, my first two interventions would have been meaningless, and I'd never be taken seriously again.

"We're cold!" the one starting with S half-shouted at me. "It's, like, five degrees out here."

Well it's a good thing I'm a fucking wizard! I thought.

I heard Celeste's voice in my head. "We're like ducks on a pond," she always said, "kicking and kicking below the surface, but perfectly composed on top."

But it became a battle of wills. Max stood, presumably as a gesture of solidarity, but didn't move. The one starting with S and I stared each other down. Other attendees stopped what they were doing just to witness this sudden test of his salesmanship skills. I got to play the role of the ridiculous micromanager who had to make an ordeal out of things as seemingly minor as heater placement, because none of them could fathom the deliberate precision that had gone into every detail of the experience they were currently complaining about. They wouldn't notice that they had edible food in front of them and implements with which to eat it, and that it was served on an appealingly decorated table, at a venue where they had been dropped off by a large moving vehicle that would later pick them up, and that they didn't have to pay for any of it. They wouldn't notice that there were entertainers to entertain them, and bartenders to make them drinks, and someone watching over it all to make sure they didn't do something stupid and inadvertently kill themselves. They would only notice the part that didn't work, and then draw everyone else's attention to it, ruining all the parts that were working in order to mold this one unsatisfactory aspect to their individual whims.

When the guy whose name started with S went for the heater a final time, the frustration and embarrassment rose up through my toes and my legs, into my stomach, through my lungs and my rapidly beating heart, and into my face.

I looked directly into his eyes and screamed, "Put it down! And don't touch it again!"

This was quite out of character for me and really unusual behavior for a Level 1. Everything went silent. Max chuckled quietly. The one starting with S looked at me like I was a raving lunatic.

Once both guys sat down, I went back to my table, red-faced. Gus gave me a sulky look—clearly he was still upset about his unimpressive donkey entrance—and went back to his conversation. Jamie Aaronson approached.

"Halley," she said, "the president would like me to tell you how inappropriate that was."

I didn't know what to say, but I wished for the day I had enough seniority to flip her the bird without consequence. "I'm sorry," I replied.

She cleared her throat. "I know you're up for a Level 2 assignment, and you're not going to get it acting like that. You need to work on being nicer."

Within minutes of the heater incident, a regional sales manager from Texas knelt down next to me, breath smelling like tequila and lime, and shouted in my ear, "Halley, come quick! The bar's out of margaritas!"

I went to the bar, and the managing bartender lifted his arms in resignation. He had no way of getting more tequila before the end of the event. I volunteered to drive to a store, since I had come to the winery by way of no-reverse rental car. On the back of a cocktail napkin, he drew me a picture of the route to the nearest supermarket. It appeared to be close by. As I jogged out to the car, keys in hand, two sales reps from Tennessee stopped me to say they were cold and ready to go. When would the buses be there?

Every time you complain, God kills a puppy, I thought.

Dinner was only halfway finished, and after dinner there would be a band, so the buses weren't supposed to be there until ten o'clock. It was eight-thirty. But I told them I'd take care of it. The women wandered off to look around.

I had almost made it to the car when the manager of the winery came running out, arms flailing.

"Excuse me! Excuse me!" he shouted after me. He had an impressive unibrow that rose and fell as he shouted.

"Miguel?" I said, turning toward him.

"The gate." He pointed behind us, panting. "It's locked."

"Okay . . ." I said.

He gestured for me to follow him. A margarita-shaped clock ticked in my mind, but I walked with him back up the dirt path to the entrance. He carried a flashlight to light the ground in front of us. Instead of going through the archway to the courtyard, we walked around the side of the house where there was another archway, blocked by a wrought iron gate. It was so quiet. The party noise was a distant chorus, a cricket song. I wanted to curl up and hide in that darkness and never go back.

"Here, see? Someone closed it," Miguel said, pointing to the gate.

"Someone from my group?"

He nodded. "This gate has to stay open. It's an emergency exit."

I had no idea why any of my attendees would be all the way over here in the first place, or why they would fiddle with a gate. It was one of those unsolvable mysteries of the universe. The mystery of the phantom gate-closer.

"I'm sorry," I said to Miguel. "I'll make sure it doesn't happen again."

He nodded, and we walked back around to the front where I sprinted to my car before anyone could ask me any more questions.

I followed the bartender's napkin map through the starlit countryside, dialed the lead motor coach driver from my cell phone, and simultaneously imagined all sorts of terrible things going wrong at the winery during my absence. The driver picked up on the fourth ring.

"Eric?" I said.

"Yes, Pumpkin?" I didn't know why he called me Pumpkin, but I let it go.

"Could you please start sending buses back? Some of the attendees are ready to go."

"Sure thing, Pumpkin," he said. "It'll take at least thirty minutes to get there though."

"Whatever it takes," I said.

I curbed the car at the store, hoping no one would notice. I wasn't taking any risk that I would have to back out of a parking space. I ran to the liquor aisle and bought every bottle of tequila they had, balancing them in my arms on the way back out to the car. Then I floored it back to the party.

A few people were huddled together under the archway as I walked through to the courtyard. They had called a taxi because they were "freezing to death." Two of them were the complainers from Tennessee. I sidestepped them to get to the bar and, in my haste, lost hold of one of the bottles of tequila in my arms. It smashed on the ground in a loud shatter, unleashing the bitter, woody perfume of Jose Cuervo into the air. Miguel came out of the building and scowled. But I had to get the intact bottles to the bartender before Gus noticed that the margaritas had run out. Maybe he already had. I ran ahead and promised to be back quickly, my right palm out in a gesture of apologetic submission. When I came back Miguel had already taken a broom and dustpan and cleaned up the glass, and he told me to go away.

As I stood near the courtyard's entrance, it seemed like there was something I was supposed to be doing, but I couldn't remember what. The after-dinner performers, a local band, had started setting up on a stage adjacent to the bar. They were all in good spirits despite the chill in the air. The first empty bus arrived, and the group of people huddled under the archway (whose taxi never came) rushed to get on. Dessert was being served in the courtyard, but people started getting up to leave as soon as they heard wheels crunching over gravel. About half of the group did seem to be having fun, which fractionally redeemed me. The band started to play. Despite the fact that I was paying them to be there, I felt guilty that no one really watched them.

As more buses arrived, more people got up to leave. In twenty minutes, all of the attendees had gone. The band manager asked me if I wanted the band to keep playing. Waitstaff collected dishes and pulled linens off the tables. The bartender packed up all the unopened bottles of tequila I'd just needlessly fetched from the store.

"Sure, one more song," I said.

I grabbed an untouched crème caramel from one of the vacant tables, pulled a chair up in front of the stage, and took a big bite. The band played a cover of "Hotel California," and I ate my dessert in solitude.

7

EARLIER THAT SAME evening, Celeste had finally arrived in San Francisco. She'd had just enough time to fetch her tire-marked Tumi from the baggage carousel and get a cab to the hotel before it was time to set up for the after-party. She checked in and changed clothes, gulped down a few gulps of mineral water from a glass bottle bearing a paper neck-tag that said "$7.00," and headed for the elevator, where she pushed P for penthouse.

It was among the more elegant penthouses we had ever rented, with long picture windows and velvet curtains the color of blood. There were ornate gueridons holding silver candelabras and huge vases of fresh white hydrangeas perched on polished sideboards.

Celeste had hired the penthouse for Gus to host "after-dinner drinks with a few friends," and she spent the next two hours moving furniture, showing the DJ and karaoke machine guys where to set up, and stocking the pantry with liquor and mixers. Gus always demanded that no hotel staff be present at his parties; the attendees would make their own drinks, thankyouverymuch, so as to have no potential witnesses to the inevitable debauchery.

I texted Celeste to let her know that the group would arrive early; the first bus left a full hour before scheduled. She wrote back to let me know everything was ready. By nine-thirty our people, already tipsy from copious margaritas and seemingly hungry for chaos, started streaming in through the penthouse's double doors.

The suite was large enough for thirty or forty people to fit comfortably among its various rooms. But for the seventy or eighty that showed up, the entryway resembled a Vegas night club—bodies so densely packed together you could barely move. I went up to check on Celeste, but when I saw the mayhem I turned back toward the elevator. Celeste liked these parties, where, according to her, she could watch "rich people get drunk and make poor-people decisions." But they made me feel uncommonly lonely. They reminded me just how much of an outsider I was, and how desperately I wanted to be an insider.

I'd just pressed the down arrow when Max Bateman approached.

"You didn't have to yell at us earlier, Halley," he said. "I think you owe S—and me—an apology."

I was silent for a moment, and I'm sure my face flushed. I considered ignoring him.

"You owe us an apology," he repeated. "S— isn't here at the moment, but you can apologize to me. I'll pass the message along."

"Max." I laughed uncomfortably.

"You're being really unprofessional," he said. "You embarrassed us in front of a bunch of people. Just say you're sorry, and we'll call it even."

My narrow shot at Level 2 still lingered in the distance.

And I wanted him to go away. So I swallowed my embarrassment and my pride and said I was sorry.

"That's better, Halley," he said in his most managerial tone. The elevator doors opened, and I stepped inside, bound to spend the rest of the night thinking of all the things I should have said.

I reached my room, closed the door behind me with a sigh of relief, and became myself again. It was luxuriously quiet. Phil Collins swam in tranquil circles inside his travel aquarium. Housekeeping had turned the bed down and the hotel catering department had sent me a box of chocolates. I stretched my tired, sore body under the covers and savored with anticipation the six hours of uninterrupted sleep that lay ahead. Delicious exquisite sleep. I wanted to inhale it like an ambrosial fog. I stared at the ceiling in the dark, listening to hotel sounds. Muffled hallway conversations. Intermittent banging from unknown origins. The ringing of my cell phone. I considered letting it go to voicemail.

"Hello?" I said.

"Halley? This is Jacques Dubois." He cleared his throat then, as if he was about to say something really important. "My room is right next to the outdoor waterfall of the hotel, and it is very noisy. I am trying to sleep. I cannot. Will you ask the hotel to turn this waterfall off?"

I was silent for a pause. "Okay," I said, "I'll see what I can do."

He hung up.

I lay there for a few minutes, on the verge of sleep. The phone rang again.

"Hello?" I answered.

"Halley?" a young man's voice asked.

"Yes?"

"What time is breakfast in the morning?"

I mentally cursed Molly for not getting my agenda booklets done.

"Seven," I said.

"Okay," he said, and then his tone changed. "So . . . what're you doing?"

I hung up.

Five minutes later, the phone rang again.

"Hello?" I said in an exasperated voice.

"Miss, this is Jordi from the front desk. I am calling to tell you that one of your meeting attendees, Mr. Darren Clevenger, was just sent by ambulance to the hospital."

"What?" I said, sitting up. "Is he okay?"

Jordi didn't know what the emergency was, only that Darren wasn't dead. He gave me directions to the hospital, which was about ten minutes away. I rose heavily and put my clothes back on. I pulled my hair into a ponytail, didn't bother with makeup, and told Phil Collins I'd be back. As I walked through the dimly lit lobby, noticing the group of French and Korean managers huddled together out front, smoking cigarettes, it occurred to me that I should tell Gus what was happening, so I took the elevator back up to the penthouse.

By the time I got there, the group had already drunk all of the liquor Celeste had stocked for the entire duration of the meeting. When I stepped off the elevator, hotel banquet staff had just arrived to deliver more. I watched their faces as Celeste guided them to the pantry, surveying the damage the group had done. People danced on tables and chaises. A few people in the hall were playing bumper cars with stolen laundry carts, captains steering the carts from behind while passengers sitting in baskets that usually held soiled sheets and towels screamed happily. A picture had fallen off the wall and lay broken on the floor. Max had ordered twenty room service pizzas and expensed them, and half-eaten pieces of pizza lay facedown on rugs. Someone urinated into an aluminum umbrella stand in the corner, bracing himself against the wall with his shoulder. People sat in a circle, playing a drinking game with a whole bottle of Johnnie Walker Blue. I heard what sounded like two people having sex in one of the closets.

This was the after-hours version of our world, a place of blind, careless destruction, where the liquor and all its consequences were paid for by somebody else. We were primates, dripping with chemical lust for the only two things in the universe that mattered: sex and power.

According to company veterans, Findlay hadn't started out this way. Its evolution had been complex. Austerity had been the dogma of the founding generation and, even in the midst of wild success, business had been an economical affair. The founders possessed an innate vigilance, a frugality that came from knowing what it was like to live without. They passed their philosophies on to the second generation, and the second generation followed suit. But the second generation was decades removed from the hardships that had shaped the founders, and so restraint would never be part of their DNA. They were a bit spoiled. And by the time the third generation came along, all evidence of thrift was beginning to disappear. Rampant prosperity had been the standard for so long that even the founders, many of whom were still around, had begun to forget how they'd gotten there. They all had the sense that they would never die.

But that was only one piece of it. It's easy to write mischief off as pure moral decay, but that wasn't the whole story. Generation 3 may have been spoiled and decadent, but their work environment also had a completely different set of challenges than the founders had. When the founders started, there was almost no competition for their products. They didn't have mobile phones or email or websites. Information didn't yet move at the speed of thought. They had not yet embarked upon a global venture that required them to be "on" twenty-four hours a day. Their personal lives and their work lives were still separate, whereas Generation 3 came of age in a world that created more information in a week than humanity had created in its first two hundred millennia. Reputations could be made and broken at the speed of a Tweet. Socialization went digital, and someone was always watching. The founding work ethic had been preserved, but it was no longer a matter of working from nine to five and going home. The phones stayed on. And as the world spun faster, so did everyone's need for escape. Kicking back and having a few drinks was their chance to turn it all off. The harder they worked, the more they used those phones. The more they used those phones, the more money they made, and the more they needed to escape. The more professional by day, the more debauched by night. Morals loosened. Bank accounts overflowed. The parties got bigger. And they had us—their Service Staff—to clean up the messes.

Next to the fireplace in the living room, Gus had his arm around a blonde sales rep sitting on his lap, a Level 2 named Lauren Miller. Lauren was a new rep from Los Angeles whose claim to fame was appearing on *MTV's Spring Break* in college and, whilst dancing on a platform in the middle of a swimming pool, getting accidentally kicked in the head by 50 Cent. We'd all heard her tell the story at least a dozen times. Celeste referred to her as "turkey-on-white" because when she came to meetings she always demanded plain turkey sandwiches on plain white bread for every meal, which we always made and kept in a cooler for her under the hospitality desk.

Gus and Lauren sang a duet of "Let It Be" on karaoke and had a whole group sing-a-long thing happening with the others gathered around. All of Gus's paranoia and sulkiness disappeared when he drank, and the old hedonist in him came out. I leaned in to tell him about Darren. He lowered the microphone a couple inches, mouthed an "okay," and went back to singing. Almost immediately he would forget I had spoken to him, and when he found out secondhand the following day about the ambulance and the hospital, he would ask me irritably why I hadn't briefed him.

I followed the blue GPS arrow toward the hospital, eyes darting back and forth from screen to road, trying to imagine what could have possibly happened to Darren. This wasn't the first time a meeting attendee had been rushed to an emergency room. At a dinner activity in a bowling alley in Atlanta, Georgia, a woman tripped on the slick wood floor and cracked the back of her head open. Another woman, during an awards banquet, complained that her head was "exploding" and promptly had a stroke on the hotel terrace. During a different sales meeting, a guy went into cardiac arrest on the floor in the hotel hallway. I hoped this wasn't going to be one of those nights.

My phone rang, and I had to fish it out of my coat pocket.

"Hello?"

"Hey, Halley!" a voice bubbled. "Can you tell me what time breakfast is tomorrow morning?"

"Seven," I said.

I drove past ground-lit pear trees, the occasional saxophone player, strings of red paper lanterns floating above the street. San Francisco was awake with fluorescent energy. People meandered the streets and crowded in front of bars. I turned the radio off and rolled the windows down, letting the cool air and the noise clear my head. I was no longer tired when I walked through the sliding glass door of the sterile white emergency room.

The nurse at the window informed me that Darren had come in with heart attack symptoms. He would describe it all to me later in more detail. It had started at the welcome reception, a bit of nausea he attributed to just being tired. On the return bus, jostling over bumps in the dark, he sat dizzily in a window seat next to a sales rep from Oklahoma, who talked nonstop about her new blog. That was when the sweating began, and he wondered if maybe he was getting the flu. Drunken bus conversations seemed to echo in his ears. The walls started closing in. He prayed he would just make it back to his hotel room without vomiting. He thought of how much he wanted to be home in his quiet apartment reading a book. He began to lose his breath. By the time he reached his hotel room he knew that something was seriously wrong.

His chest seized painfully; his heart palpitated. He called the front desk with the hope that they had someone on staff who could come and take a look at him, maybe listen to his heart. But the receptionist needed to play it safe, so he called the ambulance. Two huge men entered Darren's room with a first aid kit and a red plastic backboard. They asked him questions, which he answered politely. He wondered silently if his condition was serious enough to warrant this, and simultaneously hoped it wasn't and it was: he wanted to go back to bed, but he also didn't want to look like an idiot boy crying wolf. They strapped him onto the backboard and carried him to the freight elevator, which was being held open by several hotel house-keepers who'd gathered to help if they could. Soon he was closing his eyes to the bright interior ambulance lights as they raced through the California night.

Darren had had a panic attack, the nurse said. He was doing fine but they wanted to keep him on watch for a couple hours. I could go back to the hotel and wait for their call or I could stay. I stopped by his curtained bed to tell him I was there, and then went to sit in the waiting room. My phone rang.

"Hello?"

I could hear party noise in the background. "Halleeeey!" someone said.

"Yes?" I said.

"What time does breakfast start?"

"Seven."

Darren was finally released at 4:00 a.m. We shuffled out to the Fiat side by side, both of us bleary-eyed. He apolo-gized a few times, but neither of us really felt like talking. I put the key in the ignition, and then remembered about the gearshift.

"God damn it," I mumbled.

"What?" he said nervously.

"I don't suppose you happen to know how to put a car like this in reverse?"

"Seriously?" he replied. He looked at me like I was about to tell a joke.

I didn't flinch.

He looked down for a second, put his hand under the gearshift and lifted up on something I couldn't see. And the shifter moved smoothly across and up to R.

"Gah! How did you do that?"

"There's a little lever under there," he said, and he moved it up and down a few times with his two middle fingers.

"Oh my god, Darren, thank you!" I said.

"No problem."

"No, really," I said with a deep sigh. "Thanks."

He looked out the window as I drove. I thought maybe he'd fallen asleep until he spoke. "Did you tell Gus?"

I wasn't sure if my response would be pleasing or displeasing to him. "Yeah," I said.

He cleared his throat uncomfortably. "I'm not a total wuss, you know."

"Okay," I said.

He paused. "It's just . . . well, all this. It's great, don't get me wrong. But . . . sometimes I get the feeling that I could drop dead and no one would notice."

"I know exactly what you mean," I said.

Twenty minutes later I arrived back to my quiet room, bone-bushed. I would have given anything to lie down and sleep for twenty-four straight hours. I sat on the edge of the bed contemplating defection. But, France. So I got in the shower. I put my contacts back into stinging, bloodshot eyes. I pulled on my business suit and went down to the vast, empty meeting room. The first hungover attendee who showed up for breakfast an hour later drank a full glass of orange juice and then vomited all over the floor in front of my hospitality desk.

8

"HALLEY FAUST?" THE woman said. She wore the white button-down shirt and black vest of hotel staff. A dented and worn cardboard box was perched on the shiny gold luggage cart she pushed in my direction.

"Yes?" I said.

"This package was delivered for you."

It was my box from Ohio. That evil goddamned demon. So Molly had sent the box after all. Of course she would; that way she couldn't be blamed for not sending it. But she'd timed it so that it would arrive precisely when I didn't need it anymore, after I'd already gone to the trouble of having everything reprinted. And there wasn't a damn thing I could do about it.

"Thanks," I said. I wanted to kick the thing down the hall, blow it to smithereens. Instead, I chucked the box under the hospitality desk's maroon skirt.

The hospitality desk sat in the expansive atrium outside the general session room, where Celeste and I would be stationed during the meeting, being hospitable. The ceiling rose three levels, with surrounding windows into all the meeting spaces. It was like a reverse panopticon; at any given moment, I knew someone was watching me.

All morning I'd been there to direct confused people to where they needed to go, in the absence of printed agendas. At least thirty people had been late, a cacophony of opening and closing door latches. Anthony Kale, the company president—Level 8—hated the disruption, everyone reveling in the delicious, self-righteous relief that it wasn't them as they turned around in their seats to check the identity of the next tardy schmuck. No doubt Anthony was formulating a new policy about locking the doors at 8:00 a.m., planning for the Service Staff to enforce it.

Now the morning session had gotten underway, and tales of networking and personal branding and increasing productivity through effective onboarding drifted through door cracks. The atrium was empty, so I went downstairs to confirm lunch timing with the banquet captain. As I traversed the lobby, Stuart Nadeau from Canada—whose death Darren had predicted a few months back—limped in from the street, missing a trouser leg. On the outside, he looked as boring and conservative as they come—case in point, this morning he was still wearing his name badge from the welcome dinner—but he was always getting into some kind of trouble. My favorite Stuart story was the one from the Nashville Marriott. He shit himself one night and, perhaps out of embarrassment, locked his diarrhea-filled underwear in his hotel room safe before checking out the next morning. I guess he thought the hotel wouldn't be able to get the safe open without his password, and the soiled garment would be preserved there for all eternity. But he was wrong. That was a nice little surprise for hotel housekeeping. They had to declare his room a biohazard and bring in the guys with the plastic hazmat suits.

I stared at Stuart's missing trouser leg. "What happened to you?" I asked. He looked like he'd been attacked by a wild animal.

When he saw me, he speed-limped over to the elevator and disappeared behind slowly-closing doors, submerging himself in our ever-deepening ocean of company secrets. I didn't see him again for the rest of the day.

I reviewed the lunch and dinner orders with the captain while the hotel manager, in his elegant charcoal suit and purple tie, approached to express some concerns about the penthouse.

"Yes, we'll pay for the damages," I said. "Just add it to our master bill." It was the same conversation Celeste and I had with hotel managers at almost every meeting. For all of Findlay management's preoccupation with status and sales, they were much less concerned about budgets and property damage. Gus called it "the price of doing business."

"I think we'll remove any valuable items from the suite before your group comes back again tonight, if that's okay," he said, nervously twisting one of his cuff links.

"Of course," I said.

When I returned to the hospitality desk, Celeste was there looking well-rested in a vintage blue pinstripe. But I could tell she hadn't slept much because she'd pulled her black hair into a slick ponytail, something she only did when she was too tired to shower.

"What time did they finally wrap up last night?"

She looked reflexively at her watch. "Around four. You should've seen the place." She grimaced.

"I heard. The hotel manager just cornered me in the lobby." Now it was my turn to make a face. "I told him we'd pay for it. They might have to replace the carpet. Who ordered the pizzas?"

"Max. I swear, that guy can get anything through an expense report. I told him he'd have to pay for the pizzas himself, since we'd already paid for everyone's dinner."

"That must have gone over well."

"Yeah, he laughed, picked up the phone right in front of me and charged it all to his room. In the end I let him do it because I figured fewer people would get alcohol poisoning if they ate more."

"Best laid plans. Housekeeping was down here at 7:30 a.m. with their wet vac." I motioned with my eyes. "Right there."

"Ew. Sorry," she said.

We powered up our laptops and began checking our email, using these moments of relative calm to get caught up on other things. I loved the music of Celeste's fingernails tapping computer keys. Click, click, click, click. She paused to ruminate on something and leaned back in her brass banquet chair, kicking the cardboard under the table.

"Ah, I see the box finally got delivered," she said.

"A lot of good it did, after I scrambled to get everything reprinted at the last minute."

"How did you get around the agenda issue? There doesn't seem to be any mayhem."

"Oh, there was mayhem. Then I made a slide of the agenda and gave it to the A/V guys. They've been projecting it on the screens during all the breaks."

"Nice," she said. I took this as a compliment and mentally forgave her for laughing when I was sick.

We heard the general session room door open, and Jamie Aaronson came jogging out.

"If you are unable to reply to me in a timely manner," she said to Celeste, "you should assign someone else who can!"

I glanced at her with one raised eyebrow.

Celeste looked down at her phone. Jamie had called seven times in the last two minutes.

She looked at Jamie and smiled. "What can I do for you?"

"I need to make sure Anthony and Gus aren't sitting at the same table tonight. Did you put Anthony at my table like I told you?"

Celeste flipped her binder open to the dinner tab and pulled out an email Jamie had written on the subject, reading the list of vice presidents and their spouses aloud. "You asked for Dave Thompson, Steve Carlson, Sandy Carlson, Harold Stein, Donna Stein, Marco Crescendi, and Caroline Aft to be at your table."

"No, Celeste. I'm *sure* I told you to put Anthony at my table. I was afraid this would happen. And you know how Gus gets on his nerves . . ."

"It's no problem, Jamie. I can fix it. Who would you like to bump?"

Jamie exhaled loudly. "No one. Just *add* an extra seat."

"Sure, we'll do that."

Jamie marched back into the meeting room and pulled the door closed behind her.

"One of these days I'm going to snap and kill her," Celeste said. "I hope T.J.Maxx runs out of mom-jeans and Great Clips cuts her bangs too short."

"I hope she gets stuck in the elevator during a fire drill with that really awkward guy from third floor."

"I hope she chokes on a sandwich at lunch and Gus has to give her mouth-to-mouth."

"You are vicious," I said.

Banquet staff arrived to set up for the morning coffee

break. Among big brass coffee dispensers, they set trays of blueberry and lavender-honey parfaits. The double doors to the meeting room opened and attendees flooded out in various directions, heading toward bathrooms, elevators, food, and the hospitality desk. A line formed, every dissatisfied attendee coming to tell us of their troubles. Seven attendees asked us to change their departure flights and ground transportation to different times. Two attendees told us the meeting room was too cold. One attendee said the meeting room was too hot. Thirteen attendees wanted to change their afternoon activities. Gus asked Celeste to change his spa appointment from a shiatsu massage to a Swedish massage.

My phone rang.

"Hi Halley," Molly's voice chirped in my ear.

"Halley," the next person in line said, "the A/V tech said he needs to talk to you."

"Molly," I said into the phone, "I can't talk right now. Can I call you back?"

As if she hadn't heard me, Molly said, "Did you get the box I sent?"

"Did you get that, Halley?" the person in line said. "About the A/V guy? He asked if you'd come into the meeting room."

I nodded. "I'll call you back, okay, Molly?" I hung up.

Half a second later, the phone rang again.

"I know you would never do something as unprofessional as hang up on me," Molly said sweetly, "so that must have been a mistake. Now, are you ready to talk like a grown-up?"

"Halley," the next guy in line said impatiently, "there are no hangers in the closet in my hotel room. How am I supposed to steam my suit jacket for tonight?"

"Molly, I can't talk right now. It's the morning coffee break, and I have a line at the hospitality desk."

"Oh?" she said. "Is your job a little too much for you to handle?"

"Miss Faust," the banquet captain said from behind me, "can I order more coffee? You're close to running out."

I nodded to the banquet captain.

"I have to go, Molly." I hung up.

The phone rang again and again, but I let it go to voicemail.

"You should call hotel housekeeping; they can get you some hangers," I said to the no-hanger guy.

"Nice dress, by the way," the no-hanger guy said to me. "But I liked the outfit you were wearing yesterday better."

"Halley, there's no more coffee," Jamie said. "Can you order some more?"

"Turkey-on-white, two o'clock," Celeste said under her breath.

"I'm leaving that one for you," I said, chuckling softly as I walked away.

Lauren Miller approached. "I'm looking for Halley," she said.

"She just went to deal with coffee," Celeste replied. "Are you here for your sandwich?"

"Yes."

Celeste reached into a cooler under the desk and produced one of the sandwiches wrapped in waxed paper. "Made them myself," she said with an evil smile.

She hadn't actually made the sandwiches, I had. Before the welcome dinner I had walked down the street to a convenience store for shaved turkey and Wonder Bread.

"You must really love your job," Lauren said. "I wish I could sit around all day and just make sandwiches."

"Really?" Celeste said. "I wish I could sit around all day and just eat the sandwiches."

"Celeste, what activity did I sign up for?" It was the regional manager from Texas who'd complained about the margaritas running out last night.

Celeste consulted her binder. "You're on the list for a city tour," she said.

"I'm sick," the man said. "I'm going to have to cancel."

Celeste put on her most sympathetic face. "Company policy is that if you cancel, you have to pay for it out of pocket."

"But I'm sick," the guy said, becoming perturbed.

"Sorry, the presid—"

The man cut her off. "I never even heard about that policy. You can't just go around setting policies and not telling people about them."

"I sent you an email," Celeste said.

"Yeah, nobody reads those," the man replied. "If it's an important policy, you should tell me verbally, not send it in an email. Look, here's Jamie, I'll ask her. Jamie!"

Jamie walked over with a cup of freshly refilled coffee in hand. "Hey, Norm."

"Jamie, I'm sick, and Celeste is telling me that if I cancel my city tour I have to pay for it out of pocket. I'm wondering if you can intervene."

Jamie paused for a fraction of a second, recalling her own ironclad edict. But she couldn't resist being the hero. She waved her hand breezily and looked at Celeste. "If he's sick, Celeste, of course he can cancel. We aren't going to make people pay for their canceled activities if they're sick."

Norm looked at Celeste with lifted brow, as if she'd made some embarrassing mistake, then walked away.

Jamie turned to me. "Halley, I got a call from Molly. She

said she tried to reach you and you hung up on her? Twice?"

I looked up to gather my thoughts. "I . . . I don't think that's what happened." I glanced at Celeste, hoping for some solidarity, but she looked away.

"Well, she's really upset," Jamie said. "You need to call her and apologize, and then you need to work on being nicer."

9

OUR GALA NIGHTS were like elaborate wedding receptions: cocktails, dinner, and dancing with four hundred of your closest non-friends. We were the brides and Findlay was the groom, and we celebrated our marriage to him over and over again. We decorated and sent invitations. We chose catering and florals and linens. We hired DJs and bartenders. We picked out our dresses. We walked in with a sense of breathy glamour, each of us performing ourselves precisely as we hoped we would be seen.

The ballroom had large windows offering a 180-degree view of San Francisco, and double doors leading out to a rooftop terrace. I'd hired a local astronomer to set up a telescope on the terrace for guided stargazing. As the astronomer circled the heavens with a green laser pointer, attendees took turns standing on a ladder, facedown in the telescope's eyepiece, studying Corvus and Crater.

It was even colder that night than the night before, but the cold wouldn't be a problem this time. The attendees could stay in the ballroom or walk back to their hotel rooms at will, or they could sit around the gas fireplace on the opposite side of the terrace. There would be no transportation to worry about, no timing issues. I surveyed white tablecloths and olive leaf centerpieces, made sure canapés came out on time. The DJ had a playlist of oldies for dinner, then funk to coax people into dancing. Sales reps in smooth black suits and frothy cocktail dresses settled at their assigned tables. From across the room their eyes and their laughter seemed to glow.

Celeste stopped by to check in but didn't say much. A few minutes later she left to set up the after-party. I wondered—not in a panicky, emotional sort of way but with the scientific detachment of the overconfident—whether Celeste and I were growing apart. But what an absurd thought. A fifteen-year friendship can withstand a bit of tame competition and a few petty annoyances. We'd had worse. I took a seat at Gus's bustling corner table and listened half-heartedly to the unceasing communal chatter.

"Originally they were used to cover the sherry glass to keep the flies out," someone said.

"No, that can't be true. Really?"

A waiter passed from person to person, filling our wine glasses with a spicy Syrah.

"That's what 'tapas' means. 'To cover.' They started as just slices of meat."

"I thought they were originally strong cheeses to *cover* the taste of bad wine."

I turned to the person next to me, a regional sales manager from Belgium. "So, how is work going?" I asked, attempting to participate.

She looked at me as if I was a kangaroo who'd just spoken her first human words.

"I have been meaning to ask you, Halley," she said, "can

you put me on a later shuttle to the airport? Seven in the morning is just too early."

"Sure," I said. She turned to talk to someone else.

The seat on the other side of me was empty, so I went back to my silence.

"Did anyone else go to the tasting this afternoon?" the Belgian said to the rest of the table.

"How was it?"

"I'd like to go back to Chappelet and buy a case of that Cab to take home."

"Stag's Leap. That's what you want."

"We tried one called Rubicon that was pretty good."

"I'm telling you, go for the Stag's Leap."

As my mind drifted, a man approached our table. He sat in the empty seat next to me as if he knew he belonged there, but his presence changed the taste in the air from "off" to "on." I recognized him from pictures, although we hadn't met. Thomas Rousseau. My chest tightened. Right on cue, a waiter placed a plated entrée in front of him. Rousseau removed the napkin that was folded in the empty goblet, lifted his knife and fork, and began to cut into a piece of chicken.

We had been expecting his arrival all afternoon. Rousseau was Findlay's most important client globally, the president of a big distribution company in France and our keynote speaker for the meeting. In that room of people his face, although relatively plain if you'd seen him anonymously on the street, glowed with the appeal of wealth and celebrity. I glanced up at him, with that exhilaration you get when you finally meet someone in person whose pictures you've seen so many times. His features were lanky and pale. He had short, prematurely silver hair and full lips. His laugh-lined eyes were small behind square wire-rimmed glasses, but they were a startling shade of ice blue.

"Everyone knows the best tapas bar in Barcelona is Quimet I Quimet on Poeta Cabanyes," someone said.

I shifted nervously in my chair.

"I don't know, I really like Bar del Pla by the Picasso Museum."

"They do have good tomato bread, Gus."

"Have you been to La Cova Fumada?"

Rousseau ate silently and listened to the conversation. He glanced at me a couple times with a puzzled expression, as if he was trying to place me.

"Is that on La Rambla?" they continued.

"I don't know, I've only been there once."

"It's near the seaside. Barceloneta."

"Oh yeah. I stayed in the W Hotel over there once."

"They have a nice rooftop bar."

"The best rooftop bar is in Athens. You can see all the way to the Colosseum."

"I think you mean the Acropolis."

"Yes, that's right. The Acropolis."

"I love Greek food."

A couple people got up to replenish their mixed drinks at the bar. Gus shouted to Rousseau from across the table. "Hey, Frog. How was your flight?"

Rousseau smiled. "Who're you calling Frog? Don't you know who I am?"

Gus licked his teeth. "Are you feeling the jet lag or are you going to party with us tonight?"

"We'll see," Rousseau said.

"Well, man is not a camel," Gus said, signaling the waiter for another glass of wine. He revived the tapas discussion.

Rousseau didn't say much to anyone else, but he didn't

seem shy or uncomfortable either. His silence filled me with anticipation. I glanced over as he accidentally flung a chunk of chicken off his plate onto the tablecloth. He reached over and retrieved it absentmindedly and set it on a cocktail napkin. His hands were beautiful and clean.

He looked at me and said, "You saw that, right?"

I laughed obligingly.

"Just making sure you're paying attention," he said, straight-faced.

I looked sideways at him, and he watched me for a few long seconds. I was back in high school, and he was that impossibly cool guy. Reality seemed to pass through him and come out bigger, as if he breathed another air. I wanted to stare at him until I detected all of his flaws.

From the next table we overheard Lauren Miller utter the phrase "thinking about taking a tapeworm."

"I don't know why more people don't do it," she said.

"I did that lemonade cleanse, and it totally worked," the woman next to her said. "I mean, I had a headache for a while, but I think that's normal. It went away after a few days."

"I started a fast last week," another woman chimed in. "I can't eat any food for nine days, and I can only drink my own urine."

She was, in fact, drinking a glass of yellowish liquid. The table went silent for a few seconds.

"I'm telling you, a tapeworm is the way to go," Lauren said.

Rousseau looked at me as if we were in cahoots. "When she ends up with a wicked case of neurocysticercosis," he said, "I know a good neurologist."

I didn't know what that meant, but I laughed anyway. The idea of someone being in cahoots with me, a Level 1, was significant. My own family was not in cahoots with me. Celeste was really the only one. Maybe Darren too. We were always on one side of the desk while our "guests" remained on the other side. It was a rare thing indeed for one of them to voluntarily cross over to our side. Especially someone like Thomas Rousseau.

"I . . . thought you were French," I said, then felt stupid for saying it.

"I live in Paris," he said. "Hence the frog jokes."

"But you don't have an accent."

He took another bite. "My mother was American. My father was French. I was born in Dayton."

"You were born in *Dayton*? As in, Dayton, Ohio?" It couldn't be. Dayton was where people like me were born. Exciting people came from somewhere else.

Rousseau finished chewing. "Yes, Dayton, Ohio. That's how I got connected to Findlay."

"So . . . how did you get out? I've been trying for years."

He laughed. "My family moved to Paris when I was sixteen, to be closer to my grandparents."

This was a marvel to me. Suddenly I wanted to know everything about him, what it was like for him in Dayton, how it felt to leave, how he'd become president of his company, what Paris was like, whether he'd found happiness.

Beautiful chocolate desserts—molded layers of mousse and ganache—appeared in front of us. I was too nervous to eat, so I pushed the dessert away. Rousseau looked back at me again. "Do you ever get tired of traveling with these people?"

"Why? Do I look tired?"

"I just meant," he said, taking up his spoon. "I can see you're not a salesperson."

"Oh. No, I'm service staff." I hated saying it, revealing the filth of my caste. Surely it would change his impression of me. But he didn't seem affected.

"Ever think about doing something else? Surely there are other jobs that would get you out of Dayton."

"Well, I almost joined the Peace Corps after college," I said.

He took a bite of chocolate as the espressos and the ports were delivered. "Why didn't you?"

"One of my best friends. He joined a year earlier and got assigned to Uganda. He kept in touch by email the whole time, and one day he sent a picture of this humongous snake he killed outside the hut he was living in." I stopped, assuming the rest of the story was self-evident.

Rousseau leaned forward. "And . . ."

"And it was a huge snake! Like, six feet long."

"You didn't join the Peace Corps because of a snake?" He smiled.

"Yeah I'm terrified of snakes. I don't even like seeing them on TV."

"Sounds Freudian."

I took a sip of port. "I never thought about it that way. I'll have to stop telling people that story."

He laughed and wiped his face with a napkin. "Well at least you get to travel a bit with this job anyway. Do you ever make it over to Europe?"

"No. But I'm up for a position in France. I'll find out at the end of this meeting if I've gotten it."

"Oh, I hope you do," he said.

I reddened. "Really?"

"Yeah. You'll like it there."

"Oh," I said, understanding. He was just being nice. "I hope so."

"I've lived in Paris for twenty years, and I still love it. In Paris ugliness is beautiful. The simplest food is the best you've ever eaten. At least once a day you see someone totally captivating and something about them stays with you and follows you around . . . and then eventually you realize it's Paris."

I paused for a moment to let the words settle in, turning them over in my head. "It sounds perfect."

"Being an expat changes everything though. I never really felt like I fit in in Dayton, and I thought going to France would fix it. But what I eventually found was that I wasn't quite French, and I wasn't quite American anymore either. I was something in between."

He looked over at me, and a tiny glimmer of connection passed between us like an electrical charge.

"But, you carve your own space," he said, turning back to the remnants of his dessert. "Right?"

I thought about that for a while. I'd always believed that a place existed somewhere in the world that was exactly right for me, someplace where I belonged. I just needed to find it. It had never occurred to me that this might not be the case, and I didn't quite believe it.

"No, I actually enjoy a good sneeze," Gus said loudly, and the others erupted in laughter. I had stopped paying attention to the table chatter and had no idea what he was talking about. The company president, Anthony Kale, came up behind Rousseau and put a hand on his shoulder, which startled Rousseau so violently that he shouted and involuntarily tossed his napkin in the air, causing me to choke on the water I was drinking.

"Thomas, glad you made it." Anthony thrust his hand forward and Rousseau shook it obligingly. "We are really looking forward to your lecture tomorrow."

"Thank you. I'm glad to be here," Rousseau said. "How are Annabella and the kids?"

"They're fine. Please pass our regards on to Chloe."

"I'll do that," he said.

I glanced down and noticed the silver band on Rousseau's finger. So he was married. And yet whatever real life he had outside of this place didn't seem fully real to me. In that moment, this room seemed to contain the entirety of the universe.

I was still coughing when Anthony paused to scowl at me meaningfully. Findlay had a "no fraternization with clients" policy, and his look said I'd better keep it professional. He walked away.

"My god, he came out of nowhere!" Rousseau whispered. "Like a ninja."

I smiled at him and was silent.

"So, where were we?" he said.

"I don't remember." I took another drink of wine and tried to think of something impersonal and benign to talk about. "Are you related to Rousseau, the philosopher?"

"I don't know," he said. "Probably somewhere down the line. What was his shtick again?"

"I think he talked about goodness existing in nature. That it was the decadence of society that corrupted people. Right?"

"Don't ask me." He poured himself more wine and passed the bottle over to me, diluting my port with Syrah. I didn't mind.

"Don't you have a PhD or something?" I said, taking a sip.

"Yes, but I try not to think too much. You know, Pythagoras wouldn't eat beans because he thought they had souls."

"Okay, well I'm not sitting alone in the dark collecting urine in jars or anything."

"That's lucky for you. If you did you'd probably be talking to that woman over there instead of me."

I smiled.

"But I want to hear more about the Peace Corps," he said. "It's such a different path than corporate work; I'm trying to figure out what drew you to it."

"I don't know, I thought for a while it might be where I belonged." I paused for a second to think about how to say what I meant, so thoroughly conscious of every feeling. Anxiety, elation, stomach-churning admiration. I experienced every thought twice: once from inside my head, and once from outside looking down at myself in judgment. Time seemed to move too slowly and too quickly at the same time. "I'm always looking for *it*," I said. "Sometimes I'm not really sure what *it* is. A place, maybe. Or a person . . . That probably sounds stupid."

"I don't think so. We're all looking for *it*."

Tiny points of connection. What was it, exactly? His sense of humor? His penetrating, understanding eyes? Or was it something more mystical than that, part of some unobservable category of human experience that defies comprehension? All I can really say is that in that world, where most people passed one another without really seeing, he saw me. And it happened almost immediately, which was the first time anything like that had ever happened to me.

Others gradually moved onto the dance floor or trickled out to the terrace, and we were left among empty plates, wadded up napkins, half-drunk glasses of wine. Gus gave me a warning glance when he left the table, and I reminded myself to keep it all in check. But I didn't walk away. Rousseau and I talked and talked, about travel and getting out of Dayton, about family, and Findlay lore. Eventually, we walked out to the terrace, and he sat next to me on a padded bench. The night started to shimmer, and in a disappearing cloud of spicy cigar smoke I tilted my head back and looked at the stars. We never faced each other, only sat like that, side by side in the thoughtful velvet dark, unspeaking, as if words would have burst that evanescent yolk of happiness that descends upon my kind so rarely.

10

I tried to hold on to that feeling, but by morning it'd faded away with the wine buzz. Getting back to business as usual—proving myself when, just last night, for a couple hours, I'd been enough—felt tedious and wrong. I rose from my hotel bed at 5:30 a.m. and stood naked and hungover in front of the mirror. What was in this body? Why did it have to be so hungry for everything in the world? I looked over at Phil Collins. He didn't seem to have the answer either.

The shower was hot and relentless. I'd entered that stage of exhaustion where everything starts moving in slow motion, floating. I watched the water fall in thick lines down my abdomen. Steam drifted and curled around the ceiling's recessed light. I felt like laughing and crying at the same time, and suddenly I wanted to leap out of my skin, to kick loose the weakness and take control of myself. I wanted to feel solid and strong, but I craved resignation.

The lobby was still dim when I stepped out of the elevator. Outside the sky was dark. It was the most quiet time of day, that hour after the late-night drinkers have gone to bed and before the nine-to-fivers get up for work. In hotels it is especially quiet at that time. The heels of my shoes clicking on the marble floor echoed in the silence. I didn't meet another person on my way to the meeting room, not even hotel staff, and it gave me the gratifying and also frighteningly post-apocalyptic sense that I was the only one left.

I walked along the thinly carpeted corridor that had already become so familiar. Flipped on the lights. The meeting room was cavernous and cold. It looked chintzy without any people in it, painted white and gold with an elaborately patterned carpet. Hotel housekeepers had come through during the night and removed candy wrappers and empty water bottles from the tables. I walked down the rows and straightened chairs, enveloped in solitude that felt as infinite as death.

I sat at the hospitality desk, checked my email, and waited for the first attendees to arrive for breakfast. I envied them, being the recipients of the hospitality instead of the provider of the hospitality. Waking up stress-free, maybe a little annoyed at having to listen to lectures all day, bumbling downstairs and eating breakfast without a care. Rousseau would deliver his lecture later that morning, and I sent him a reminder about the room location. I was surprised to see his response, half-expecting the entire previous night to have been a dream.

"I knew it," he wrote. "You're one of *those* people."

"What people?"

"The ones who get up at 5:00 a.m."

"Well someone has to manage things around here. We wouldn't want Jamie's coffee to be late."

"See you in a minute," he said.

His words were birds flying through me.

Gus passed the hospitality desk wordlessly on his way into the meeting room to get mic'd up for the first session. From my seat I heard the audiovisual tech start the sound check. I watched hotel banquet staff remove lids and plastic wrap from fruit trays and chafing dishes of scrambled eggs and bacon. The hallway started coming to life.

Crowds soon gathered around coffee stations, filling breakfast plates, filing in and out of restrooms. I stayed behind the desk to answer questions. Rousseau stepped off the elevator, flanked by three sales managers all trying to keep his attention. He passed my desk in a cloud of prestige, looked into my eyes and said, "Hey." His eyes slightly wrinkled at the corners, as if we were in on the same secret. If my insides could melt and flow like candle wax from my pores, in that moment, they would have.

Gus walked up to my desk, adjusting the lavalier on his lapel. "Halley," he said, "can you and Celeste sit in on this next session? We're going to talk about the Tantalus, and it might be a good lecture for you two to hear."

"Sure," I said.

I picked up the phone to dial Celeste, but she stepped off the elevator before the line started ringing. Gus drifted back through the meeting room doors, and I motioned for Celeste to follow. We grabbed cups of coffee, Celeste's black and mine with a generous amount of half-and-half and a sprinkle of cinnamon, and took seats in the back. It was a packed house, hundreds of stars hovering in a vast solar system. Their energies were different colors. Different shapes, different sizes. That's how existence felt to me. Those I knew rose in the sky, became bigger. The Celestes were orange glowing orbs, the Clives, ultramarine supernovas. There were all manner of lesser constellations, some barely visible, like bit parts in a movie, the kind that seemed to evaporate into nothingness when they walked off the screen. But Rousseau was the center. He blazed with a brilliance that eclipsed the sun. If his spirit could have a form and a face, it would have been the size of the building in which we stood. Of course it couldn't, and it didn't; our minds and hearts would remain hidden inside these bodies. You never see the magnitude of a soul. You only get some vague idea of it.

Gus walked on stage to some booming classic rock tune he'd chosen. He was manic and giddy, snapping his fingers to the music and basking in every invisible wave of energy and attention radiating in his direction. The A/V tech faded the entrance music and the room applauded. Whether we were clapping for what had just happened or for what was to come, I couldn't rightly say.

"Now," Gus began, never quite making eye contact, "I'm going to introduce you to an exciting new product. You'll learn more about it when we officially launch next year, but I'll give you a taste now so you know what's coming."

The audience leaned forward, eager to leap over the barrier separating us from our cult leader who would deliver us from mediocrity. We were on a mission to change the world, and Gus's sheer magnetism assured us that the promise of greatness was out there, a butterfly we could catch as long as we had the right net.

A spotlight followed him as he walked back and forth across the stage. "I'm going to start with a little story," he said. "Once upon a time there were two business executives. Let's call them Jim Crook and Biff Crazos."

His pause indicated we should laugh, and we obeyed.

"Their business model is top-down: they create products they and their engineers determine are useful, and then put those products on the market for anyone who is interested in buying. They do a fair amount of research, of course: they pull together focus groups, they test concepts and conduct competitive analyses. But in the end, they rely mostly on the capacity of their team to innovate, and they also rely on the consumer to notice their product in the marketplace and buy it.

"Now, enter an executive named Gus. Gus takes a bottom-up approach to business. Instead of asking his team to come up with ideas, Gus finds out exactly what consumers want. Then his team uses that information to design products. Once designed, Gus's team precisely targets the consumers who most want the product they're selling. Knowing what people want—what they really, truly want—is the key to motivating them. It's not about us, it's about the people."

He gestured toward the audience, moved by his own magnanimity, and they burst into applause. Gus took a sip of water from a slim glass.

"The question is," he continued, "where does one get this information? How do we know what the people want? Well, ladies and gentlemen, that's what the Tantalus will do. Now, this is all proprietary, and I know a couple of executives who would love nothing more than to get their hands on this technology, so I'm not going to reveal any more than that. But if our projections are correct, the Tantalus is going to revolutionize consumerism. And that means our future together is bright."

On cue, they applauded again, as Gus stood godlike, marveling at his ability to command.

Rousseau's style of speaking was completely different

from Gus's. He wasn't a showman. His manner was intimate and conversational; he was talking only to you. He told us what was new in the industry, what was coming soon, what was missing. He talked about how useful the Tantalus would be in people's everyday lives. He made us feel noble; we were making a difference.

I felt a complex longing as I watched him. I wanted to be what he was, to be the one on stage being respected and adored. I wanted to be him, and I wanted to belong to him.

When the talk was finished and Rousseau had answered all the questions, I rose from my seat and walked out. He'd scheduled an early flight, giving himself just enough time to deliver his lecture and leave. The car we'd hired to transfer him back to the airport was sitting outside the hotel's front entrance. I waited to make sure he found his driver.

"Hey, there you are," he said when he spotted me in the atrium.

"I liked your lecture," I said.

"Oh, well don't tell anyone, but this is my eighth time delivering it. I've had time to practice."

"Ah, and here we thought we were special."

He looked at me, and I looked at my feet.

"Do you have your luggage?" I asked.

"I left my bag in my room. Are you walking me out?"

"I was going to. I can meet you downstairs."

"That's okay, it'll only take a minute. Ride up with me."

"Oh," I said.

"Is that weird?" he asked. He said it so straightforwardly and with such self-assurance that I believed nothing he said could have possibly been weird.

"No-er," I bumbled.

Damn it. No-er? What the hell was that? He smiled. We boarded the hotel elevator. He pushed the 9 button. I was sidetracked, worrying about the no-er. Why couldn't I have just said "no"? And then there we were, enclosed by lighted brushed steel on all four sides, a ball of energy hanging in the air between us like a thunderstorm. Neither of us said anything. We arrived at the ninth floor and I waited by the elevator for him to return. He came back pulling a small black suitcase on wheels.

We re-entered the elevator. I pushed the L button. I stood against the adjacent wall, afraid to look up at him, afraid he would see all the way down into me, my deranged mind, the depth of my adoration. Then I saw his right shoe advance toward me, and then his left. His hands rose to the wall on either side of me. I closed my eyes. His face brushed against my face. He breathed a deep breath in, then back out again, hesitating. He kissed my jaw, and an electric jolt went straight through me. And then I felt his lips on my collarbone. Earth was put on pause. His mouth warmed my skin. All I could think about was how badly I wanted him to kiss my mouth. Then the doors opened to the lobby, and in a second he was gone. The faint smell of him lingered in the air inside the elevator. It felt silent and empty, as if a vacuum had opened up and sucked all the life out of it.

11

I'd liked Rousseau's kiss in direct proportion to the shame I felt for liking it, and I was embarrassed by the shame. It was the shame of a child, a novice, and I was supposed to be an adult. I wanted to go on with my day as if nothing had happened, and I felt that I could. And there was the real turmoil, because the child in me—bound by the fear of the cosmic punishment that awaited me should I violate such clear and firm absolutes—said that I was supposed to be disturbed by what I'd done; I was supposed to feel terrible and promise I'd never do it again. He was married! And a client! But I didn't feel terrible. I didn't feel like I thought people who kissed married men—married clients!—should feel. Instead I was newly aware of how easy it was to do bad things and remain intact, and that awareness began to shift the boundaries of my universe. I got the disquieting and not unwelcome sense that there was some unseen current slicing through me, shaping me into something darker. I could do anything, and life would go on.

All at once my sense of urgency over the product launch was reborn, bigger and brighter than ever. Rousseau's life, Rousseau's world: I wanted to let it mold me into someone exactly like him. I imagined myself as that person. Someone whose energy matched Rousseau's energy. Someone a little bit untouchable, from whom a sort of seductive certainty would emanate in beautiful waves. It had been her in the elevator with Rousseau that day. Now the scene became much more interesting, like a movie where the bit actress is replaced with a star. She wouldn't be awkward or nervous. She'd be steady. Aloof and unsexed, face betraying nothing. No provincial fears caging her in. He might even be a little scared of her. Standing there beside her, his hand would brush against her hand and the force of her distance would turn that one small touch into something explosive and extraordinary. And when she looked at him, when he pushed her against the wall, when she kissed his mouth, when he picked her up, when she wrapped her legs around him, the world would ignite. Then the elevator door would open and she would go back to her life. No regrets. Such a complete and impervious thing. I wanted to be her so badly that the taste of it burned my mouth.

All afternoon my mind wandered, searching for a way to get there, to reach Level 2, to go to France and see Rousseau again. Then, as I reviewed the meeting's departure transportation schedule, an idea came to me. It was a vile idea. The most underhanded, deceitful idea I'd ever had. I dismissed it almost as soon as I thought it. But I kept hearing the echo of it again and again, like a song I couldn't get out of my head. Gradually I let it work on me, let it weigh the choices that would decide my fate. I could be the same polite old Halley, dripping with existential fear and self-consciousness. Halley Faust, preoccupied with being likable while everything I'd ever wanted went to someone more tenacious. Or I could be the strong, fearless, take-matters-into-her-own-hands person I'd wanted to be in the shower that morning.

I closed my eyes, picked up the phone and called the transportation company.

The next morning, hotel staff and audiovisual technicians had the Sisyphean tasks of tearing down staging and lights, switching the rooms for the next group. Tearing and building, building and tearing. Every day, never moving forward. It put me in a dreary mood. I packed leftover demo kits and marketing materials into boxes to send back where they came from. Celeste came in, clearly agitated.

"You're not going to believe this," she said, eyes glistening. "The limo never showed up to get Gus and the other execs. I had to call them cabs, and some of them didn't have cash so I had to run to an ATM; it was a nightmare."

My stomach fell, and I looked down at the floor. "That's awful. Did you call the transportation company?"

"Yeah, they were confused. Fucking idiots. They thought I canceled the car. They must have misunderstood when I called to update the other transportation yesterday."

The sound of the packing tape dispenser cut through the room as I raked it across a box. "I'm sure everyone will get over it," I said.

She rubbed her eyes with her fingers. "I don't know, they looked furious. You know how they always want to be early."

I looked her in the eye and then looked away again. "Did you tell them it was the transportation company that messed up? It wasn't your fault."

"No," she said tiredly, "then it just sounds like I'm making excuses. Anyway, it *is* my fault because I didn't reconfirm that pickup. Stupid."

The fact that she didn't suspect my treachery was so excruciating I almost confessed everything. Suddenly I regretted all of it, every little betrayal, every moment we'd spent questioning one another since the day Gus had announced the product launch. I wanted to take it all back.

"What's up with you?" she asked. "You're acting kind of weird."

"Nothing," I said.

She crouched down to the floor and started packing a stack of miscellaneous pamphlets into an empty box, waiting me out.

"Well, I spent a couple hours talking to Thomas Rousseau the other night. At the gala."

"As in *the* Thomas Rousseau? Wow. What happened?"

I thought of the kiss and a breath of heat ran through me. "It was like we knew each other in another life or something."

Celeste turned to see if anyone was within earshot. "You're not getting involved with him are you? You know that'll get you fired."

I sighed and picked at an old shipping label. "It wasn't like that. I'll probably never see him again."

She smiled. "You're actually thinking about it!"

"No, I'm not."

"Sweet, innocent little Halley who never does anything bad suddenly wants to have an affair with a married man who happens to be the company's most important client. I never thought I'd see the day."

"No, I don't! I just like him, that's all."

Celeste studied me for a few seconds. "Let's go out tonight," she said. "We could use a night out."

Her bright-eyed openness, as if everything was the same as it had always been, tormented me with guilt. "I don't feel like it," I said.

"Come on. It'll take our minds off things."

"I can't, Celeste. I'm on the 7:00 a.m. back to Cincinnati tomorrow. And you know how Phil Collins gets nervous about going through the X-ray machine. I think I should . . ."

"Look. We've been under too much stress lately." She shoved the box she was packing aside. "Tonight we're going to live."

I briefly imagined us committing some insane crime and then driving off a cliff like Thelma and Louise. Tempting.

I sighed. "I can't."

"Okay. Well . . . I just wanted to say I'm sorry I've been kind of a jerk lately." She stared at the floor. "I really wanted to go to France, but . . ."

"Maybe we should both just quit," I said, changing the subject. "Let's quit this job and move away."

"I'm being serious," she said. She grabbed my hand and held it, like she used to do when we were kids, and for a moment I was transported back in time. A wave of self-loathing hit me so hard I burst into tears. I wanted to leave, or get into a fight, or drive off that cliff. Anything but this. Celeste mistook the tears for happiness and came in for a hug, and I pulled away. I wiped my eyes with grubby fingers, got up, and walked out of the room.

12

"How was your flight?" my mom asked. I held Phil Collins's travel aquarium firmly under one arm as I pulled my suitcase toward her familiar plum-colored sedan in the freezing-cold parking garage.

"It was fine," I said. "We watched a movie."

Musty heat blew from the defroster and the light rock radio station played Celine Dion. It was remarkable how business trips always made Dayton's relative poverty feel oppressive and filthy. How vulgar my mother's red nail polish looked in the winter light. I felt a guilty shame for her that made me want to hide my eyes.

"I brought you back some Dandelion chocolate," I said.

"Oh. They put dandelions in chocolate?" She chuckled softly. "That sounds like something they'd do in California. Your dad will eat it."

I shifted in my seat. "I don't think they put dandelions in it."

"Then why do they call it that?"

"I think it's just the name of the store," I said, taking the bars out of my bag. "Here, why don't you just try one?"

"No, thanks," she said. "But I'm sure Dad will love them."

I studied her while her eyes focused on the road ahead. I'd been back in Ohio for twenty minutes and we were already on that same old merry-go-round. I should have been content to keep things like this for myself. If she didn't want them, I didn't need to share them. But I did need to share them. Alone they felt less real.

"Why won't you just try it?" I half-shouted.

A silent wave of tension filled the car. She gave me an icy look.

I started to scan the ingredients on the wrapper and wondered, petulantly, how my heart could contain so much life that she would never know. To think that anyone could spend so much time studying your cries and your gestures and still have no idea who you really were was bewildering. It was one of those childhood absolutes, that mothers were supposed to be penetrating, all-knowing beings. But, in our case, the more time passed, the smaller we seemed to become to one another. I felt cheated.

I gave up and put the bars back in my bag.

Neither of us spoke for most of the ride back to Dayton. We passed pro-life billboards and one-pump gas stations. A red and white cement truck swirled down the highway like a fat candy cane. There was my old high school. Here were the derelict cars that hadn't moved in a decade. I searched a ragged cornfield for the spot where I'd had my first kiss, damp and exhilarated and unaware of a future outside of that moment. They floated up to me, memories and smells like scraps rising from a shipwreck. Trips to the mall when we used to beg Mom to let us sit in the massage chairs at the Sharper Image. Riding in the rusty bed of my dad's pickup truck, the side-wind so strong it blew your hair straight over your face. The way an orange Popsicle stick smells after you've eaten the Popsicle. Nights full of imagining princesses and castles, writing our names in the air with sparklers and believing in a world of infinite light, so big and mysterious it couldn't be contained. I'd just begun to edge far enough past all of it that the first complicated traces of nostalgia twisted within me. It wasn't nostalgia for this place. It was nostalgia for who I'd been, for the imagined future that I still hoped would one day match up with reality.

"Uncle Larry and Aunt Jo said they want to come visit you if you move to Europe," my mom said a little more brightly.

"No way," I replied without thinking.

She glanced sideways at me.

"Remember the last trip we took with them?" I said. "When he touched that painting in the museum and set off the alarms?"

My mom pursed her lips and stared at the road.

The air outside smelled like freezer burn and auto mechanic fingers. We got a table near the front of the Cracker Barrel and ordered two Diet Cokes. My parents loved Cracker Barrel. It was one of the only restaurants that my dad hadn't given what he called "the axe" for some permutation of unacceptable food, bad service, or steep prices. I started playing with the golf tee game in the middle of the table while my mom decided whether to order from the breakfast or the lunch menu. A toddler at the next table buried his face in his mother's chest as if she was the source of all good feelings in the world. I pulled Phil Collins's food out of my purse and sprinkled a few flakes into his travel aquarium. Still skittish from the trip, he emerged from his castle, looked around, and then went back in again. Probably the scary farm kitsch hanging on the walls didn't help.

"Mike is in town," my mom said. "I saw his mom at the store yesterday."

"Hmm," I said.

"Are you going to meet up with him?"

I sighed. "No, probably not."

"Why not?" she said.

"Because he's not the right person for me. And spending time with him will just lead him on, and then I'll have to let him down again."

She looked thoughtful for a second, and I wondered if she might break character and tell me that I was a good person, or at least good enough, and that I deserved to get what I wanted. Instead, she said, "Mike is a great guy. What do you think it is about you that causes you to be like this?"

I looked at her tiredly. "I don't know. What do you think it is?"

"I don't know either. Your sister never had these kinds of problems."

"Don't worry," I said. "I'm fine."

I finished the golf tee game with three remaining and started over again.

She took a drink of her Diet Coke. "You know your dad is drinking about ten Cokes a day now."

I laughed. "Why?"

"He read on the internet they dissolve kidney stones."

"Probably *cause* kidney stones is more like it," I said, sipping through my straw.

She sighed, unrolling her silverware bundle and arranging the paper napkin on her lap. "Well," she said, "someone wouldn't go to all the trouble of putting it on the internet if there wasn't some truth to it."

I turned my attention back to the golf tee game and hopped the last one over. "Look. It says here I'm a genius."

"I've never seen anyone do that without cheating," she replied with a half-smile.

The next morning Gus called me to his office. My bowels tightened as I crossed the gray speckled carpet, the floating walls smelling of wood cleaner. I crossed and uncrossed my legs, waiting next to Poor Charlene's desk. I avoided eye contact with the cappuccino machine the way people afraid of heights won't look over the edge of tall buildings for fear they might accidentally throw themselves off. A few long moments later Gus's door opened a crack, and I stood. I passed the windows with their king's-eye view of the parking lot and sat in one of the wing-back chairs while Gus finished typing something on his computer. My pulse pounded in my ears.

"Give me just . . . one . . . more . . . second . . . Halley." He tapped another key. "There." He turned to face me.

"Oh, you look nice today," he said, scanning my hunter green shirtdress up and down.

I choked out a "thanks."

"Did you have a good flight back?"

"Sure," I said. "Yeah, uneventful."

"That was some meeting," he said. "Did you hear about the trouble with our limo?" It may have been my imagination, but he seemed to be eyeing me as if this were some kind of inside joke.

"Yes," I said.

His mouth formed a wicked grin, tongue flashing between his tooth gap, then flattened again.

"Halley, we want you to join the launch team. I am officially offering you the position."

I let out a breath. "What?"

I lost some of what he was saying, preoccupied with how to adequately express myself. Should I give him a hug? Shake hands? Was "thank you" enough? Should I gush about how much this was going to change my life, or was that unprofessional?

"We'll need you to be ready to move in two weeks. Can you do that?"

"Okay," I said. "I mean, yes, absolutely, I can do that."

I tried not to giggle like an idiot.

"Do you need time to think about it? Keep in mind that you'll be taking a risk. We will have to backfill your position here. I can promise you that you'll have a job when the launch is over, but it might not be a job you want."

"Oh," I said. "No, I don't need any time."

He continued as if I hadn't spoken. "If the launch goes well—and we have every reason to think it will—you can have the Level 3 position that I mentioned before."

I crossed my legs again. Holy shit. I could be a Level 3.

"Of course we have to wait and see. There are others who want that position too."

I thought of Molly. For certain she'd be jockeying for it. Then my thoughts sobered. "What about Celeste?"

"I know. Well, it was a tough decision. Maybe something else will come up for her. You should plan to bring her over for the final event in Paris next year, to help you on-site. We'll need all of our best people there."

I nodded.

He cleared his throat. "That's settled then. HR will get all the paperwork to you. They already have a new cell phone for you, and you'll be getting your company car when you move in to your new apartment in France. They're also working on our visas—oh, did I tell you who else will be on the team? It'll be you, me, and Darren, of course, plus Max Bateman and Lauren Miller. The company is putting us up in a town called Biot. It's cheaper than living in a big city like Paris or Barcelona, and it's close to an international airport. They originally wanted to put us in the Heidelberg facility, but I asked that we be a bit isolated from the rest of the corporate nonsense so we can actually get things done.

"Anyway," he continued, "HR will talk to you about insurance, shipping your stuff, everything in your expat package. Your pay will stay the same, but you'll get a cost-of-living allowance and an expat bonus, and Findlay will do a tax equalization for you, so you won't be paying any more taxes than what you would have been paying here."

He studied me for a few seconds, then decided we were done here. "If you don't have any other questions for me, then I'll see you in France. I leave tomorrow. Travel will book your ticket; just give them a call."

It happened so fast. I rose from the chair and floated out of his office in a state of semi-disbelief. Even after what I'd done in San Francisco, part of me still figured Celeste would get the job. I wasn't lucky enough to land an opportunity like this. I almost believed this might be a practical joke, my just desserts for the transportation company thing. Any minute Gus was going to come back out of his office and say, "Heh, just kidding, we're taking Celeste after all."

But he didn't. And suddenly what I'd done to Celeste became bigger. It was more than one betrayal. It was the rest of our lives.

The office looked different to me now. Was it my imagination, or was Poor Charlene's face a little bit less friendly? The air in the building felt a little chillier. I felt like a dead woman walking, this seeming coolness of the world's gaze along with the fear and the relief and the anticipation of soon leaving it all behind.

I almost bumped into Baldwin Frank, standing in front of Gus's cappuccino machine. Chad Johnson stood beside him.

"What are you doing, man?" Chad whispered. "Are you nuts?"

Baldwin didn't reply, didn't even look around to see who was looking. With a sure hand, he shoved his Kelley School of Business coffee cup under the nozzle, toggled through the drink options, and pushed a button.

It took me a few seconds to register what was happening here. Baldwin Frank, using Gus's off-limits cappuccino machine. I wanted to shake him. What the heck was he thinking? Poor Charlene stared at him with the horror of someone witnessing a rape. Chad and I looked away, then back, then away again. Baldwin offered no explanation besides a look of desperate, end-of-your-rope menace. I stepped back slowly for fear I might appear complicit. The coffee finished making with a satisfying "scree," and Baldwin pulled the cup to his lips and took a sip. This appeared to steady him, and he took another, bigger drink. We stared. And just when I thought he'd gotten away with it, that maybe the world I knew wasn't the world at all, Gus poked his head out into the hallway, locked eyes on Baldwin, and called him into his office.

"Baldwin Frank just got canned," Darren said when I saw him in the hallway. "Something about a direct-to-consumer sales idea that lost the company a bunch of money."

Word traveled fast. "He drank Gus's coffee," I said.

"No way!" Darren shouted, then lowered his voice. "Really?"

"I was there; I saw it happen. Poor guy. He had this crazy look in his eye."

"Damn," Darren said, scratching his fingers together.

I still couldn't figure out why he'd done it. Baldwin knew as well as anyone else what the rules were. Temporary insanity? Problems on the home front? I wondered if the whole ordeal should mean something.

Celeste was hanging up the phone when I got back to our cubicle.

"Well," she said, "the transportation company still insists I canceled that car. Leona says she spoke to me on the phone, and that I told her to do it."

I didn't say anything. The fluorescent lights overhead felt uncommonly bright. She turned to look at me.

"Was that . . ." She paused. "Were you just meeting with Gus?"

The area around us went silent and I could tell everyone in the vicinity was listening to us now.

"Yes," I said.

"What did he say?"

I braced myself, knowing this was going to hurt. My eyes squinted into a sad grimace. "He gave me the job."

"Oh," she said, sitting back in her chair. "That's great. Congratulations, Hal. We'll have to go and celebrate . . ."

Her eyes narrowed, and she looked out into space. Then straight back at me, realization darkening her features.

"No," she said slowly.

I looked down at the floor.

"The car company," she said. "Tell me it wasn't you. You'd never do something like that to me."

The moment was upon me so quickly. My mind wound

in circles and I couldn't think fast enough to lie. If I had she wouldn't have believed me anyway. She knew me.

"You wouldn't do that, right?" she whispered. "Halley?"

"I'm sorry," I said. "I'm so sorry, Celeste."

I wanted to take it all back. Everything I'd ever done wrong, every lie I'd ever told, every mean thought I'd ever had, every hurtful thing I'd ever said. I wanted to do some extra nice stuff that very minute to convince her I was still the same old me. I looked into her eyes and saw the sea change, and I knew our relationship would never be the same again, and the seeming finality of it was almost unbearable. I thought of the day in sixth grade when Celeste braided strands of our hair together and made me wear them as friendship bracelets. And sophomore year when her dad caught us trying to pierce our belly buttons in the downstairs bathroom with nothing but a sewing needle and ice cubes. And my first day at Findlay, when Celeste left a strawberry cupcake on my desk.

A fat tear rolled down her cheek. "Get the fuck out," she said. "I hope I never see you again."

It knocked the wind out of me. I fell heavily into my swivel chair as panic stabbed me in the chest. It's astonishing, the human capacity for catastrophic harm. That we can spend decades building grand palaces and then, in a matter of minutes, shatter them all to pieces. Celeste rose from her chair, packed her laptop into her bag along with a couple files, and grabbed her coat.

"You are a fucking monster," she said without looking at me and walked out. She didn't say where she was going—maybe another part of the building, or maybe she took some time off and went home—but she didn't come back. It would be a long time until I saw her again.

13

THE NIGHT BEFORE I left Ohio, suitcases packed and waiting by the door, I pulled my hair into a ponytail, tugged on a pair of jeans and a black sweater. The highways were congested with construction and it took me longer than normal to get out to my parents' subdivision. Gentry Quarters. The name always made me roll my eyes. If you have to call yourself gentry, you probably aren't gentry. Two sheriff cars were leaving the subdivision as I pulled in. I groaned when I saw my uncle Larry's Ford parked in front of my parents' house. Apparently when she'd said family dinner, my mother had meant extended family too.

Dry, savory heat wafted in my direction when I opened the door, the smell of fried chicken and Lawry's Seasoned Salt. I could hear the oil popping as my mom dropped the flour-dusted breasts into the electric skillet. I stood by the refrigerator with its plastic fruit and vegetable magnets. The house was alive with voices and feet. My dad sat at the dining room table—which my mom had extended by pushing a folding card table up next to it—double-fisting two cans of Coca-Cola and listening to Uncle Larry's latest get-rich-quick scheme. Granny, with her hair done up like the top of a cartoon ice cream cone, stood at the counter peeling potatoes and dropping them into a pot of water. Aunt Jo stirred a pan of gravy, because we couldn't have a meal without gravy. My sister Lindsay peeled biscuits out of a can (the kind you have to tap on the counter and wait, cringing, for it to pop open like a jack-in-the-box) and lined them up on a cookie sheet. My brother Luke was absent, probably in his room playing video games.

"Hey Halley," Aunt Jo said when I stepped through the door. She put down her paring knife, wiped her hands on a towel, and crossed the room to give me a hug.

"Hi," I said, sounding more energetic than I felt. "It smells good in here."

"It should be ready soon," my mom said.

"Go tell Grandpa you're here," Granny shouted. "He's in the other room."

"Are you sure I can't help?" I said.

"No, no, there's nothing else to do," my mom said.

I bent down to snuggle the dog, who vigorously licked my palm. Then I shuffled past the dining room table and into the living room. My grandpa snored on the couch with his head back and his mouth open. On the TV across from him, there was some nature show about bears mating. Two huge brown grizzlies were going at it, humping away. I was struck by the awkwardness that would ensue if my grandpa woke up at that very moment, and I walked out.

"He's sleeping," I said to Granny.

"What?" she replied. She turned to face me so she could see my lips move.

"Jesus, Mom," my mother said under her breath, rolling her eyes.

"HE'S SLEEPING," I repeated, louder.

"Well, wake him up," Granny shouted.

"That's okay, I can talk to him during dinner."

She clucked. "I'll get him. He needs to take his pills anyway." She shuffled away, and a few seconds later I heard her say, "Heavens to Betsy, Mert, what are you watching?"

"You r'member that ol' man, used t'come around with that horse-drawn ice cream cart?" Grandpa asked, pointing his fork at my grandmother. "Only flavors he had were chocolate an' vanilla, an' they both tast'd like horse." He chuckled at his own memory.

"Did you hear about Krissy Taylor, Halley?" my mom asked as she passed the bowl of gravy to Uncle Larry. "Just got married."

"Good for her," I said. In ninth grade Celeste took some photos of me for a photography project, and in one of the photos I had my head down, smelling a flower. Krissy Taylor stole the negative from the school darkroom, superimposed a penis where the flower was, and circulated the prints all over school. My parents knew about this, of course—knew that Krissy Taylor was a vicious bully—but they were in denial, as if it was a stain on my character they'd rather believe didn't exist. Both of my parents had been popular in school, just like my siblings.

"Your sister was invited to the wedding, but she had to go to Justin's family reunion that weekend," my mom continued.

"I probably wouldn't have gone anyway," Lindsay said between bites. "I'm not very close with those girls anymore; we were only friends because of cheerleading."

"She married Jason Bunt, so her last name is Bunt now,"

my mom said. "Krissy Bunt."

"I can think of a word that rhymes with Bunt that describes her better," I said.

"What?" Granny shouted from across the table, straining to hear.

"Halley Marie Faust!" my mom said.

"When are you getting married, Halley?" Aunt Jo said. "Your mother said you have a boyfriend here in town."

"He's not my boyfriend," I said. "We broke up, like six months ago."

My mom and sister glanced over at me with the disregard of people who've witnessed all of your most embarrassing moments.

"I'll tell you something," my dad chimed in. "All a man wants is a woman who'll take care of him and won't nag him. You're a pretty good cook, Halley." He gave my hand a supportive pat. "You shouldn't have any trouble."

"Lindsay, have you and Justin decided where you're having your wedding?" I asked, changing the subject.

"At church?" she said, like it was the dumbest question ever.

"Oh, I meant the reception."

She swallowed a drink of iced tea. "Yeah, I think we're gonna have it at the park."

I looked down at the diamonds on her ring finger and felt the slightest twinge of envy.

"There's a place in town where we can rent all the tables and chairs," my mom said. She smiled proudly at my dad.

Granny pulled a partially chewed piece of meat out of her mouth and fed it to the dog.

"Them Taylors been livin' up at ol' Roger Ziebert's place," my Grandpa said to no one in particular. "You remember? That ol' house on the hill? Fixed it up pretty nice, looks like a different place now. I used to go there an Roger's mother'd let us pick apples off that apple tree. Place was in shambles back then . . ."

"We're still looking for the dress," my mom said.

"She took care of it best she could, I 'magine," Grandpa continued, "but, you know, after ol' Herb died, she couldn' keep up on the yard work. I used to mow their lawn for a nickel. Can you believe that, Halley? A nickel . . ." He winked at me, and I smiled into my mashed potatoes.

"I think I'm going to make most of the food," my mom said. "Some of the ladies from church have offered to help out too. David said we could use the church kitchen, isn't that nice?"

Aunt Jo nodded.

"What's ol' Harrison up to these days, Larry?" Grandpa asked.

"Oh, he's still trucking along," Uncle Larry replied.

"I'm not going to attempt a cake though," my mom said, stage-laughing.

"I know a woman in Avon that makes beautiful cakes. Cheap too," Aunt Jo said. "Well, cheaper than most, at least."

"He's a tough ol' bird," Grandpa said. "I was sure sorry to hear about that cancer. Jus' sorry to hear it."

"He seems to be hanging in there," Uncle Larry said. "They've got him on those radiation treatments."

"What do you know about that, Halley?" Grandpa asked.

"Not much," I said. "Sorry, Grandpa."

"Well you better start findin' out. One o' these days it'll be me in there, and I might be needin' to call you up!" he said with a wheezy laugh.

"Mert, tell Halley about France," Granny said.

That was all the prompting Grandpa needed to start spinning his yarn. Everyone always said my grandfather had "the gift of gab." I've never been sure whether to be sad or relieved that this gift wasn't passed down to me.

". . . Operation Overlord," he said, "they sent us—'Ol' Reliables,' they called us—a few days after D-Day to take the peninsula so they could capture Cherbourg. Hadn't slept a wink in two days with all them planes flyin' over. I was one o' the guys landed on Utah Beach. Course, after bein' up 'ere in England with all them movies 'n dances, France looked purty shabby to me . . ."

Luke and Lindsay's eyes glazed over, but everyone else at the table appeared rapt as this relic of the Greatest Generation recounted the hallowed past. Their smiling eyes revealed a desire to return to a time none of them could remember. Uncle Larry forked another piece of chicken and silently offered the plate to Aunt Jo, who took it from his hands and set it delicately back down on the table.

". . . I tell ya, Halley, my feet never been so wet for so long in all m' life. You just take some good socks with ya when ya go honey, you're gonna need 'em. And I'd steer clear of the mutton if y'can . . ."

My mom and Aunt Jo collected our empty plates and took them to the sink to wash. Granny carried a fresh sugar cream pie to the table and cut it into thick, custardy wedges sprinkled with nutmeg that brought to mind all my favorite things about Ohio. The hot summertime smell of old car back seats. The rainbow glint of sunlight off jars of garden green beans and pickled peppers in my grandparents' root cellar. Holding my mother's strong, fine-boned hand as we traversed the Olive Garden parking lot for all-you-can-eat breadsticks. Now that I was really leaving, I felt a little sad.

As the end of the evening drew nearer, everyone was

nicer, I guess because we knew we wouldn't be seeing each other again for a while. Why couldn't it have been this way always?

"Be careful over there," Granny said. Her open arms smelled like soft, powdery gardenias. "Don't talk to strangers."

"Love you, sweetheart," Grandpa said, pecking me on the cheek.

Aunt Jo squeezed my hand. "Have fun, honey. Send us a postcard."

"Don't do anything I wouldn't do," Uncle Larry said with an awkward wave.

My brother walked around the table and hugged me for maybe the second time in his entire life. "Bring me back something cool," he snickered.

My sister smiled up from her spot on the floor. "Send me your new address so I can send you a wedding invitation."

"Okay, I will," I said.

"Work hard, Hal," my dad said with watery eyes, pulling me in close. "You know, anything can be achieved through honest hard work."

"I hope you're happy," my mom added. She wrapped her thin arms around me and kissed me on the forehead.

The next morning, a few hours before my flight, I popped in to the office to finish the last of my HR paperwork. I dismantled what was left of my portion of the cubicle, filling the wastepaper basket with discarded postcards and receipts whose sentimental value I couldn't recall. I wrote a parting email to Celeste, telling her I was sorry again, that I couldn't believe what I'd done, that I'd been scared I'd never amount to anything and I'd panicked, that I thought she'd get the job anyway. I told her I wished I could see her again before I left so I could say all this in person, and that I'd make it up to her somehow. A second after I hit send, an email from Thomas Rousseau appeared in my inbox, and my chest nearly exploded. It was the first word I'd received since the elevator.

"Hey you," the email said. "I've been wondering about the verdict on the job in France."

I replied immediately. "I got it. I'm leaving this afternoon."

He wrote me right back. "Congratulations! That's great."

"Thanks," I replied.

"You'll have to start practicing your French."

"I know. We're living in a town called Biot."

"Oh yes, near Cannes. I haven't been there, but I've driven past it. That's a nice area. Maybe I'll see you there someday."

Maybe I'll see you there. I read the words over and over again, closed the email, opened it back up, and read it again. I read it until I was full to the brim, until the words no longer had any meaning.

I gave Phil Collins a few sprinkles of food and then headed down to HR. Dave the HR guy had two documents for me to sign, and an unmarked cardboard box containing a shiny new cell phone with an international plan. I thanked him as if he had bought me the phone out of his own pocket, and he "you're welcomed" me likewise. I carried the box back with me to my desk, ready to say goodbye to my cubicle, grab Phil Collins, and head for the airport. Then I saw the knife. It didn't register at first, what I was looking at. A black-handled jackknife sticking straight up out of my desktop, its blade impaling the lifeless body of Phil Collins. My sweet, innocent little Phil Collins. My friend. Murdered in cold blood.

PART TWO

14

I FELT SICK as I made my way through the airport. My head ached from crying. Celeste hated me; Phil Collins was dead. Sidestepping crowded Newark gates, I felt the lack of him, the weight of his bowl I would no longer carry. I had no idea who had murdered him. I didn't recognize the knife. What kind of twisted fuck stabs a goldfish? There were people at Findlay who didn't like me, to be sure. Molly. Jamie. Celeste. Disgruntled San Francisco meeting attendees, maybe. But I couldn't imagine any of them stabbing Phil Collins. It was a degree of cutthroat I didn't know existed among our ranks, and I was ready to call a truce.

If this was Level 2, it already wasn't all it was cracked up to be.

All throughout the flight from Cincinnati to Newark, a kid had kicked the back of my seat to the beat of his Leapfrog jingle while I sat in anguish, trying to roll myself into as small a human capsule as possible and disappear. Now the feeling had set in, the one you get when you find yourself at that crossroads between your own discomfort and someone else's, when you start to notice all the ways in which life is a dance between cattle and butcher.

"Well, if it isn't Halley Faust," a voice said behind me. "Who'd you have to fuck to get this job?"

I turned. "Hey Max."

He flashed a testosterone-fueled grin. "No, really though. You and Gus?"

"What?"

Max raised his hands innocently. "Don't get mad. That's just what I heard."

I shifted my weight from one foot to the other. "What's just what you heard?"

"Nothing," he said. "Never mind."

"Whatever." I partially smiled, feigning an indifference I did not feel. Max was now a Level 4, and I felt an acute sense of inferiority next to him. Although I found him despicable in almost every way, I wanted him to like me.

I pulled my carry-on over to a row of plastic seats and dropped my purse heavily. I'd been unwilling to leave anything important in my checked bag so my purse weighed about twenty pounds. Lauren approached, looking fresh. Level 3 looked good on her. I was jealous.

"Where's Darren?" Lauren asked over the din of a gate announcement. "Wasn't he on your first flight?"

"He said he was going to find something to eat," I said.

She picked at the chipped edge of one of her finger-nails. "I wouldn't eat anything in this airport."

I almost made a wisecrack about turkey sandwiches, but I didn't have the energy.

Lauren turned back to me. "Did they tell you what kind of cars we'll be getting in France? Mine had better be at least an Audi. I heard Gus's getting a BMW."

"I heard Volkswagens," I said.

"Ugh," said Lauren.

"I heard they're thinking about giving us one of the company jets," said Max. "We're going to be traveling a lot, and Gus has a pilot's license."

"They should," Lauren said. "We're practically giving up our whole lives to do this."

It seemed they had been appointed under different conditions than me.

"Oh my god," Lauren continued, "I already miss my boyfriend so much."

"Boyfriend?" Max said.

"Well, we just started dating about a month ago, but it has been so intense. Like, we're already talking about getting married."

Max's bored eyes glanced idly around the building, so Lauren turned to me.

"That's nice," I said.

"I've already written him three letters. I brought different perfumes to spray them with. There's one that smells like vanilla for when I want to be romantic . . . then another one that smells flowery for when I'm talking about the wedding . . . and one that has a strong sandalwood smell for when we discuss travel plans . . . and another one that's citrusy for when I'm feeling cheerful . . ."

"How about one that smells like barbecued ribs?" Max said. "I'm hungry."

Darren approached, carrying a giant pretzel and The Backpack. "Hey guys."

"I hope our condos are nice," Max said as if Darren hadn't said anything.

"I told Gus I'll need an extra bedroom," Lauren added excitedly. "I have a ton of people coming to visit." She shifted away from the wall as a beeping golf cart carrying two handicapped travelers pushed through the crowded terminal walkway. Next to us, a girl of eleven or twelve crouched behind a seat and flung Tic Tacs at people while her guardians argued.

"I'm going to miss my kite club," Darren said, chewing a bite of pretzel. "I brought two of my kites. That close to the Mediterranean . . . should have some good wind."

Max looked at Darren, as if for the first time. "Hey Darren, what all is in The Backpack anyway?"

"Documents," he said. "Mostly plans for new devices."

"Give us a peek?" Lauren said.

"Can't," Darren said, taking another bite. "Gus said that if anyone tries to open it, they're automatically fired. Also I have permission to taze them."

Lauren stepped backward.

"Don't worry, I put the Taser in my checked bag."

Max changed the subject. "Is it true that Gus commissions his own live porn?"

Darren looked at the floor and smiled. "I'm not saying anything."

Lauren's eyes sparked. "Is it true he has glacial ice shipped from Greenland to put in his drinks, and he wipes his ass with orange blossoms from Spain?" she asked. "I heard that from one of the RMs."

"Is it true that he keeps a tranny mistress in Rome?" Max continued.

"Ew," Lauren squealed. "Thanks, Max. Now I'll never get that image out of my head."

"Come on, Darren," Max said. "Just blink twice if it's true."

"Nah, I'm not saying anything."

"Lame," Lauren said. "I'm going to get a Frappuccino."

"I'll go with you," Max said. "I can expense it."

I sat down and propped my feet up on my carry-on. Two gate agents wearing blue vests and plastic credentials around their necks walked behind the clean gray counter and began tapping keyboards. One of them swiped her badge through a slot on the wall and passed through the boarding door, returning a minute later. The other one began calling names over the intercom system. "Jacinda Moore, please approach the check-in desk at gate seventy-three for your seat assignment."

Darren finished his pretzel and wadded the paper into a ball, picked up The Backpack and walked to the nearest trash can to throw the paper away, almost tripping over the feet of an old man sleeping at the end of our row.

Another announcement boomed through the air above our heads. A line began to form at the counter where the gate agents stood. The upgrade list flashed onto the screen behind them, and I glanced over it idly, hoping that by some stroke of luck I might be on it. I wasn't.

One of the gate agents picked up the microphone again, her voice like a pre-recorded airline robot. "Ladies and gentlemen, in a few minutes we will begin boarding flight thirty-two with direct service to Nice."

My heart fluttered.

"We will board this flight by zone, beginning with zone one. Please remain seated until your zone is called."

People started clustering around the gate, stepping in front of each other, as if our orientation within this crowd defined our relative superiority and inferiority in life.

"We will now begin preboarding flight thirty-two with direct service to Nice."

I made my way to the back of the cluster.

"What are you doing?" Max said from behind me.

"What?" I said, turning. He was sipping something

from a large cardboard cup.

"You're in first class with us, right?" he said. "You can skip ahead to the front."

Lauren walked up behind him and looked at both of us nervously, as if we might be talking about her.

"No, Darren and I are in coach. We're only Level 2."

"Oh," he smirked and pushed his way through the crowd. "First class," I heard him say. "First class, coming through. I'm an American."

When my zone was called, I inched my way slowly to the front, presented my ticket, continued down the jet bridge and onto the plane. I found an open space in one of the overhead compartments, stowed my carry-on, and sat in my assigned window seat.

The seat next to me was empty and I hoped with a level of vigor incommensurate to the situation that it would stay that way. Give me SARS, take away my phone, but please don't force me into awkwardly close proximity to a complete stranger. But the flight was full, and just as the flight attendant began the introductory announcements, a guy emerged in the aisle and sat next to me. He had long, gray, stringy hair and stank of stale cigarettes. He belched up smoke-and-rotten-Chinese-food-flavored wind for everyone in the vicinity to inhale and didn't seem to care or even notice. I felt naked and permeable as the smell entered my nose, its molecules violating my body. The man put his bag on the floor and part of it was on my side, touching my right leg. When he wasn't looking I nudged it over. Not because I really cared about it being there, but because he represented a world that would have swallowed me whole if I'd let it.

I looked through plexiglass at the sun setting in the distance, the accordion folds of the jet bridge and the detritus of human existence, grime and black curly hairs, stuck in the corners of the window. I scrolled through the selection of in-flight movies and settled on one. We ascended, our bodies jostling, subject to our own fragile mortality, and eventually leveled out. Ephemeral specks floating above the crust of the earth.

Soon dinner was served on plastic trays. I picked through the pile of pasty ravioli. Wilty lettuce. The brownie was decent. I wondered if Lauren asked them for turkey sandwiches. She was probably the kind of person who didn't eat on planes. I could imagine her up in first class, being presented with champagne and warm nuts, breasts of pheasant on hand-painted china, and turning it all down. True luxury is having enough abundance to decline.

I woke up as we began our descent. Flight attendants were passing through collecting dirty breakfast trays and empty water bottles. The guy next to me quietly farted under his blue airplane blanket. We all languished in a cloud of miscellaneous human stench. When the plane had safely parked at the gate in Nice, I speed-walked as fast as I could up the jet bridge and didn't slow down until I got to an open space where I could breathe.

15

THEN I WALKED into my dream. Sunshine. Palm trees.
Sparkling blue sea. The Nice airport was full of Hermès
bags and Ferragamo shoes and Longines watches. Giant
clothing ads with thin, sexy men pouting in gray suits. The
language, though unintelligible to me, sounded glamorous
and beautiful. From a café called Paul, the smell of golden,
buttery pastries. I wanted to consume all of it until my soul
became saturated with its aura. A chauffeur-driven SUV
picked us up at the warm, sunny curb outside of baggage
claim. Darren, Lauren, Max, and I quaked with anticipation as we sped toward Biot, our new home, watching the
beauty of the French Riviera flood past. Even Max, by far
the coolest of our crew, was excited.

Soon the driver was pulling through a remote-activated
gate and into a posh resort complex next to a well-main-
tained golf course. The buildings were all parchment-col-
ored stucco and clay tile roofs. Silvery olive trees bordered
the swimming pool, framed by green hills on the horizon.
As each of us was dropped off at our assigned condo, the

rest of us jumped out of the car to take a look. Each condo was different, each individually owned and furnished and rented to Findlay by a property management office on the other side of the golf course. Max's place was owned by a British bachelor with a fondness for sports memorabilia. Lauren's place (which, as she'd requested, had an extra bedroom) was light and airy and owned by Parisians. Darren's place appeared to be owned by monks but was actually owned by an old Polish couple. It had no pictures on the walls and very little furniture, only a small twin bed, a table, and a chair. Gus would tell him he could buy some furniture and put it on his expense account, but Darren, thinking perhaps this was some kind of test, would say he didn't mind. And we didn't know who owned my place, but it was quintessentially Provençal: sunny yellow walls, rustic furniture, quilts, and a big pot of lavender next to the front door. I had a large terrace dotted with hedges and olive trees, overlooking the golf course. The minute I walked in the door I wanted to stay forever.

Gus emailed that afternoon and asked us to come to his place for a five o'clock meeting. I had enough time to wash the film of travel grime off my body in the claw-foot tub, hang my suits in the perfumy closet, and take a quick nap on the toile de Jouy-covered bed. Around 4:30 p.m., I set out across the golf course. The air near the cart path smelled like green onions. Wild rosemary grew in the rocks around the sand traps. I listened for voices screaming "fore!" in myriad European accents, prepared to hit the ground if I had to.

Lauren jogged toward me in painted-on black Lycra, and I tried not to stare at her perfectly sculpted body, fearful of violating some kind of coworker privacy code.

"Are you heading to Gus's?" she said, stopping to walk

with me. "It's amazing here, huh?"

"I love it," I said.

"Max said that Gus wishes we'd gone to Barcelona instead."

"Why?"

She looked around and lowered her voice as if the golf course might be bugged. "Apparently Gus and Clive take two of their Italian clients there every year to go to this high-end brothel they all like. They buy the whole place out for a weekend and set it up like a game of hide-and-seek. Max said they divide the prostitutes into teams, half good and half evil. Then they hide a Rolex somewhere in the brothel and whichever guy finds it first gets to keep it. The guys wear tuxedos and carry laser guns, and the "evil" prostitutes kidnap them and the "good" ones help them escape. So it's like laser tag but with lots of sex and tying people up."

"Wow." I kicked a pebble as I walked.

"Yeah. Boys."

"So you're a runner, huh?" I asked, changing the subject. "I should be doing the same thing." It was complete BS; I hated running.

"Oh, you should come with me some time," she said eagerly.

Crap. "Sure, that'd be great," I said.

"I'm not a long-distance jogger, just a few miles normally," Lauren said. "But it looks like it's mostly uphill here, so, good for the glutes."

Great, I thought. Now I would have to start avoiding her.

"Okay, well, tell Gus I'll be there in a few minutes," she said and took off again. I flashed a quick wave, and she smiled, knowing we weren't friends but pretending we were.

I stopped to assess where I was, not entirely sure I was walking in the right direction. The place Gus had described in his email appeared to be just over the next hill.

My phone buzzed in my pocket, and I checked it. An email from Rousseau. I smiled giddily.

"How is the place?" it said.

"Beautiful," I typed and hit send.

"When are you going to invite me to visit?" he wrote back.

It was a thrilling and unexpected question. I stopped walking and sat down on the grass by a tree. Rousseau writing to me again—that was surprise enough. Rousseau suggesting we actually meet—that was someone else's life. I didn't know how to respond. What did he want? Did he actually care about me? Or was I just a diversion? Was I overthinking? I wanted to give him what he wanted. I also wanted not to ruin this, whatever it was, either by smothering or by neglect. I wondered about his marriage. Did she know he was writing to me, that he'd kissed me? They were European; maybe they were more open-minded than Americans about things like that. Or maybe they loved each other so uniquely and so completely that he could never love anyone else, and I was nothing to him. Maybe this was all nothing. I fell back on our San Francisco repartee.

"Never," I wrote. "Biot doesn't allow Rousseaus. I checked."

"Ha," he replied. "Five bucks says Gus invites me down before the end of the month."

I stood and started walking again. "You must be special."

"I am."

"Aren't you supposed to be working?" I wrote.

"I'm at work right now, I'll have you know. Desperately

struggling to stay awake at a very boring meeting."

"What would they do if you just got up and walked out?"

"Give me dirty looks," he replied.

"Do it."

"You are a bad influence." I could feel his smile coming through the digital screen. It gave me butterflies.

I put the phone back in my pocket, hiked the steep hill at the edge of the third hole and, slightly out of breath, walked past the clubhouse. The afternoon sun washed the pink bricks of the sidewalk so brightly they looked white. I passed through a metal gate leading to a small courtyard, boozy with honeysuckle. It was cool in the shade. Inside the door there was a stack of paintings leaning against the wall. From the sounds of the voices echoing off the tile floor, Max was already there.

". . . not here to do that," I heard him say in a raised voice.

"You don't need to do anything," I heard Gus reply. "You just need to know how to motivate people to do good work for you. Didn't you ever read Huck Finn?"

I knocked on the edge of the doorway where I stood, to let them know I was there.

"Who is it?" Gus shouted.

I announced myself. Gus emerged in the hallway singing welcomes, motioned for me to follow him inside, and then meandered into his white and stainless steel kitchen. It was a strange feeling being inside Gus's house— too intimate—even if it was a rental. Gus wasn't quite a real person to me, and I wasn't sure I wanted him to be. Also, it was hard to look at him now and not picture him in a bow tie chasing hookers with a laser gun.

"What are all these?" I asked, pointing to the stacks

next to the door.

He set a bottle of chardonnay on the kitchen counter. "Paintings I shipped from the States."

I wondered if they were expensive, and then mentally answered my own question.

Gus opened the bottle and side-eyed me. "I couldn't leave them in Ohio; somebody might steal them. I know those thugs Tim Cook and Jeff Bezos have my house under surveillance. I'll be damned if they're going to get within thirty feet of these babies."

I looked around the kitchen. "Can I do anything to help you?"

He poured three glasses of wine and put them on a tray.

"Sure," he said. "You can carry this into the other room. Thanks."

I followed Gus into his cavernous living room and immediately noticed the cappuccino machine—the shiny black Jura from outside his office—sitting on a sideboard. Of course he wouldn't leave that behind to be abused in his absence. I set the tray down on the table and handed Max a glass of wine. Max looked at me as if I'd ruined something by showing up, but I was too busy looking around to care much. Gus's place was nicer than any of ours, full of art and exotic plants and relics from Gus's extensive travels. A menagerie of Veblen goods I hadn't even known existed. One wall of the living room was entirely made of glass in order to showcase the pristine Ducati parked in the all-white adjoining garage. There was what appeared to be an alligator-hide bar, stacked with bottles of liquor, the kind that, I learned, was bottled after being poured over women's bare breasts. He even had a remote-controlled toilet in the guest bath, complete with foot heater.

"Not a bad life, eh?" Max said. He looked voracious, as

if he might open his mouth and suck the paint off the walls.

"Was this already here before he moved in?" I asked, motioning to the glass wall.

"I had some adjustments made before I got here," Gus said. "Nothing extreme." His eyes met mine for a second and a ghost of a smile twitched on his mouth, as that of a person trying to appear nonchalant while searching my face for envy.

More knocks at the door announced the arrival of Darren and Lauren, along with a fresh gust of honeysuckle air. Darren dropped The Backpack gingerly to the floor and took a seat at Gus's glass dining room table next to Lauren, who had changed from her running clothes into a burgundy wrap dress. Max and I picked up our glasses and joined them there.

"Did you have a nice run?" Max said.

Lauren's lips fluttered into a small smile when he looked at her. "Yeah, it helps with the jet lag."

I poured Lauren and Darren each a glass of wine while Gus opened another bottle. He set it on the table, then crossed the room, picked up a thin-handled coffee cup and made himself a cappuccino from the shiny, black machine. He didn't offer the rest of us one and we didn't ask. I wondered, though, why it was that Gus was so liberal with the wine, and yet so stingy with the cappuccinos.

"Okay, guys," Gus said, taking his seat at the head of the table. "Thanks for coming out. This shouldn't take too long, but I want to at least establish everyone's roles so we can get started. Just a reminder that all of you will be eligible to advance if you do well here. I'll decide after the launch whether you'll stay at your current level or move up. So do a good job, and your future at Findlay will be bright."

I looked at the eyes around the table. If there were ever

five more ravenous people in a room together they would have eaten each other.

"This is April," Gus said. "The launch is in January. So we have nine months. The home office sent us these launch plans, one for each of you." He nodded to Darren, who immediately pulled a stack of binders out of The Backpack and passed them around. We flipped through pages of basic charts ("a product launch has three phases: strategy, development, and execution"), a calendar of vague and obvious benchmarks we were expected to hit ("launch to customers on January 15"), and some product data so technical that none of us could decipher it. Thanks a lot, home office geniuses. It appeared we were going to be inventing this wheel from scratch. All we really knew was that we had this product, the Tantalus, and that it needed to be introduced to our sales force and customers in a big and memorable way that simultaneously educated and attracted. Tasks like generating timelines and producing sales pitches and drafting training plans still existed in the ambiguous realm of "somebody else does it."

"So, where was I?" Gus said. "Yes, yes, roles and responsibilities. Max will be the Executive Marketing Manager. Darren and Halley are support staff. And Lauren, you'll be in charge of training the sales team."

Lauren asked, "What's my title?"

"I don't know," Gus replied. "We haven't gotten that far. Max, what do you think?"

"Hmm . . ." Max said, "Director of Sales Training?"

Gus shook his head. "Clive will freak out if anyone has the phrase 'Director of Sales' in their title."

Max leaned back, linked his hands behind his head, and looked at the ceiling. "Okay, how about Sales Training Director?"

"That doesn't make sense," Lauren said. "In everyone else's title the 'Director' part comes before the thing they're directing. It sounds weird for mine to come at the end; people will wonder if there's something wrong with me."

Max rolled his eyes. "How about Director of Training for Sales?"

Darren gulped his wine and poured himself another glass.

"I don't like the 'for' in there," Lauren said.

"Let's just call you 'Director of Training,'" Gus said. "Will that work?"

Lauren thought about this for a moment, clearly displeased, but eventually relented. "Fine," she said, lips pursed.

That was all we accomplished that day.

16

THE NEXT DAY, my new car was delivered. I gathered my keys and my bag and locked up on my way out, pinching a fingerful of lavender from the pot by the door. The warm camel-colored interior of the Passat smelled like new leather. I rolled down the windows and wound through the narrow country roads, past roadside fruit stands and red-awninged boulangeries and billboard ads for French mobile phone companies with big white bubble letters. I negotiated the scary roundabout in front of a store called Le Clerc, tiny cars flying at full speed through the tiny exit and into the parking lot like they were on rails. I got honked at, yelled at, gestured and stared at for my slow driving and my fear of picking the wrong lane.

I didn't have a Euro coin to rent a shopping cart, so I pulled a blue plastic wheelie basket around the store, gathering cheeses and baguettes, fruit and chestnuts, and working to block out the smell of freshly bleached dead lake and bait shop emanating from the *poisson* section. At the checkout, the cashier chucked the items down the conveyor belt at me, not a grocery bag in sight. And as it dawned on me—watching other patrons unfurl rumpled plastic sacks and pack their own groceries—that unlimited free grocery sacks and pimple-faced high schoolers standing at the end of the chute packing those sacks for me (and, at certain stores, even carrying them to my car!) were a privilege that I'd always taken for granted, the checkout girl lifted my clear plastic bag of apricots and spoke to me in words I did not understand.

"*Blah blah blah blah blah.*"

"*Vous parlez Anglais?*" This was practically the only French phrase I knew.

"*Non,*" she replied. I took that as a "no."

I was a deer in the headlights with no idea what to do next. The clock ticked.

"*Blah blah,*" the girl said.

There were a few awkward seconds in which we both stared each other down. She held the bag up in the air and dropped it down onto her other palm in demonstration, but I was as confounded as ever.

"*BLAH BLAH!*" the girl said, progressively louder, as if my problem was simply bad hearing. I stared. So did other people, actually, considering that this person was now shouting at me.

The girl kept performing the same bag-dropping motion over and over again, and my face burned with embarrassment. I felt the acute loneliness that comes with knowing you are the only person in the world in this exact situation at this exact moment.

Eventually a guy standing behind me in line said, "You need to *weigh* them," as if speaking to a small child.

D'oh. I hadn't even noticed the weigh and label stations.

I wanted to tell the checkout girl never mind, I could go without the fruit, just keep it. I was holding up a long line of disgruntled French people. But I didn't know how to say that. Or even mime it. I stood for a second longer. The checkout girl shoved the bags of produce into my hands, smiled patiently, and waved at me to go, *go now,* to weigh this stuff and come back when I was done.

"It's okay?" I asked. "All these people are waiting . . ." I trailed off as she waved me away. I looked back at the other customers, who clearly thought I was *tres stupide.*

I ran back to the produce section, dropped the bags individually onto the scale, pressed the corresponding picture button, affixed the paper label sticker to the side of each bag, and ran headlong back to the checkout where the line of customers and the checkout girl were still waiting.

Groceries tossed, unbagged, back into the wheelie basket, I handed the girl my American credit card. And then it was declined. Mortification complete.

The bank had frozen my account for suspected fraudulent activity, because no Dayton girl would be using her credit card at a grocery store in France. I had no other way of paying for my stuff. I lifted my arms in resignation and apologized to the cashier, who blinked at me in disbelief, then I abandoned my groceries and left, wishing I had a mask to hide my face. This was not the European romance I'd imagined. This was an episode of *Looney Tunes* and I was Pepé Le Pew and France was the cat who thought I smelled bad. My childish dreams of this place—the cafés, the purple fields of lavender, riding through the countryside on a vintage bicycle with a basketful of fresh baguettes—died right then and there. I would have gone back to Dayton immediately, back to Celeste and Phil Collins and Level 1, if I could've.

"So far, living with Lauren and Gus and Max is like

being marooned on Gilligan's Island with a bunch of Mrs. Howells. I've only been here for a couple weeks, and all day long I'm getting emails from them. 'Halley, my dishwasher isn't working.' 'Halley, find me a restaurant for dinner tonight.' And, my personal favorite, 'Halley, there's a cat outside my apartment that won't go away,'" I wrote.

"What do they want you to do about it?" Rousseau wrote back.

"I don't know," I replied. "I've been forwarding all their emails to the property manager."

"Stop being so competent, darling, and maybe they'll leave you alone."

"Yeah, good plan. That'll show them."

I put my phone on the side of the bed to finish drying my hair, then picked it back up again to read his last message. Stop being so competent, *darling* . . . There were so many things I wanted to say to him. So many questions I wanted to ask. It was all still so new, but the existence of him, always there on my phone, keeping me company, believing I was significant, was the only thing preventing me from going to pieces right now. When Rousseau and I conversed, for those moments I got to bask in the sunshine of my best self. I looked forward to his messages with a glad sparkle that contained all my previously held affection for Phil Collins, my complex attachment to Celeste, my need for the stability that I'd never noticed Dayton and my family provided. But I was playing a dangerous game; I knew I was. How long would it take for Gus or Anthony to find out about this? And what could I possibly ever mean to him?

I stepped into a black and gray-striped maxi dress and swiped some mascara over my eyelashes. Then I picked up the phone again and began to type.

"Do you talk to everyone the way you talk to me?"

"What do you mean?" he replied.

It wasn't the response I expected, and I squirmed.

"Just that if Gus found out I was talking to you like this, I'd probably be in trouble," I wrote.

"Well I'm not going to tell him, if that's what you're worried about."

"I'm not worried," I typed, then reconsidered. Eventually I would have to say it, so I might as well say it now. "I guess I am worried. It's not just the work thing. I've never been friends like this with a man who is married before." It must have sounded so provincial, but at least it was true.

"Oh, are you upset about that?"

"Aren't you?"

"No," he wrote. "I hope that doesn't sound bad. I don't know, it seems like I've known you all my life or something."

I got that same shimmery feeling I'd had sitting next to him in San Francisco, as if he'd reached through the screen and brushed my neck with his fingers.

"And the answer is no," he wrote, "I don't talk to everyone the way I talk to you. Frankly, I don't talk much to anyone at all. Just you."

When I realized what he was saying I almost lost my mind with joy. So this was something then.

"I have been so nervous," I confessed, "wondering how to read you."

"You make me nervous too, but in a good way," he replied. "I was so depressed the day I left San Francisco. I know it's not ideal, and I don't want to get you in trouble, but I hope we can keep talking."

"Of course," I said. I would slay dragons to keep talking to him. He made me feel, for the first time, as if I'd transcended ordinary life.

17

W<small>E</small> <small>FINALLY</small> <small>GOT</small> through the long-winded introductory welcomes, the thank-yous for dialing in, and the managerial "allow me to say a few words" portion of our first conference call and got down to business.

"Maybe we could make it rocket-themed," Max said. "You know, like an *actual* launch. And we could set off a rocket at DEVO."

DEVO was short for Device Expo—the largest devices trade show in the world, where we would launch the Tantalus in January. Launching at a big trade show was a strategic move, guaranteeing us a captive audience of our most important customers.

"I don't think they'll let us set off a rocket at DEVO," I said. "In fact, no more ideas involving fire."

"What if we curtain off part of the booth and have sound effects like people are building something?" Chad Johnson, one of the brand managers, said. "Everyone will be wondering, 'What's Findlay building in there?' Then we unveil it."

"But what are we going to unveil?" Max asked.

"The device—the Tantalus," Chad said, as if this should be obvious.

Max cleared his throat condescendingly. "Well, it's awfully small. That seems kind of gimmicky. Won't it look weird if we pull back the curtain after all that jackhammering, and all that's sitting there is this little Tantalus?"

"Oh, but setting off rockets isn't gimmicky?"

"What if we get Gus to jump out of a giant cake?" Molly squealed.

No one spoke for a moment, as, I assume, we were all picturing this in our heads.

"There is no way in hell he would do that," Max said. "But you could jump out of a cake, Molly." Max snickered in a way that made all of us want to join whatever team he was on.

"I would do it. I'd jump out of a cake," Molly replied. "Put it on the list, Halley."

I did not put it on the list.

"Okay," Max said, "how about a champagne toast? Halley, can we get those guys who cut the corks off with swords?"

"No swords," I said. "No weapons in the trade show hall. No loud noises, no banners hung from the ceiling, no roving signage, no outside catering, no activity outside the booth footprint. You know the rules, Max. They can't give any exhibitors an unfair advantage."

"Maybe we should get Gus to give a speech!" said Molly.

"Yes, I have that on the list. But we still need a theme," I said, attempting to bring the conversation back around. "The graphics, logos, print pieces and the booth design are all going to incorporate the theme, so let's establish that first."

No one said anything.

"It would help if we knew exactly how the Tantalus works," Chad said. "Are they ever going to give us this 'proprietary information' Gus keeps mentioning?"

"We're not engineering the Tantalus here, we're just selling it," Max said. "We have enough information. We know it's cutting edge new technology that reveals what people want most. What more do we need to know?"

"And state of the art," added James Blakely, the new brand manager who'd just replaced Baldwin Frank. "It's going to revolutionize consumerism."

"Okay," I said. "So, cutting edge, state of the art. Visually, I'm thinking . . . black . . . metal."

"A camera," someone said.

"Mechanical parts," someone else said. "An engine."

"A Ferrari."

"Guns?"

"Airplanes."

"Ozzy Osbourne."

I didn't even know who was talking anymore. I left the phone on speaker and got up from my dining room table to pour myself another glass of wine.

"Killer whales!" That one came from Molly.

"A clock," I said.

"Black widow spiders!"

"Wait a minute," James said. "Whoever said clock, I like that."

"I was thinking about a digital alarm clock," I said. "Like what you'd see on the side of a ticking time bomb."

There was a long pause.

"Like a countdown clock," I said.

"Yeah . . . I like that," James said, trailing off.

"We could use it to generate buzz," I said. "Picture just

a clock, counting down. But no explanation. No one will know what it means; they'll just see the date and time of the launch. So they'll know something is about to happen when the countdown gets to zero . . . something big . . . they just won't know what."

"Do *we* know what?" Max said. "What are we counting down to?"

"The launch."

"Well yeah," he said, "but something has to happen."

"We could set off fireworks," Chad said.

"Not allowed," I replied.

"Not even little ones? I think they allow little ones."

"I'll find out." I put it on the list. *Little fireworks*.

"What if we fabricated a giant model of the Tantalus and put it in the middle of the booth," I said. "Then we could do the unveiling thing like Chad suggested."

"Sounds gimmicky," Max said.

"What if we got people to wear T-shirts with the countdown programmed into them on a timer?" I said. "Then when the clock hit zero, they'd all break into dance, like a flash mob."

"Where would we get these people?" James said.

"I don't know," I said. "They could be anyone. We could even recruit people off the street."

"Great," Chad chimed in, "some French hobo is going to be walking around in a Tantalus shirt."

"That's going to damage our brand," James said.

"We could always hire a streaker," I said. "That would get everyone's attention."

That one may have been the wine talking.

"Molly," I said, "do you think you could get the designer to mock up some countdown clock images and get them to all of us in the next couple weeks?"

"I'll have to run it by Gus, Halley," she said, clearly irritated that we didn't choose her killer whale idea. "Or, maybe I should let you run it by him, since the two of you are so . . . close." She chuckled for good measure, and everyone else was uncomfortably silent.

"Sure, I can check with him," I said, pretending I didn't know what she meant.

18

WE PASSED OUR time in a blur of unproductive meetings. We met over meals and wine. We got many detailed accounts of the harm Tim Cook and Jeff Bezos might inflict on Gus in the future and why they were not to be trusted.

On a Wednesday Gus asked me to meet him for lunch at the clubhouse. The Mediterranean air was warm on the terrace. If you looked past the golf course and its perimeter of pale condos you could see a slice of bright blue sea in the distance. By noon the pastel polos and Bermuda shorts filled every table.

Gus and I both ordered the caprese sandwich, mostly because we liked the channel-cut fries. I had begun to memorize the necessary French restaurant phrases—*Une table pour deux* (Table for two). *L'addition s'il vous plait* (Check, please). *Un verre de vin blanc pour moi, merci* (A glass of white wine for me, thanks)—while Gus thought that if he just spoke English with a French accent it was the same as speaking French. The waiters already knew that he

141

took his Coke Light with ice and no lemon and that I liked Dijon mustard with my fries, so we didn't need to say much anyway.

Gus looked perturbed. "Lauren is having cat problems," he said, gleeking a tiny spurt of Coke Light through his tooth gap.

"That gray cat?"

He sucked down the last few drops of his drink and waved to the waiter for a refill. "Do you think maybe it's a spy cat?"

I coughed to keep myself from laughing. "What's a spy cat?"

"I was just thinking that thing that looks like a growth on the side of its face might not be a growth at all. Maybe Cook and Bezos implanted a camera in there," he said, stony-faced.

"I don't know. That seems . . . extreme," I said.

"These guys are ruthless. They even got to my wife. Why do you think I got divorced?"

"You divorced your wife because of Tim Cook and Jeff Bezos?"

"I divorced my wife because she was a spy. Like that cat."

Our food arrived. "*Bon appétit*," the waiter said casually. Gus opened a little glass bottle of ketchup and reached for his knife.

I forked a fry and dipped it in mustard. "I think the cat was here before we got here. I've mentioned it to Fleur in the property management office a few times. She said they keep the cats around to control the mice."

"Well, I told Darren to keep an extra close watch on The Backpack just in case."

Gus's knife made a pinging sound as he thrust it in and

out of the ketchup bottle.

My phone beeped, and I paused to check it. A text from Rousseau. "Wish you were here," he said.

"Stop teasing me," I typed back. "I'm at lunch with Gus."

Gus held a corner of his sandwich, ready to take a bite. "How about Paris, the launch? Everything going okay?"

I silenced my phone and shoved it back in my pocket. "Well," I said, "it's hard to get anything done when everyone has to agree."

Gus cleared his throat. "That's part of being a good manager, Halley," he said.

I stared at my plate. "That's the thing though. I'm not actually a manager. I'm only a Level 2. I'm more like . . . a notetaker. I can't force people to agree, but I also can't make any decisions."

"Well," he said, waving to the waiter for another Coke Light, "I'll leave it to your judgment. But you're responsible for outcomes, so you're going to have to find a way to do what needs to be done. Don't let us down."

It was the kind of advice that wasn't helpful at all. I didn't say anything. The sun burned hotly on the back of my neck; I'd been afraid to attempt a trip to a French pharmacy, so I didn't have any sunscreen.

Gus held his sandwich up as if he was speaking into a microphone. "Halley, let me tell you something. You are going places. If you can make this project a success, you'll move right up the Findlay ladder, I promise you that. You'll be a manager in no time."

It was like he knew exactly what I wanted, exactly what I needed to hear.

"Really?" I said.

"Really." He took another bite of his sandwich. "So I

know you'll do whatever you have to do to be successful."

"I will," I said.

"Good. Now, I've decided I want to give the speech at the launch event in the booth. This is my project and I want to be the one to roll it out. So put me on the agenda for the launch event."

"Okay." I wrote it in my binder.

His phone rang. He glanced at the number, then jumped out of his chair. "Gotta go," he said, tossing his napkin on the seat. "Do you mind signing the check?"

"Okay."

He activated the phone, and I heard him whisper "*ciao bella*" into the mouthpiece. I waited for the bill and wondered what that was all about.

I checked to see if my own phone bore a reply from Rousseau. It did. There on the screen: "Come on. Just let me be in love with you."

I tucked the phone back into my pocket, slightly more gently this time, as if it had become an avatar of him. As if he was secretly mine.

We all took seats in Gus's living room. He set a new pack of our favorite Speculoos cookies on the coffee table, and we tore into them as if we hadn't just eaten a few minutes ago.

"Max, you go first," Gus said over the cellophane din.

"Thanks, Gus," Max said. "I'm going to Brussels for a couple days, then to London, and then to Berlin. I'll be meeting with sales managers. I leave on Sunday."

Lauren looked at Max with a sly half-smile and bit into a cookie. "I'm going too," she said.

Max snickered. "That's right, I almost forgot. Lauren is coming."

She rolled her eyes.

Darren looked up from his binder. "While you're in Brussels, Max, could you drop in on Simon Phloss? Gus and I spoke with him yesterday and he has some ideas that might help us with the sales training. I started working on the—"

"Darren, my boy," Gus said, "would you mind getting us some wine? I could really use a glass."

Darren hopped out of his seat, put his binder down, and jogged away to the kitchen. We heard the opening and closing of cabinet doors, the *thunk* of the wine bottle uncorking, the *thwash* of the pour.

Gus leaned back in his chair. "Okay, Lauren, do you have anything to add?"

"Well, while we're traveling I'm meeting with product managers to get some help understanding the data, so I can incorporate it into the sales training."

"Sounds reasonable," Gus said.

Darren returned with glasses of wine for everyone.

Gus looked up. "Darren, do you mind grabbing the napkins?"

"Yeah, I was just about to do that," Darren said. He disappeared again and returned with a stack of white cloth napkins.

Gus sipped his wine. "Okay, Halley, what's happening with you?"

"I'm still trying to establish the theme, then I'll start working on the booth."

"Why are we getting a booth?" Lauren asked. "Shouldn't we have a pavilion?"

"They don't have pavilions at DEVO," I said.

Max straightened. "Maybe they can construct one for us. Find out if they can build us one."

I made a note in my binder.

"How many podium talks are they giving us?" Gus asked.

"None," I said. "They're giving us a luncheon symposium."

Gus clicked his tongue. "No," he said, "we want podium talks. At least two."

"Two?" Max jumped in. "I think we should get six. We have a lot to present."

"Yes, six," Gus said.

I made a note.

"I have a question," Max said. "Can we put the launch meeting at a Hilton? I'd like to get the points."

I made a note.

19

"I DON'T LIKE the countdown clock idea," Chad said.

"I don't either," Max added.

We were on our third group conference call, and still no launch theme. Whatever idea we came up with, someone didn't like it. Max didn't like any idea that wasn't his.

I sighed. "Maybe instead of focusing on the newness of the technology, we should tie the theme to what the technology does. What do you think?"

"So, something aspirational?" Chad asked. "Tantalus is making dreams come true, it's giving people what they want most . . . that sort of thing?"

"Yeah," I said.

"What if, at the launch, we staged one of those paper lantern shows?" Max said. "I've seen them in Vegas; you're supposed to make a wish and set the lantern on fire and it floats up into the sky."

"Great," Chad said. "Drunk people and fire. Good idea, Max."

"Thanks," Max said.

"We can't light things on fire at DEVO," I said. "But I'll put it on the list for the gala."

"Why don't we just make it French-themed and plaster pictures of the launch team all over the booth," Chad said, chuckling. "You're living the dream, right? I'm surprised you came back from the beach long enough to take this call."

"Don't make me fire your ass," Max said. "Unless you'd rather go collect unemployment with Baldwin."

"Whatever, Bateman, I don't report to you. Besides, I was just kidding."

"Okay," I said. "Let's keep thinking. Wishes. Dreams. Findlay is giving you everything you've ever wanted. What comes to mind?"

"Rainbows!" Molly said.

"Ferraris."

"Princesses!"

"Sleep."

"Castles!"

"Sex."

"Money."

"Disney!"

"What if we hire an illusionist?" James said.

"To do what?" Max grumbled. "What do illusions have to do with dreams?"

"You know, dreams, magic, magicians . . ." James trailed off. "No?"

We ended the call exactly as we'd started it: without a theme.

I got up from my chair and crossed the cold tile in bare feet to move a load of soggy laundry from the washing machine to the dryer, then poured myself a glass of water and looked at the clock. 6 p.m. At least the logistics of the launch were in motion. There would be a trade show booth where we would showcase the Tantalus and stage the launch, a gala to entertain our most important clients, a luncheon symposium with expert testimonials about Tantalus's features and benefits, multiple dinners to meet with clients one-on-one, six sponsored lectures in the conference general session, a sales meeting to get the reps fired up to sell, and an array of banners, media spots, and advertisements. All I needed to do now was book the gala space, contract the hotel for the sales meeting, send a save-the-date to the audiovisual company, line up a motor coach vendor, and get everyone to *settle on a theme*. And then I could start working on the details.

I sat back down at my computer and scrolled through emails. I was beginning to develop a love-hate relation-ship with working from home. Sure, I could go multiple days without wearing pants. But, no office was more unre-lenting than my condo. No manager was more implacable than the voice inside my head. *You're not good enough*, the voice whispered. *You're not working hard enough. You're a fraud. They're all going to find out you're a fraud.* It didn't help that people back in the Dayton office bellyached about our team in Biot, supposedly sunbathing and living large on Findlay's dime. When you're a Level 1, you imagine that they'll applaud your success when you get to Level 2, that they'll finally respect you. But instead, they go from barely noticing you to hating you. Because now you're a threat. Now you have something they want.

Later that night I sat up in bed, three pillows stuffed behind my back, while Rousseau and I played our usual game of conversation volleyball.

"I would punch a baby for some Mexican food right now," I texted.

"Forget that," he replied, "you're in France. Do you like

oysters?"

"I've never had one that wasn't fried."

"Someday I'll take you to this place in Paris. Best oysters in the world." He added, "Hemingway used to go there."

I mulled this over, the idea of going somewhere public with him. Not just the way it would feel to be near him, but how it would feel to be seen by his side.

"I think I killed most of the fruit flies in my kitchen," I typed. "I used the swat method. Very effective. It's like a fruit fly holocaust around here. I left the dead ones out as an example for the others."

"How very Saddam Hussein of you," he replied. "How's work? Settle on a theme yet?"

"Plenty of ideas floating around. Most of them involving combustion."

"Ah."

"What about you, how was your board meeting and dinner thing?"

"Well, the chairman was in top form."

"I hope you fired a series of questions that were impossible to answer, and then slyly gave him the finger while coughing."

"I didn't. I was too busy daydreaming about San Francisco."

I smiled. "Oh really?"

"I was thinking about when I first saw you, at the dinner table. I thought you were the most authentic person I've ever seen. Everyone else at dinners like that always has this plastered-on smile and a list of conversation starters in their pocket. But you were so real. You blushed every time I asked you a personal question. There was a guilelessness about you that I almost never see in people."

"Is that a nice way of telling me I'm a yokel?"

"I'm serious. Talking to you made me remember what it felt like to be like that. Before the world crushed it out of me. I wanted to talk to you forever. Then there was the elevator."

I sunk down lower, willing him to keep going. More of this. I wanted more. "I think that was my favorite part," I replied.

"In the elevator," he wrote, "I wanted to smell your hair."

I shifted in bed again and started to hear a noise. It came from the hallway outside the bedroom door, which was closed. At first I ignored it, thinking it was the condo settling, or maybe the wind. But it was more of a scratching sound, not very windlike. When it didn't stop, I quit typing and listened. The noise seemed to move across the room, at times sounding in different places, eventually landing in the wall behind me. It was one of those horror movie moments when I should've just cut my losses and bailed, but I went to investigate instead. I slipped on a pair of rubber wellies and leather winter gloves and pulled a flashlight out of the bedside table that I might use as a weapon if need be. My mind cycled through all the possible origins of the sound, from serial killers outside the door to little animals eating the carpet. I crept across the room and decided it was definitely coming from the region of the bed, a queen-sized outfit made of two twin-sized mattresses pushed together. I started to take the quilt and the sheets off and pull the mattresses apart, and as I did, three tiny brown field mice scattered across the floor.

"GAH!" I screamed. I couldn't decide which was more disturbing, the scampering mice themselves, or the fact that I'd been unwittingly sleeping atop a rodent village for weeks. I imagined them consuming me, one tiny nibble at a time.

There was nothing to jump onto, and I didn't want to step on a squishy mouse, so I stood with feet planted, alone and screaming, flailing my arms in the air in terror. I stood like that for a long time, debating with myself about what to do. Obviously I couldn't stand there forever. I could call someone, but it was late.

Stepping carefully, shaking every article thoroughly, I packed a bag with enough stuff to get me through the next two days. The following morning I would call Fleur in the property management office, but that night, sufficiently traumatized, I checked myself into the hotel across the golf course and resumed my work in a plush white hotel bed, sans rodents.

20

"Some mice got in bed with me tonight," I said.

"Like, *in* your bed?" my mom said. Seeing her face in the Skype window made me surprisingly homesick.

"Yup."

"Jeez, they've got you living in squalor."

To her, living in France was the same as living in Somalia. If I wasn't the U.S., it must be the third world. I felt defensive all of a sudden.

"Actually, it's a pretty nice place," I said.

"Can't be that nice if it's full of rats."

"I think they were just mice and, so far, I only saw three."

"Where there's three, there's a hundred," she said. "What'd you do?"

"I left. I'm at the hotel across the golf course."

"You really should just come home." She said it with the tone of someone who'd just won a bet.

I could, I thought. *I could leave.* There was nothing stopping me. I had chosen this path, and all I had to do was

153

turn around. But if I did go back, who would I be then? The same ordinary old Halley from Dayton, Ohio. Unwed sister. Level 1 daughter. Nobody from nowhere.

"I can't," I said.

My mom cleared her throat. "Well, you missed a new Faust family first last weekend. Your father got smacked by the sample lady at Sam's Club." She rolled her eyes.

"What? Did he know her?"

"I'll let him tell you about it," she said. She got up from the table and shouted "Lewis!" out the back door.

My brother walked into the frame and looked for something in the refrigerator, then noticed my face on the computer and did a doubletake. He stepped closer until his head filled my screen.

"What's going on with your hair?" he said. "You look like Ted Nugent."

I didn't respond.

He chuckled, and I heard the *pssschlk* of his soda can opening. "See you later," he said and walked away.

Then I saw my dad's tall figure come into view. He looked like he'd put on a few pounds. He stopped at a cabinet and took out a drinking glass, walked to the sink and filled it with water from the faucet. He took a long drink, wiped his brow with the side of his arm, and then walked over to the computer and sat down.

"Hey Hal," he said.

"Hey. What's with the water—are you off the Coke kidney stone treatment now?"

"Yeah, I overdid it on the Cokes. Can't stand the sight of the stuff anymore."

He made a face, and I laughed.

"What else is going on?" I asked.

He reached up to scratch his face stubble. "Well, let's

see. Mr. Wheaten died. You remember Bill Wheaten, the pharmacist? He used to give you suckers when you were a little girl."

It took me a few seconds to recall the man's face. "What happened to him? He wasn't that old, was he?"

"No, it was pretty tragic. He was driving across the train tracks and got hit by a train. His wife and daughter were in the car too. They all died."

"Jeez, that's horrible."

My dad sat back in his chair, then leaned forward again. "Yeah, that family is cursed. It's the weirdest thing, his grandfather got hit by a train in his horse and buggy back in the 1930s. He was a farmer during the depression, you know. Raised pigs. Lived right down the road from here. And then his son, Bill's father, got hit by a train in his car back in the early 70s. They say he was drunk driving, but I'm not sure I believe it. He was as nice as they come, that guy. Levi was his name. I knew him when he was in school; he was in the same class as your Aunt Jo. Then Bill's brother got hit by a train about ten years ago. Really cursed, I tell you. Bill has another brother, and by god if I was him I'd be buying up life insurance policies and getting right with the Lord."

I got the feeling there was a significant life lesson I should take away from this story, but I couldn't quite figure out what it was.

"That's a pretty big coincidence," I said.

"Yep." He took another drink of water.

"What's this I hear about the Sam's Club sample lady?" I cracked a smile.

He sighed. "Well, this lady was set up at the kiosk in the frozen foods section giving out free samples of those little sausages. You know, the ones that look like tiny hot dogs?"

"Yeah."

"Well I tried one and it was pretty good, so I went back for a second one. And I ate the second one, and I thought, 'Man, this is really good,' so I went back for a third one, and the lady smacked me."

I grinned. "What did you do?"

"Well, I guess I stood there sort of surprised for a second, and then I apologized. Your mother felt so bad she bought two big boxes of the sausages and made sure the sample lady saw her put them in the cart. Guess we'll be having sausages at every family dinner for the next six months."

I glanced out the window of my hotel room, which looked out onto the third hole of the golf course. There was some movement on the green that caught my attention, two shadows that looked familiar.

"Dad, can I let you go?" I said, getting up.

"You be careful over there. And keep working hard. It'll pay off in the end."

"I will," I said.

I turned the lights off in my room and opened the window, letting my eyes adjust to the dark. The full moon came out from behind a cloud and turned the grass silver. And there, next to the third hole pin, I saw Max and Lauren, vigorously kissing. Wasn't she engaged to some guy back in California? Were they drunk? They swayed a little, but that could have been a factor of their height difference. Max held her face with the palms of his hands like he was afraid someone might show up at any minute and snatch her away.

I watched them, hoping they'd do something really scandalous. Actually, I was envious. It had been a long time since anyone had kissed me like that. Max reached over and pulled the flagstick out of its cup and whipped Lauren on the ass with it. She jumped back and shouted something I couldn't hear, and he began chasing her around, poking her in the back with the flag. Then he tripped and fell, and the flag went flying. He rolled over onto his back. She coughed with laughter and fell down next to him.

I continued to stare like a nosy neighbor, picturing myself in her place. A pressure built in my chest as I imagined the ripples of barbaric joy in their kisses and jumps and falls. I willed him to kiss her again, put his hands on her. My hand pressed against the glass. Then Max looked up. He stopped what he was doing and stared in my direction, and then Lauren did too, squinting. I quickly shuffled the curtains back into place, leaving the lovers to the vagaries of the night.

21

"Why do we even need a theme?" Molly asked sweetly, as if she was only trying to help.

What followed was the sound of my head exploding. It was our fourth attempt at establishing a theme, and now we had to stop and have a conversation about whether or not it was necessary to establish a theme.

"You can't run a campaign without a theme," Chad pointed out.

"Why do we need to run a campaign? Can't we just do the launch?"

Max sighed. "How are people going to know what we're launching?"

"We'll tell them it's the Tantalus," Molly replied.

"How will they know how the Tantalus fits into the context of their own lives?" Max asked. "How will we even get their attention to tell them?"

"The campaign," Chad suggested.

"Right," Max said.

"Okay, so back to the fireworks," I said. "They told me

we could have them at the gala but not at the booth."

"We need them at the booth," Max said matter-of-factly.

"They won't let us have them at the booth."

Max's voice flattened. "You need to play hardball, Halley."

"How can I play hardball? We don't have any leverage."

"Threaten to pull out of DEVO next year."

"We're a Platinum sponsor, that's not even something I can decide. They'll just laugh in my face."

"You're overcivilized," Max said.

"What . . .?" I didn't even know what he meant by that. "Why don't *you* call them?"

"Not my job," Max replied. "I'm here to think up the ideas. You're here to execute them."

I began to reminisce about a simpler time when I was a Level 1. Sitting in my happy little cubicle, listening to Celeste's latest travel story, watching Phil Collins blow bubbles. I missed them so much I almost cried. Now I had twice the workload, an off-limits married client as my only friend, and I had to deal with Max.

"If you're the ideas man, why are we still debating the theme?" I said. "Why don't you come up with one?"

"Fine," Max said.

Everyone was silent for a few seconds.

"Well?" I said.

"I will announce the theme when I'm ready, Halley."

"Fine," I said.

It was Friday afternoon, and the exterminator had cleared my condo of rodents. I headed to Le Clerc to buy some cheese, because maybe cheese would temporarily ameliorate my increasing inability to control any aspect of my life. These days I couldn't seem to get enough cheese.

Cheese was the source of all that was good and right in the world. Actually, there was something about French food in general that had begun to elicit addictive tendencies in me. Considering I'd spent the first twenty-three years of my life in a place where gravy was a food group, I guess I needed to make up for lost time.

I was standing in front of the dairy case trying to decide between a *Cabecou* and a *Brie de Melun*, when the cheese lady approached and spoke to me in words I didn't understand.

"*Blah blah blah, blah blah?*"

I flipped through my dictionary, but I didn't even know where to start. The cheese lady smiled, pulled a knife out of her apron, sliced off a little piece of the *Cabecou* and offered it to me. I popped it into my mouth. It was tart and creamy.

I pointed to the *Brie de Melun*, and she sliced off a little piece and offered it up. Mmm.

When I looked up again, she was holding a new slice on the end of the knife. *Don't mind if I do,* I thought. But when I reached for it she snatched the knife back and clicked her tongue at me sharply, as did the guy standing next to me, whom she had actually been offering the cheese to. *Oh my god*, I thought, *I'm becoming my father.*

Before I had a chance to feel the deep psychic consequences of this realization, I picked up four random hunks of cheese, put them in my basket, and walked away. I could throw myself a little cheese party later.

My phone buzzed with a text. I parked my shopping basket next to the charcuterie to read it.

"Come to Paris," Rousseau had written.

We both knew I couldn't go. "What will we do?" I replied.

"Visit museums," he wrote. "Drink wine."

"Let's drink wine *in* a museum," I typed.

"I think that's forbidden," he replied.

I smiled. "Well that hasn't stopped us so far."

"You're right," he wrote. "So why aren't you here?"

I sidestepped a woman who reached behind me to grab a salami. "Why do I have to come up there? It's nicer down here."

"Am I invited?"

He wasn't being serious, right? We were just bantering like we always did.

"Of course," I replied.

"Well that's settled, then," he wrote.

I walked to the checkout, packed the groceries into my reusable plastic sack, paid with cash from the surplus I now carried with me at all times, and headed for my car. When I arrived back to my condo I was already thinking about calls I needed to make and emails I needed to send. The air inside was damp and warm, and I could smell the trash that needed to be taken out. I put the hunks of cheese on a plate and ate mouthfuls as I typed. My hunger was vacant and compulsive, a giant vacuous hole. I ate thoughtlessly, making room inside my head for more urgent things. Before I knew it I'd polished off the entire plate, and I continued pecking and scrolling until it was time to eat again.

Thunder woke me up, then rain. The room was dark, and I walked over to the desk to read the fifty or so emails that had rolled in since I'd dozed off. The computer screen glowed eerily on the wall behind me.

Around the thirty-fourth email, I heard a knock at the front door. Assuming it was Lauren or Max coming to complain about a cat or a broken appliance or their inability to find a ride to the airport on Sunday, I pretended I wasn't home. But a minute later I heard the knock again. Louder this time. I mumbled an obscenity, pushed back in my chair, stood and walked to the front door. Opened it. No one was there.

I was about to sit back down when I heard shoes on the terrace. A figure moved in the dark, past the sliding glass door that faced the golf course. Adrenaline. Did 9-1-1 work here? I grabbed for my phone on the table. Then I looked right into the oceanic eyes of Thomas Rousseau.

I crossed the room, flipped the lock and pulled the sliding door aside, and there he was. The sight of him filled my body with electric light.

"Oh my god, you scared me to death."

"Oh," he said. His face sank and he leaned against the door jamb.

"What are you doing here?" I said. "I thought you were joking earlier."

I took his hand and tried to pull him inside, but he resisted. He was soaked, and drops of water ran down his temples and stuck on the ends of his hair and to the lenses of his glasses. The door was still open and thin slivers of rain like millions of tiny needles misted the tile floor.

So many questions ran through my head. "Would you please tell me what's going on?"

"Stop it," he said. "This isn't the way I pictured it would be. Give me a minute."

It was surreal, seeing him here like this. I stood next to him, watching his face. Then I reached out and touched his arm, pulling him toward me into a hug so full of feelings that it took my breath away. It had been weeks since I'd had a real hug. I was becoming a companionship camel. When I was full, I didn't notice I was full. It didn't occur to me that

I might someday be empty. But when I was empty, I began to fear deep in my bones that I would never be full again. I began to notice how loneliness sent me burrowing into myself in ways that magnified all other feelings. Sadness became depression, happiness became exuberance, and fear became terror when there were no friends, no family, no normal life to temper them.

Rousseau's embrace was magic; I could barely catch my breath. His hair dripped on the side of my face, and the warm wet of his clothes dampened my front.

"I just . . ." he began. "This is stupid, I know. I'm sorry."

I closed the sliding glass door behind him and we sat down across from each other at the dining room table.

"How did you get here?" I asked, running my fingers nervously over the knotty polished wood.

He hunched over, elbow on the table, and rested his forehead on his hand. "I took the last flight from Paris."

"Does Chloe know where you are?"

"No," he said. "I'm supposed to be in Milan for the weekend."

"Wait, what? You're lying to your wife now?" I was simultaneously angry and curious and elated about it. What we were doing was wrong; I knew it was. And, for god's sake, I could get FIRED. But he was here, and he was mine, and I wanted him with dizzying fire.

"I can go, if you want me to," he said.

"Right. Back to the airport at almost midnight in the pouring rain," I said. He looked up at me, a little mortified, and I realized I was being harsh.

"Where's your bag?" I said, more gently.

He nodded toward the wall behind me. "I left it by the front door. When you didn't answer I thought maybe you weren't home. Sorry for scaring you."

I gave him an indulgent look and moved toward the door.

"What were you picturing?" I asked, turning back to him.

"What?"

"You said this wasn't the way you pictured it would be. I was just wondering what you were picturing."

"I don't know," he said.

We were awkward together. I was still so anxious around him. In person we were practically strangers, no devices there to mask the distance between us. In person he was still *the* Thomas Rousseau, and I was still a Level 2. I had imagined him in so many different ways since San Francisco, and none of them were quite true to life.

I opened the front door, and he took his bag from where it was parked on the sidewalk. He carried it upstairs and put it on the floor in my bedroom, which was dark and stuffy and smelled faintly of perfume. He didn't turn the light on. I stood in the doorway while he removed his belt and his wallet, peeled his wet shirt and jeans off, and tossed them to me. I carried them downstairs to the laundry room, the image of him in a t-shirt, socks, and black Hugo Boss boxer briefs burned on my retinas. Before I put his jeans in to dry, I checked the pockets and pulled out the stub of his plane ticket. I tucked it into the front pocket of my capris.

When I returned to the bedroom, Rousseau had cracked open the doors to the balcony so the blustery wind could blow in. He was sitting shirtless on the side of the bed, facing the open door. The muscles in his back shifted as he leaned on his hands.

"I see why you like this place," he said, watching the storm.

I stood against the wall, thinking. What now,

Halley Faust? Rousseau was forbidden fruit. Sure, I had daydreamed about him, but the daydreams were cloudy and girlish, not the flesh and consequences there in front of me. We were standing on the edge of an abyss, both of us knowing we were going to tumble over from the momentum set in motion months before. I understood in that moment that the torment and excitement of resisting temptation might be more gratifying than actually succumbing to it. Up until then there had been curiosity between us, and no small amount of anticipation, but our exchanges were still simple and innocuous. We could still sleep at night. As I began to undress, knowing what was about to happen and wanting it to happen, part of me wanted him to resist me, wanted to wake up in a bed that was still safe and good, knowing we had not bent the fragile elements to our temporary pleasure. But I also wanted to see him fall, to savor the inextinguishable humanity of something grand and beautiful falling apart.

My phone rang, and we both turned to look at it. The number on the caller ID belonged to the Dayton office. It was like they had some kind of morality radar.

"Sorry, I have to take this," I said. I picked it up.

"Halley, I have a message from the president," Jamie Aaronson said.

I wondered if she started all of her phone calls that way, just to make sure people paid attention.

"Jamie," I said, "this isn't a great time."

"Oh, sorry, did I interrupt something? Tell Gus I said hi."

I didn't reply.

"I just called to tell you that Anthony has decided he will be the one to announce the Tantalus launch in the DEVO booth. Please have everything ready for him."

"I can't. Gus already said he's doing it."

Jamie didn't say anything for a few seconds. "Halley. Anthony is the *president*. He trumps Gus. If Anthony wants to be the speaker, he's the speaker. Just make the arrangements."

"Alright. Gotta go," I said, and hung up.

I silenced the phone and put it back on the nightstand. "Sorry about that," I said.

While I'd been talking, Rousseau had stretched out on the bed with his hands behind his head. He stared up at the ceiling like we were two bunkmates at summer camp about to have our nightly chat, and it began to dawn on me, the complete absurdity of all this. Thomas Rousseau was in my bed! How did I get here? I began to laugh. The laughter gurgled up out of me from some untapped place and it just kept coming and coming. Soon Rousseau was laughing too, but neither of us knew exactly why.

"That's it," he said. "You've finally lost your mind."

I could barely catch my breath. "What are you doing here?"

He propped himself up on an elbow and studied me with curious amusement. There was that same shameless certainty he'd had in San Francisco, watching me to see what I'd do next. But it was his humanness that disarmed me. It was there in his eyes, some lost thing he searched for with the earnestness of a child. I quieted. He moved toward me, pausing an inch from my skin, like he'd done that day in the elevator. I inhaled the rich damp smell of him. He closed his eyes when he kissed me, as if willing the world to stop existing as he knew it.

We sank into each other then: a slow, agonizing shipwreck. I saw in an instant that forbidden love is a force that destroys everything. This wasn't the peaceful, selfless love that happy people talked about. This love was like drowning, gasping for breath while sinking deeper and deeper into blackness. We wanted to be so far inside of each other that we could never be separated again, our embodied isolation dissolved by fusion. That ferocious, insatiable appetite for him, all of him, ran through every cavern of me; we craved each other like two starving heathens. Could that even be called love? It seemed like more. It was something bigger, more profound. Something written into the cosmos millions of years before we were born.

I didn't sleep at all that night. I stared at the walls and the ceiling blanketed in shadows. At the faint light coming through the balcony window. The air outside was peaceful and I wanted to melt into that peace, become a part of it. But it was just outside my reach.

22

IN THE MORNING we drove to Cannes with the windows down. The summer sky was clean. Our fingers touched on the arm rest. I parked where I always parked, on the Croissette down by La Roseraie, and we walked. We passed crepe stands and gelato stands, arcades and carousels, squatty Peugeots and Smart cars crammed together in an endless train. Chubby old women sat on blue enameled chairs with dogs on leashes, looking at the sea. The bright turquoise water sparkled in the sun. The marina was lined with low concrete walls where a few tourists sat eating ice cream cones. There were monstrous yachts parked side by side like an inventory of surrogate penises. Big. Bigger. Biggest. We watched the tanned, white-polo-shirted boys who leaned out from their virtual planets, wiping salt-water droplets from pristine hulls with cloth diapers while their Arabian and British and Russian employers tried on Chanel sunglasses in town. I still wanted to live in their world. Surely these people never felt pain.

Rousseau took hold of my hand. I smiled at him, and

then I smiled at this, at us. Us. The idea of it filled me with repressed glee.

"I had another grocery store debacle yesterday," I said, chuckling.

"Jesus, you need a Sherpa."

"I'm afraid I'm becoming my father."

Rousseau laughed. "I know the feeling," he said. When he looked at me his eyes warmed, crinkling at the edges. There, in the sunshine of his gaze, I was my favorite version of myself.

"Really?" I said. "I didn't think you had parents; I've always assumed you were hatched from the head of Zeus or something."

"Nope, I've got real parents. They live in Normandy now, and I am more like my father every day. Just give in to it. It's going to happen whether you like it or not."

"You probably have really amazing, cool parents."

He stared at the ground. "You might be surprised."

"Well, mine are not cool. So, for me, becoming them is kind of an emergency. All my life, my number one goal has been to not be like them."

"What are they like?"

I thought about this for a while. "I don't know. I guess they're just . . . ordinary. They don't ever try anything new; they just eat the same meals and watch the same TV shows over and over again."

"And you were the abnormal one because you wanted to get out of Dayton. Or did you want to get out of Dayton because you wanted to be abnormal?"

"Maybe both?" I said.

"Maybe both."

"It makes me feel like a jerk to say it out loud. It's just . . . ordinary people don't make history. Nobody ever writes stories about ordinary people. I just want to do something special. Something . . . exceptional. Otherwise, what is life but a big hamster wheel, and what are we doing besides going through the motions?"

"I know exactly what you mean."

Rousseau smiled and swung my hand in high arcs back and forth, and I felt it acutely in my bones, the sense that certain people have born into them a direct line to your soul. I'd lived with my parents for eighteen years and they'd never seen me the way he saw me. Their lenses had bent me this way and that, projecting onto me visions of what they thought I ought to be, not because they didn't look, or because they were shallow or ignorant about the world, but simply because some mechanism in their souls was calibrated to see someone else, while Rousseau's was programmed for mine. I could see how crass I'd always been, shouting to be heard among none who could, because here was someone who listened so thoroughly that I barely had to whisper a word, move an inch, and he understood.

We decided to go for pizza and wine. There was a restaurant by the old port called La Pizza, a paper table-cloth kind of place. We sat outside facing the marina and watched the boats in their cerulean still life. The air had already begun to sizzle, but there was a breeze. I listened to Rousseau place our order in perfect French and tried to memorize what he'd said, although I should have written it down because it faded almost immediately. We shared a carafe of cold Cote de Provence. Then our pizzas came in huge crescents bigger than plates, Rousseau's a *napolitaine* and mine a *margherita*. The waitress recited the requisite "*bon appétit*" before retreating.

"So what was your grocery store debacle yesterday?" he asked.

I told him how I'd reached for someone else's cheese at Le Clerc.

He seasoned his pizza with olive oil and took a big bite. "That doesn't sound so bad."

"Well, I'd just had a conversation with my dad about how he got slapped by the Sam's Club sample lady for taking too many samples, so I was mortified."

Rousseau laughed. "The one off of 75? My neighbor used to work there."

I tried to picture that. Rousseau as a kid in a working class American neighborhood. It didn't compute. "It still amazes me that you grew up in Dayton," I said.

"Why?" he said. "Do I seem pretentious?"

"No, not at all. It's just that people who are really accomplished always seem to be from New York or London or Chicago, someplace like that. Almost all of the people I know from Dayton are still there doing the same boring things they've always done."

Rousseau looked amused, then thoughtful. "You never know where you're going to find someone you like, could happen anywhere. That's the only thing worth living for, in my opinion."

After lunch we stopped at a fromagerie for some cheese to take home. Old men played Pétanque on dirt *terrains* near the Palais des Festivals. We strolled through a street market and looked at cheap paintings of the seaside. I could already imagine our life together, the unbearable joy of getting to walk with him like this anytime I wanted. The idea of it was as surreal as waking up to find out I was the queen of England, but now that I'd gotten a taste of it I couldn't fathom not having him. The horizon—that not-quite-describable conglomeration of dreams I was currently pursuing, the reaching of which would bring about supreme and everlasting happiness—shifted focus. This—being here, in this place, with him—this was the very definition of exceptional.

"So, now that you know all about my dad," I said, "you have to tell me about yours. How are you like him?"

Rousseau grimaced and withdrew. I wondered if I should change the subject. Then he said "My father has never been faithful to my mother. I used to hate him for it, as a kid. And now here I am, doing what he did, and it doesn't seem like such a crime anymore."

I don't know what I was expecting, but it wasn't that. We walked along silently for a while.

"Did something happen between you and Chloe?" I said. It was something I'd been curious about for months but had never been able to ask.

The question seemed to snap Rousseau back to the present. "What do you mean?"

"Well," I continued nervously, "you must have loved her at some point, to have married her. Did it just fade over time?"

"No, not really," he said. "I mean, I still feel pretty much the same way about her that I always have."

"Oh," I said with an ache. "Then . . . why are you doing this?"

I wondered, as I often did, what she looked like. What she might be doing at this very moment. Sitting at lunch, probably, unsuspecting and missing him. Flames of guilty darkness licked at my feet.

Rousseau stopped to gather his thoughts.

"I don't know how to explain it." He rubbed his face with his hands. "Here," he said, "I'll give you some back-story. Imagine you're a guy in his last year of university. You've been dating the same woman for about a year, and you're having fun with her, she's a nice person. There's nothing wrong with your relationship, per se, and it's not like you're an expert on relationships anyway. You decide you want to lock this thing down because you're about to start working eighty hours a week. You want to have a family someday, and there are no guarantees you'll ever meet another woman you get along so easily with."

We walked along slowly, both looking at the ground in front of us. I feared what he was going to say, feared it would sting, and I couldn't look at his face.

"So," he continued, "you propose, she says yes, and you get married. Life is stable, but somewhere in your mind is this . . . itch. There's just a sort of constant dull sense that something is missing. You work and you have kids, and there are high points and low points. You try to give your whole heart to it. You refuse to admit to yourself that it feels . . . I don't know, empty somehow. You wake up every morning hoping to feel full, hoping you'll look over at her next to you and see the thing you've been looking for. That's what keeps you going, the hope that tomorrow morning will be different. For fifteen years. Eventually you convince yourself you're never going to find it, that this is all there is, which kind of kills you inside. This is as good as it gets, you tell yourself. And then one night . . . you're sitting at a dinner table in San Francisco, talking to this woman you've just met, and there it is. That indescribable thing you've been looking for your whole life is right there in front of you. It makes you want to start your life all over again."

He paused and looked me in the eye. "Do I care about my wife? Of course. But I never have felt and never will feel about her the way I feel about you."

His words hung in the air between us. I stopped to lean against the side of a building in the shade.

"So what does that mean for us?" I said. "It's okay, I don't need to be *married*. I've never really been the kind of person who wanted to get married. My mother harasses me about it all the time, actually."

Rousseau put his hands in his pockets. "Well . . . what do you want then?"

"I don't know. I've been happy with the way things have been between us these last few months. Can it just stay like this?"

"Really?" He eyed me skeptically. "You'll be happy with that?"

"I think so."

"I can do that," he said.

We headed back up the Croissette, under palm trees, in the direction of the car. And there, watching a sidewalk artist spray paint a neon landscape on the side of a wakeboard, were Lauren and Max. I grabbed Rousseau's hand and pulled him backward at the same moment that Lauren glanced in our direction. I couldn't tell if she saw us.

"What's happening?" Rousseau murmured.

We crossed the street and turned down an alley. "Max and Lauren," I said. I pulled him behind a dumpster that filled our nostrils with the tang of wet, rotten meat. Rousseau crouched down behind me as I peered around the corner. Lauren pulled Max by the hand, through traffic and toward our alley. We were toast.

"They didn't see us," Rousseau said. "They were twenty meters away."

"Shh. They're coming."

At the end of the alley Max huffed. "What in the hell is going on, Lauren?"

Lauren hummed and sucked in a breath. "I could've sworn I saw Halley with . . ." She looked around.

"With who?"

Rousseau moved his foot and it scratched loudly against the concrete at the same time that a car went by. I glanced back at him, wide-eyed, and he gave me an apologetic frown.

"Thomas Rousseau," Lauren said.

"As in, *the* Thomas Rousseau?" Max guffawed. "In her dreams!"

"Seriously, I swear I saw them."

"If you said you saw her with Gus I might believe you."

"Jesus, will you get off that already? She is not hooking up with Gus."

"How do you know?"

My ankles started to ache, and I considered standing up and "outing" us just to see the look on Max's face.

"Because," Lauren said, "I can just tell."

Max clapped his hands together. "Come on, let's get some gelato . . ."

They walked away. After a beat, Rousseau and I stood upright and dusted ourselves off.

"Sorry," I said, not looking at him. I wanted to say something that would erase what he'd just heard, but I couldn't think of what. I felt my Level 2 status more strongly than ever. Did he feel it too? I moved toward the mouth of the alley to examine the street. "Let's go. I think they're gone."

Rousseau took my hand, and we walked to the car.

It was our last night together for who-knows-how-long, and I tried not to think about it. I lay on my stomach in the dark and soaked up every delicious sensation of him, my adoration only increased by his complete acceptance of it. He ran his fingers in an achingly slow line down my back, across my hips and into dark places. The warmth of his mouth made my skin tingle. My body, which had always been sort of grotesque and untidy to me, with all its odd and improper parts, seemed to finally belong in the world. Every boy I'd ever known had expected women to be as flawless and accommodating as an airbrushed centerfold. But Rousseau loved the ugly things. Every fold and freckle. He loved smelling me. We defiled one another for hours. And every touch amplified my urge to take this day, this night, and pin its wings down for all eternity. I would have happily expired right then and there. Impermanence. It was a gut punch. I tried reminding myself that everything ends. I tried reminding myself that even if Rousseau was a permanent fixture in my life, our lives were still made up of seconds and minutes. That people never truly possess each other, they only possess the minutes, and some of Rousseau's minutes were mine and that should be enough. I tried reminding myself of all these things, but it didn't work. I wanted him so badly I was blind with it.

I looked over at him and said, "When you're really happy, do you ever wonder if someday you'll look back at this moment and it will have been the pinnacle of your life?"

He seemed to ponder this for a while, and gradually his features changed in a way I couldn't pinpoint, as if he'd just lost hold of the world's last remaining mystery. It was the first thing I'd ever said to him that I wanted to unsay.

In the morning, I woke up before he did, alone with my thoughts. I knew I would be lying in the same place the next morning, trying to conjure the warm feeling of his arms around me, the earthy smell of his breath on my cheek, the domestic sound of his light snore. A hot tear ran down my temple. A few short hours later, I watched from the curb as he pulled his black roller bag through the sliding glass airport doors. It would be okay, I told myself. Rousseau and I were going to stay in touch, and when I made it to Level 3, I could stay in France and it could be like this always. It would be okay. It would be okay.

I meant to keep the stub of his plane ticket, the one I'd taken from his jeans pocket two nights before. I'd taken it intending to tuck it away where I could always find it and remember. But I left it in the pocket of my capris by accident, and after I washed them I found the paper had disintegrated to nothing.

23

I SHIFTED UNCOMFORTABLY on Gus's couch.

"Wine?" he asked.

It was ten o'clock in the morning. "I'm fine, thanks," I said.

"Well, I think I'm going to have a cappuccino." He disappeared into the kitchen and returned with a cup, put it under the nozzle, toggled through the options and pushed the button. As the machine worked its magic, Gus looked around jadedly, as if it was completely normal to make yourself a cappuccino and not offer one to the person sitting on your couch.

"So," he said, balancing his cup as he sat, "how are launch preparations going? All set for my booth announcement?"

I'd been thinking about it for the last two hours. Should I tell Gus we still didn't have a theme? Should I tell him that Anthony had trumped him on the booth announcement? Would he consider me weak? Would he demand that I go back and talk to Jamie again? Or, worse, would he be so exasperated by my lack of effective "management" that he would ask Max or Lauren to take over? Would this impact his decision to give me the promotion? Would I get sent back to Dayton next year and never see Rousseau again? I decided to respond in the way that any other sane person would respond. I lied.

"Yes," I said. "All set."

A slightly amused smirk flashed across Gus's mouth, which unsettled me. Did he know something? "Good," he said. "I heard a rumor that Anthony the Wanker wanted to make the announcement. So, if he asks you to boot me, you tell him that this is my project and I'm making the announcement, no matter what."

I smiled politely and made a note about the announcement in my binder, dreading the proxy war that was about to happen between Jamie and me.

"I don't suppose you've heard from Thomas Rousseau lately?" Gus said with a twinkle. Now I was sure he knew something.

Rousseau. A montage of our last night together ran through my head like an acid, corrupting everything.

"No," I almost-shouted. "Why would I?" One of my eyes began to twitch.

"I put in a request for him to give one of our podium talks at DEVO. I told him to get in touch with you and let you know if he could do it."

"Oh," I said, visibly relieved. Jesus, Halley, settle down. "Sure, I'll watch for his call."

"Great," Gus said. He looked at me expectantly, like he was waiting for me to say something. I hoped he didn't notice my eye twitching. I wasn't built for all this skulduggery. "Is something wrong?" Gus said. "You look a little pale."

"No. Should there be?"

"Okay," he said. "I want to tell you about an idea I have. I think you're going to like it."

The idea was this: we would buy a few cases of local French wine, slap a custom-made label on each bottle, and deliver one to every person involved in the Tantalus launch, from early product research, engineering, and production all the way to execution, to celebrate our hard work. Naturally, it would be my responsibility to find the wine, buy it, coordinate with Molly to create the custom labels, and get the right quantities shipped to each of the three company offices. Gus even knew which wine he wanted. He had tried a *fabulous* rosé in Marseilles a few weeks ago, in a restaurant whose name and location he couldn't remember, from a vineyard whose name and location he couldn't remember, with a label the look of which he couldn't remember. He did remember that the wine was tasty and French and came in a square-shaped bottle. So, it was my new mission to find said tasty square rosé. Oh and, by the way, it might take a while to get the labels printed, so I should probably find the wine ASAP.

"Great idea," I said. "I'll start first thing tomorrow morning."

I went to visit a local wine shop owner whom Gus, in his zeal to keep his cabinets stocked with good wine, had recently befriended. He gave me a list of every vineyard in Provence he knew of that used square bottles. I mapped them all out on my computer and programmed the addresses into my GPS. Soon I was driving down the A8 in the summer sunshine, the bright blue Mediterranean sparkling on my left and a montage of craggy hills and periwinkle-shuttered towns on my right. Ferraris and Maseratis sped by, racing toward Aix-en-Provence. I put the windows down and breathed in the grassy air.

I was no wine expert, so I decided that the best way to tackle the project was this: upon arriving at the chateau and tasting the wine, if it didn't make me gag, I'd buy two bottles, take a photo of the label, get ordering and shipping instructions, and move on to the next destination. Taste, buy, photograph, drive. Taste, buy, photograph, drive.

"*Bonjour*," I would say to each empty tasting room, a bell hanging on the doorknob announcing my entry. The air inside them would smell deliciously similar: musty old oak and cold earth. Eventually, someone would saunter out of a back room. "*Bonjour*," I would repeat. "*Vous parlez Anglais?*"

"*Oui, un petit peu*," they would say. "How may I help?"

"I am looking for a rosé wine in a square bottle." I would stand squinty-eyed, hoping they didn't laugh at the absurdity of my request or ask me any difficult wine trivia questions.

"Yes, I will show you what I have," they would say. "Would you like a taste?"

"Sure," I would say.

After a few tastings I became a little more relaxed about all this, and by the end of the day I was downright merry. Level 2 had its perks. I drove back toward Biot, a little drunk, with twelve square bottles clanging around in the back seat and six photos on my phone. I emailed the photos to Gus in hopes that one of them would spark his memory, but none of them did. He replied that I should just pick my favorite, and I swallowed the small disappointment of having failed to deliver precisely his heart's desire.

On the way home I took an exit toward Sainte-Maxime in search of a place to have dinner. Dusk was about an hour away, and the sun-burned sky was just beginning to glisten. I wound through dense forest in the direction of the coast until I passed a painted sign along the road that said "*Restaurant Les Petits Poissons.*" I did a three-point turn and backtracked. The driveway was lined with trees like stone giants. A two-story *manoir* stood elegantly at the end, iron gates open. Around to the left there were seven café tables on a gravel patio, all of them rusty and patinaed. Downy white dandelion seeds floated across the path in front of my feet. The place felt a little strange, abandoned, but the remnants of a wine buzz were just heady enough to make it all seem like an adventure.

I sat on a rusty folding chair. Fat bees circled galvanized buckets of lavender, and I thought of Rousseau and wished he was here. I dug my phone out of my bag to send him a text, and as I typed I heard gravelly footsteps and a woman's voice say "*bonsoir Madame!*"

The woman was small and chestnut-haired with a plain, tan face. She carried a folded tablecloth, a small baguette and a drinking glass containing cutlery, which she arranged on the table in front of me.

"*Bonsoir*," she repeated.

"*Bonsoir*," I replied. I looked around, feeling another twinge of strangeness. I liked the idea of informally dining in someone's French country house, being invited in from the road and cared for like a pilgrim in an old novel where people in villages did that sort of thing. In practice though, in our post-*Texas Chainsaw Massacre* world, that kind of intimacy with strangers was a little nerve-racking.

"*Blah blah blah, n'est-ce pas?*" the woman said.

"Um . . ." I replied, digging through my bag for my dictionary. I understood part of what she said, but not all of it.

"You are American?" the woman said.

Thank god she spoke English.

"Yes," I replied.

"For the dinner, would you like fish or chicken?"

I chose fish.

The woman nodded and turned toward the house, emerging a minute later with a wooden plate of food. There was a thick slice of what she described as cheese made with the milk of her own goats. Next to the cheese was a handful of fresh figs from her own tree and a little pot of honey from her own hives. I spread things and dipped things and forgot momentarily about finishing my text to Rousseau amid hunks of crusty bread and mouthfuls of earthy rich cheese. There was a carafe of cold grenache blanc that tasted like fresh dill on my tongue. I felt brave, sitting there alone. I had time to think and breathe the air.

The woman returned again, this time with a plate of just-picked asparagus. The thin stalks had been tossed on the grill for a few seconds until they just barely tasted of smoke. Beside them she wordlessly set a bowl of dark green olive oil, half a lemon, and a box of salt.

After that, the woman was gone for a long time.

For a while the silence was pleasant. To be able to focus singularly on the tastes of the food and the warm breeze. I watched the sky behind the trees turn purple. I finished my text to Rousseau, attempting to describe the day and how much I wished he was there. He responded a minute later.

"I wish I was there too," he wrote.

I finished the last crisp spear of asparagus and drank the rest of the wine.

"You know you could *actually* be here, right?" I replied. "Just a short plane ride away."

"You make it sound so easy," he wrote.

I allowed myself to imagine for a moment what it would be like to see him whenever I wanted. "Do you think we could be happy together?" I wrote.

"Without a doubt," he replied.

"Do you ever think about it? Do you think about how it could be?" I asked. As dusk set in, my table began to feel rather lonely. I heard the high-pitched whine of mosquitoes in my ears, felt the delicate pain of their bites on my ankles.

"Yes, I think about how it could be," he wrote. "I mean, I try to. I'm so used to my life the way it is, I have a hard time imagining it being different. Maybe I'm too literal-minded."

"How do you imagine me then?"

He didn't reply for a long time. I waited, staring at the phone's screen, a flutter in my belly, as if his response would be the culmination of everything we were to one another.

"Last year, right before Christmas," he wrote, "I spent a day with my kids. They were looking at the packages under the tree and guessing what was inside each one, and they were so excited. Like, pure anticipation. And I was envious. I hadn't felt that kind of excitement about anything for a long time. Not until I met you. That's what you are to me. You're the thing I look forward to every day."

It was one of those responses that was simultaneously nice and not what I wanted to hear.

"So," he wrote, changing the subject, "have your worst fears been realized? Did anyone suspect?"

"Suspect what?"

"You know, us. Did Max and Lauren see us?"

I'd been trying not to think about it, but now that he brought it up, I noticed the coil of fear inside me like a waking serpent. All at once my wine buzz wore off, and I felt a little sick.

"I don't know," I replied. "I hope not."

"Could add some spice to your life. Pretend we're in a spy movie."

"My life is spicy enough right now. But I'm glad this is fun for you."

"Oh, it is," he wrote.

I looked around the dark patio and began to wonder if my hostess had forgotten me. I didn't want to violate whatever social code existed in that place, but I went to look for her. The big wooden door to the kitchen was unlocked and I walked inside. The place was charmingly French. A huge garlic braid hung on a hook in the burgundy wall above blue and white tile countertops overflowing with piles of fruit. A clay pitcher held olive oil, next to a stack of well-worn linens. No one was there. I came back out to the patio and walked around the back of the house, feeling the curly crunch of fallen tree bark underfoot. The back patio was vacant too. Maybe I'd have to just leave some money on the table and go.

But as I turned I heard the petite footsteps, and then the woman emerged from the trees carrying a fishing pole in one hand and a wriggling fish in the other. She approached the smoking grill and slapped the fish down, eyeballs and all. I could only guess at what kind of bloodbath would have transpired back here if I'd requested the chicken instead.

I went back to my seat again and the woman brought me another carafe of wine and a few candles. The sun was long set and the patio glowed with fireflies. I mused that a long dinner like this would have been unthinkable in Ohio. My dad would have been up asking to speak to the manager a long time ago. He would've definitely given this place "the axe."

Eventually the woman brought the whole grilled fish on another wooden plate. She left the salt box and set down a fresh lemon. "*Bon appétit*," she said, vanishing again. I peeled back the crackled skin, squeezed the lemon over the white flesh and pinched some salt from the box. It was fresh and meaty and the best fish I'd ever eaten, like a clean cube of briny smoke plucked out of the sea.

At the end I was given a bowl of ripe peaches, peeled and diced, and a little bowl of cream. I poured the cream on the peaches and swallowed them with a bitter espresso. The meal was a marvel, and if I'd had the gift of hindsight it might have occurred to me that in this moment I was living exactly the life I'd always wanted to live. But all I could think about was Rousseau's absence and the square rosé situation and the lies I'd told Gus and the possibility that Lauren and Max had seen us in Cannes. I was there and I wasn't there, preoccupied with both past and future, where my imaginary self in my imaginary life might have a dinner just like this. Where I might be someone exceptional, someone who might leave a footprint on history. I didn't know that history, while it's happening, no matter how it's retold later, feels remarkably average. I still believed that history was the stuff of books, the stuff of mythical giants, not of regular people who ate food. This night didn't count; my clock had not yet started. History wasn't happening right now, wasn't happening to me.

The next morning I chose one of the twelve square rosés as the winner and sent the bottle's measurements and some photos to Molly, for the custom label. It seemed simple enough, but around two she called me.

"Sorry to interrupt beach time," she sang. "I just have an

itsy bitsy question about this bottle."

"Okay," I said.

"Well, do you think *maybe* the bottle might be slightly truncated, and that *maybe* we might need to have one here in hand so we can make sure the label is the right size?"

"You have the measurements, but if you need the bottle I can send it."

"I'm sure your measuring is just as adequate as the rest of your work," she continued in her high pitch. I could imagine that squirrel finger puppet pointed at me, its happy black eyes boring into my soul. "I'd just feel better if I could have the bottle here, to make sure it's right."

"Sure thing," I said.

"Also, Halley, I need the booth graphic work orders."

I sighed heavily. "I can't get them to you until I have the theme, and Max is still working on it."

"I'm sure you can find a way to work around that, right? After all, they wouldn't have hired you if you couldn't manage your part of the project."

I cleared my throat. "I'll send the bottle of wine out by FedEx this afternoon."

I drove to a department store to buy packaging materials. I wrapped the wine in bubble wrap, taped it up inside a cardboard box, filled out the FedEx slips, and took it to the clubhouse to be picked up by the courier that afternoon.

A couple hours later, I received a call from the clubhouse receptionist.

"*Madame 'alley,*" she began, "in order to import wine into the United States you must go online and pay a fee. The courier cannot take the package until you have done this and printed the confirmation."

The receptionist gave me the URL for the website. I went online, used my credit card to pay the fee, printed the confirmation, drove the printed page over to the clubhouse and rescheduled the courier pickup for the following morning.

The following morning, I received a call from the receptionist.

"*Madame 'alley*," she said, "in order to export wine from France, you must go to an office in the center of Cannes and file a form and pay fourteen Euro."

"Can I email the form to them?" I asked.

"No, you must go in person," she said.

I drove to the clubhouse, retrieved the package, unpacked it at my kitchen sink, uncorked the wine, took a big harried slug and poured the rest down the drain. I wrapped the empty bottle back in the bubble wrap, filled out new slips and rescheduled the pickup for that afternoon.

The bottle was finally delivered into Molly's hands two days later.

That same day, I got a call from Gus. "Halley," he said, "I was talking to Anthony the Wanker yesterday and he thinks that if we give wine to some people in the company and not others, some people will be offended and get upset. So we either have to give wine to everyone in the company, or no one. I decided it's just too much of a hassle. So cancel the wine; we're not giving any gifts after all."

24

"HALLEY, I AM calling on behalf of the president."

"I know what you're going to say, Jamie, but . . ."

Jamie cleared her throat. "I thought I was clear the last time we spoke, that Anthony is making the announcement at the DEVO booth. But one of the other VPs told him today that Gus thinks he is making the announcement."

"Gus said it's his project, so . . ."

"This is Anthony's project. Anthony is the *president*. Every project is Anthony's project."

"Gus is giving everything to this launch," I said. "He relocated to another country! Don't you think he deserves the opportunity to stand up in front of our customers and make this announcement?"

That was the funny thing about proxy wars. We were so dedicated to our respective causes that soon it became our war too.

"Ha, that's rich," Jamie said. "You all are over there living in the lap of luxury, playing golf and going to the beach and jet setting around Europe on a company-paid vacation, while Anthony sits in an actual office, and you want to talk about what Gus deserves?"

"We're not—"

"Anthony is making that announcement. Put his name on the itinerary, or you're fired."

I wasn't sure she had the authority to fire me, but I wasn't sure she didn't have the authority.

"Fine," I said.

Rousseau's text said, "I love you so much I sometimes spontaneously vibrate." Outside my window the evening sky glowed purpley-pink over the golf course.

"How do you always know exactly the right thing to say?" I replied.

"You okay?" he wrote.

"Yeah. That wine-buying thing was a bust; Gus just pulled the plug on it. And I'm the middle man in a war between Gus and Anthony over something stupid. I feel like I'm just spinning my wheels here."

"Ah, I sensed a disturbance in the force. Well, at least you'll be fully stocked up on square rosé for a while. You'll be a hit at dinner parties."

I chuckled at the screen. The sound echoed off the tile floor of my silent living room and back into my own ears again, reshaped into something sadder.

"Indeed," I replied. "How are things going for you?" I wished I could watch his life via a series of hidden cameras like a reality TV show and know once and for all what kind of person he was, what was in store for us. Time and distance made everything about Rousseau more perfect, as I mentally relived our days together.

"You mean with my wife?" He knew that's what I was

really asking and, even though it was intrusive, he would answer.

"I don't know, we barely talk anymore," he said. "She's been sleeping in a separate room for a long time."

"Why?"

"Maybe she's seeing somebody else. Maybe she doesn't love me. I don't know. We go through phases of this every couple years."

"Why don't you just get divorced?"

"I don't want to wreck everyone's lives. We have kids. We have a family. It's easier to just let it be."

I leaned over the armrest of my chair and fished around in my purse for a bottle of Nurofen—French ibuprofen. I found the bottle and extracted two of the red capsules, replacing the cap with a satisfying snap. I didn't have any water and didn't feel like getting up to get some, so I swallowed them dry.

"So what are you going to do after the kids are grown up and out of the house?" I asked.

"That's a long time from now," he said. "I could die before then."

I rolled my eyes. "Seriously though. Let's say your kids are gone and you and I are still close. Would you be with me?"

"I don't know," he replied. "A lot could happen between now and then."

"But if we were still happy, as happy as we are now. Would you?"

"I don't know, Halley."

"Jeez. I'm not going to make you sign anything. This is hypothetical."

I went to the sink for that glass of water after all. Something, probably the pills, felt lodged in my throat. I took the glass back to my chair.

"I guess, yes," he wrote. "Hypothetically. I probably would. But no promises."

I sat back down and stared at the ceiling. What was happening to us? What was happening to me?

"You said this was going to be enough," Rousseau wrote.

"I know," I replied.

But maybe it wasn't going to be enough. My heart was beginning to resemble one of those computerized adaptive tests—as I found answers, the questions changed. What satisfied me a few weeks ago didn't satisfy me anymore. Tendrils of anxiety began to wind around the back of my neck. I had to be careful. I had the sense that my not needing more was the only thing keeping us on solid ground. But as my life got lonelier, as my job became more difficult, as I began to doubt the decisions I was making, I needed Rousseau to deliver the light.

"It's just . . . I'm afraid of losing you," I said.

If only I could stop caring so much, stop needing so much, stop wanting so much . . . I could be what Rousseau needed me to be. I could be what the company needed me to be. I could have been what Celeste had needed me to be, what my parents needed me to be. The sight of my own disgusting need spelled out on the tiny screen in front of me made me feel suddenly, grotesquely self-conscious. In my mind I saw Rousseau in all his effortless, accomplished perfection, behind glass like a beautiful instrument, while I stood next to him, something clunkier, trying too hard. I feared his response to my last note, feared he would be as disgusted by my growing desperation as I was.

I stood from the chair and took a walk around my living room, touching the yellow wall, the antique armoire, the rustic green couch, totems of my prosperity. I opened the sliding door and stepped onto the terrace to watch the last remaining light drain from the sky. Nighttime in Biot didn't smell the same as daytime in Biot. Everything intensified at night, as if a divine hand reached down to Earth and turned up the volume. The lavender misted its soapy perfume in the direction of the olive trees, whose woody, bitter bouquet swirled together with the green acrylic scent of hedges against stucco walls. I lay on a chaise and watched the inky sky until a few stars began to shine through, then I went back into the condo, which now felt stuffy with stagnant air. I picked my phone up off the floor, knowing a response from Rousseau would be waiting.

"You're not going to lose me," it said.

25

JULY AND AUGUST were hot and crowded. But by September the droves of vacationers had mostly gone home, and the balmy, bug-filled days had begun to cool. I knocked on the chalky pink door of Darren's condo and heard him shout "Come in" from inside. The door opened easily. There was something oddly comforting, almost holy, about the minimalism of his place. No trinkets to clean, no gadgets to maintain, nothing to distract the eye. Darren's only splurge had been a high quality espresso machine that rivaled Gus's, which meant that meeting at his place consisted of a tranquil table, really good coffee, and undivided attention. I sat in a wicker chair next to the window.

"I feel like I'm losing my mind," Darren said, setting the cups, spoons, and sugar cubes on the table between us. "There just isn't enough time in the day. I shouldn't even be having coffee with you right now—I have so much to do— but I need a break or my head might explode."

"What are you working on?" I stirred some sugar into my espresso.

"Everything. I'm doing most of Gus's, Lauren's, and Max's work for them. I'm writing a report for Gus for his next executive meeting. Max has me drafting the marketing plan. And Lauren talked me into 'helping her'"—he fingered air quotes—"design the sales training, but she has gradually punted the whole thing over to me. In fact, she wasn't even here half the summer; she was off touring Europe with Max."

He tossed his coffee back like a shot and then looked up, crazy-eyed.

"Last week I didn't sleep for three days straight. I feel like nothing I do is ever good enough. I'm actually thinking about hiring a freelancer—whom I would have to pay out of my own pocket—to take a few things off my plate. I haven't even had time to fly my kites!"

"Why don't you just stop? Tell them to do their own work."

"You know the answer to that," he said.

"I'm serious. What are they going to do, fire you? Think about it. You've got them all on the hook now; they need you. They can't do this without you. So, set some boundaries."

"Halley, come on. They could replace me in a second. We have to do our time. And if I don't want to do the time, there's a steady supply of new blood from business schools across the U.S. waiting to do it. If I can't hack it, if I start complaining or start making things difficult for them, there are hundreds of guys out there eager to take my place."

I picked at a hangnail on my index finger and looked at the table in thought.

"You know what bothers me the most?" Darren said. "Gus still has never made me a cappuccino from his cappuccino machine. I've actually daydreamed about sneaking into his house and making one for myself."

"No! You know what happened to Baldwin Frank. Besides, you have your own machine. It might even be nicer than Gus's."

"That's not the point," he said. "It's . . . it's the principle. I want a seat at that table."

"I do too," I said.

But maybe he was right: maybe we had to do our time. Maybe we were just spoiled millennials, too entitled, too coddled, unwilling to do the heavy lifting that our predecessors had done. I mean, really, what was so unsatisfactory about all this? We lived in a beautiful place, we had all these perks, we got to see Europe.

But it did feel like something was missing. We *were* working hard. In fact, we lived at work; we worked all the time. And what was waiting for us at the end of the passage, after we'd done our time?

As if he'd read my mind, Darren said "It's just that sometimes I wonder if we'll ever get there."

"I know what you mean," I said.

"This job . . . Level 2 . . . it's not as good as I thought it would be. I mean, I like working. I like feeling like I'm contributing, you know? But . . . I don't know, I thought it would feel different. This just isn't who I thought I would be at this point in my life."

I shrugged. "Don't ask me. I always thought I'd be a princess by now."

"Right? This isn't what they promised us!" He banged his fist on the table in mock outrage and we both laughed.

"Who are 'they' anyway?" I said. "Who made up all these stories about dreams and wishes?"

He picked up our empty cups and took them to the sink. "Probably people trying to sell something."

Then he turned back toward me, and that old glimmer was there. "But what if we're right on the edge of it . . . and if we just work a little harder we'll get there? You have no idea how much I want to succeed here. Sometimes I sit up in bed at night, wired, imagining what my life could be like. I feel like a drug addict or something."

That was all he needed to say to get us both back on track again. Because we did believe that we were bound for something more special. So we would keep jumping higher, reaching further, rearranging the pieces to make something new. And hoping.

Max and Lauren sat on opposite ends of the table and didn't look at each other. I hadn't seen them in weeks. Lauren looked stricken and stared at the floor, while Max wore his usual smirk, as if he had a secret he wanted everyone else to guess at.

"Goddamned cat," Gus muttered as he walked in. "Sitting there all slitty-eyed, like he's plotting to kill us. I tried to shoo him off and he *hissed* at me. Cook and Bezos trained him well." He drank the last dregs of his cappuccino and put the cup on the table.

Max held back laughter. "Maybe there's a mouse in your condo and he's trying to catch it. Could be a helper."

"I'll take the mouse," Gus said, lowering himself heavily onto the chair at the head of his dining room table.

The door opened and Gus screamed, "Don't let the cat in!" as Darren shuffled inside. We heard him slam the door shut.

"Jeez, what is that cat doing here?" Darren said, emerging from the entry hallway. "I thought it liked to hang out over by Lauren's apartment."

Gus's lips flattened. "It's a goddamned spy cat, that's what."

Darren unshouldered The Backpack and pulled out two huge binders, a notebook, and a pen, and arranged them on the table in front of himself. He looked up and read the very clear exclamation in Gus's eyes that said, "Why haven't you gotten the goddamned wine yet?" and stood up again.

"Wine, anyone?" he said.

We all grumbled our yeses, we'd take it if he was already going to the trouble.

"Let me help you," I said, following him into the kitchen.

"I'll come too," Lauren said.

This was a significant departure, and Max and Gus's conversation went silent as they watched Lauren leave the room. The minute you allow yourself to be reduced to a servile position in any job is the minute everyone begins to perceive you that way. Soon they'll start thinking of all kinds of menial things you can do for them, and when you seek a promotion later, they won't be able to imagine you as a manager because you carry the stench of a servant. Darren and I stood in the kitchen like statues, wondering what to say.

"What?" Lauren whispered.

We blinked. She picked at her split ends and looked at the floor, unwilling to acknowledge her shift of allegiance.

Darren opened the bottles of chardonnay while I pulled the glasses out of the cabinet. Lauren stood against the wall and watched.

We heard footsteps approach, and then Gus poked his head around the corner. "What's going on in here? It takes three people to pour some wine?"

"We're just keeping Darren company," Lauren said.

Gus frowned. "Girls. Darren is fine. Aren't you, Darren? We didn't banish him to the colonies. He's coming back."

Gus wrapped his old-man fingers around Lauren's arm and guided her out. Darren and I exchanged mocking glances before I picked up the tray of glasses and followed, Darren coming out last with two chilled bottles.

"Max was just catching me up on the marketing plan," Gus said. "Go ahead, Max, tell them what you just told me."

"Well it's a good thing we're here, because the Europeans would have totally botched this."

On Gus's face a faint blush of pleasure bloomed at this confirmation of our domination over the European savages. It was the ultimate validation of the company's enormous expenditure to bring us over here. We could see the cogs turning; he couldn't wait to share this tidbit with the executive board.

"Since the Tantalus is brand new technology," Max continued, "we can't just shove it out into the marketplace. We have to prove to the public that it's necessary and will improve their lives."

My mind wandered to thoughts of Rousseau, and Max's voice began to sound like a long string of meaningless sounds. I snapped myself back.

"Just show them the data," Gus said.

Darren moved to say something, but Max interrupted him. "Simon Phloss has been conducting some focus groups, and the participants didn't respond well to the data. Even though it ultimately benefits them, they found the Tantalus's data collection processes and predictive analytics to be manipulative and invasive. I think we should consider initiating another round of research. I can stay here to manage it."

Darren, who had done most of the work behind the

story Max was telling, opened and closed his mouth in an attempt to add comments that would go unheard. Lauren stared at Max with focused concentration, the way a chastened dog might look upon its master. I worked to tamp down an emerging rage that had begun to bubble up into my stomach. I couldn't decide exactly where to direct it; it felt more like rage for some communal sickness I couldn't name. I wished I was a robot, that I could merely exist there without any human frailties, able to completely focus on the task at hand. It was a skill the others seemed to have mastered, to butcher their more unmannerly inclinations and replace them with empty space.

"So, have you come up with a theme yet, Max?" I asked, snatching onto a rare moment of silence. "Molly keeps asking for the booth graphic work orders, and I can't send them to her until I know what the theme is going to be."

"Let's come back to that, Halley," Gus said. "We were just getting to Lauren's part next."

Lauren looked over at Darren, who flipped to his other binder. But as soon as Darren opened his mouth to speak, Lauren began reading from a sheet of paper she'd brought.

"I have a list of all the materials I think we're going to need to train the sales reps," she said. "I've been working on a slide show, which will be the main training tool. And I'm putting together booklets for each rep that contain one-sheets on features and benefits, competition, and talking points, as well as easy-to-understand explanations of the data, and a copy of each of the articles that has been published about the device."

She paused. Darren started to say "We also—" before Lauren spoke over him. "I'm ordering demo product for each rep, and I'm working on getting some branded swag to hand out. Briefcases, ties, pens."

"When will the booklets be ready?" Gus asked.

Lauren looked at Darren.

"November first," Darren said, dry-throated. He walked to the kitchen for a glass of water.

"Are you having them translated?" I asked.

Lauren hesitated, looking around. "Yes?"

"You know translation takes about six weeks," I said.

Lauren moaned loudly. "Can't anything just work? There has to be someone to do every tiny thing!"

"Okay," Gus said, "moving on. Halley, where are we on the booth announcement? I heard from one of the other VPs that Anthony thinks he's doing it."

My stomach lurched. "Uh," I stammered. "No, you're making the announcement."

My face flushed and Gus looked at me soberly. Darren looked away as if it was too uncomfortable to look me in the eye, and Max stared straight at me like a kid burning an ant with a magnifying glass.

I flipped through my binder. "I'm still waiting for the marketing managers to decide on the final booth design. The product managers need to decide which speakers they want for the podium talks and the symposium, and then I can figure out the content and timing and make all their arrangements. Clive needs to get me the attendee list for Europe and Scotty needs to get me the attendee list for the U.S. Jamie needs to get me the executive attendee list and send me the private plane info . . ."

Their eyes glazed over and Gus gave me a look that said he didn't want to know how the coffee got made.

"Basically, I just really need the theme," I said. "I can't submit the graphic work orders without it."

"Thanks for the update, Halley," Gus said mildly.

His eyes seemed to be penetrating me for weaknesses,

and the panic returned. I wondered if he secretly knew all of my inner thoughts, what I'd done to Celeste, what I'd been doing with Rousseau. Maybe they all knew. I felt the secrets like layers of concrete around my rib cage, squeezing and squeezing.

Gus looked over at Max, then back at me again. "Why don't we schedule a meeting later this week to specifically discuss the theme? Clive is flying in for a couple days, so we can do it while he's here."

"Thanks," I said. "That would be great."

"Now," Gus said. "I've been wanting to discuss my entrance to the launch gala. I'm thinking I'd like to zip line in."

"Hello?" I said into the phone. "Hello?"

My dad cleared his throat, and when he spoke his voice was thick and husky. "Hal, we need you to come home."

His tone hit me like a slap. "Why?" I asked.

"Grandpa Mert died last night."

"What?" I said, although I'd heard him clearly. I sat down heavily on the bed and stared at the rambling *toile de jouy* figures on the quilted comforter. "I mean . . . I just saw him a few months ago and he was fine. What happened?"

"He had a heart attack," my dad said. He sounded tired, but gentle. "It happened really fast, he was gone before they got to the hospital."

I didn't know what to say. It was the first time anyone I knew had died, and I didn't have the words to describe the strangeness of it. The muteness of my heart. I was supposed to cry now, to rush to the nearest airport and go home immediately and wear black and reminisce and sob at my grandfather's grave. That's what I was supposed to do.

Death was supposed to be the ultimate in awfulness, and, therefore, this news was so awful that it didn't seem like it could really be happening. It wasn't real. It couldn't be real, because this still felt just like any other day. Time did not stop; sad music did not stream through the background of our conversation. I felt nothing.

"Is everyone doing okay?" I asked.

"Yeah," he said. "Well, I don't know, maybe not. Your Granny is a mess, and your mom too. But, yeah, we're okay."

"Jeez, Dad, I'm so sorry."

"I know, honey. When can you come home?"

I paused to think. I had meetings all week. And we were finally going to nail down the theme, which would set in motion a long list of tasks for me. What would happen if I dropped everything and left? I was still on probation here, still proving myself worthy of Level 3. Even though there was a death in the family, everyone would question my dedication. It wasn't like one of my parents died; it was a grandparent, a "distant relative." And that would be the least of it: if I left now, people like Max and Molly would take over my projects while I was gone, and they'd wreck everything. I had worked so hard to get here, I could not afford to let things slide now, when I was so close to the finish line. And what good would it do to go home anyway? Grandpa was already gone. He wouldn't know if I'd attended his funeral or not. I could go and put flowers on his grave the next time I was there. It wasn't like I was such an integral part of the family anyway; most of the time they didn't even like me. No, I needed to stay.

"I don't think I can get away, Dad," I said. "Things are really hectic right now—it's really bad timing."

For a moment he didn't say anything. Then he sighed. "Okay, Hal. Will you just think about it? We'd really like you to be here."

I heard a shuffling, muffled voices, and I could feel the energy change as my mother grasped for the phone. Then her angry, pain-shaken voice.

"Halley Marie, how dare you?" she said, as if she'd been practicing the line all day, saving her ocean of vitriol for the one person upon whom she knew she'd be able to unload it.

"I—"

"You abandon your family for some job and we don't see you for months and months, and now you can't take two days out of your precious schedule to come home for your grandpa's funeral? Your grandpa who loved you?"

I could hear her tears, her choking fury, her deep, full-hearted grief. She gasped for breath. "HOW CAN YOU BE SO SELFISH?" she screamed. "DON'T YOU KNOW WHAT WE SACRIFICED FOR YOU, WHAT GRANDPA SACRIFICED?"

I heard my father shushing her as she sobbed into the phone. My eyes burned.

"We gave up everything for you," she cried. "Did you know that? You think we never wanted a different life? And I had you anyway, and Grandpa supported us. And all that time, after everything we gave up, this is what I had to look forward to?"

There was a long pause while she collected herself and I didn't dare speak a word. I listened to her cough and blow her nose.

"I have never been more disappointed in you, Halley. You think you're so important, flying around the world . . . that you're better than us. You turn your back on your family like we're nothing. We support you, we indulge you, and this is the thanks we get? You are not the child I raised. You are a bottomless pit, Halley, you just take and take and take. Don't bother coming home. Do you hear me? Just stay there in France with your new family. Don't come home at all."

26

"MY GRANDPA DIED," I wrote.

A few seconds after I hit send, the phone rang.

"Aren't you working?" I said. A phone call from him was a rarity.

"Yes, but I can talk for a few minutes," Rousseau said. "Are you okay?"

"I feel awful. My parents want me to come home and go to the funeral, but I just can't get away. Everything is so crazy right now with work. Please tell me I'm not a terrible person."

"You're not terrible," he said. "We all have to make that choice sometimes, between work and family."

"It's just the launch. After it's over I'll be able to go back to normal again. But right now I can't let anything fall through the cracks."

"I know. I really do understand."

"My parents don't. They're furious. My mom . . ." I thought again about what she'd said, and I started to cry.

"It'll be okay," Rousseau said gently. "They're just upset.

They'll come around."

Neither of us spoke for a few seconds.

"I miss you." I wished he was there to hug me. I pressed the phone closer to my face to hear the way his lips would shape the words.

"I miss you too," he said.

There. The bittersweet longing was like a hit of cocaine, laced with just enough pain to make me question what we were doing, just enough impermanence to keep me wanting more.

"Tell me things are going to change someday," I said. "Not today or tomorrow, just someday."

"You mean between us?" he asked.

"Yes."

He sighed. "I don't know," he said. "How was your meeting? Did they finally decide on a theme?"

These words, and his buoyancy when he said them, felt a little cruel. For him, everything must have been perfect. He had it all. I wanted him back in the trenches with me. I breathed deeply.

"Come on, Thomas. I just need some light at the end of the tunnel. Can you not give me that?"

I was willing to believe the words, even if they were lies, if only he would say them.

"I know," he said. "I'm sorry. Maybe I should talk to you later, after you've had some time to rest."

A sharpness sprang up inside me. "For fuck's sake," I said. "I don't need rest. Why can't we just talk about this?"

I took a breath and stared at my reflection in the sliding glass door. Way to go, Halley. Now you've ruined it. Sometimes I could sense him beginning to grow tired of me, sense myself becoming tedious, and it made me want to turn it all around. I still could. I could be what I was in the beginning, distant and easy and carefree. I had to be, because in this relationship I was the "vacation person." I wasn't allowed to be sad or upset or tedious. I might have one low moment in a week, but if that was the moment he saw, it became the totality of me, despite the fact that I may have been happy and fun during thousands of other moments he didn't see. And the more time passed, the more tedious I would become, because, as my feelings deepened, it took more of him for me to get my fix. Those sweet early months had already faded to something different.

"I'm starting to have some doubts," I said to him.

"About what?" he replied.

"Us."

He paused. "Don't say that."

"Sometimes I just don't see the point. We're hurting ourselves. You're risking your family. I'm risking my career. And for what? So we can miss each other forever?"

"Because we have to," he said.

"What does that mean?" I asked.

"I want you in my life. I need you."

"I don't know if that's enough. Long term, I mean. Put yourself in my position."

"Look, I would leave my wife for you today," he replied. "But I can't destroy my family. Not yet, at least. Maybe someday, when the kids are older. I just don't want to ruin their lives."

"I don't want to ruin anyone's life either," I said. "But what about my life, Thomas? It seems so unfair. I'm not happy."

The moment I said it, I knew it was true. In our heads it had all seemed reasonable in the beginning, like a simple math problem: love plus love equals happiness. But real life was more complicated than that. We were both silent for a minute.

"You're serious about this?" he said.

I didn't know how to respond. Saying goodbye was really the last thing I wanted. I just wanted him. The way we all want the things we can never have. We can imagine them. We can desperately try to will them into being. But, eventually, don't we have to make peace with not having them? Stop dangling them in front of our faces, torturing ourselves with the hope that anything will change?

"Can I just say one thing?" he asked.

"Sure."

"I love you."

"I know," I said.

He didn't reply.

"Let me think about it for a couple days," I said.

"Okay."

I couldn't see the future. I didn't know if I'd be better off with Rousseau in my life or not, and I was afraid to close that door and find out later that it was the wrong decision and be unable to open it back up again and regret it forever. I knew people who were full of regrets—who'd passed the prime of their lives and wished they'd loved more, wished they'd traveled more, wished they'd lived more fully, more in the moment. Wished they'd gobbled up life, rolled around in it and sucked up all of its bitters and spice. I was terrified to end up like that, to end up like my parents. Would it really be better to turn away from this? Embrace comfort and mediocrity because it was the easier thing to do? To wash all of life's sharp edges away in a tsunami of numbness? No, I wanted the scorching pain and the euphoric joy and the wild freedom. The minute I began to think of comfort, the softness of that feather bed began to feel sickly and I longed for the cold hard ground again. Life wasn't supposed to be easy and pleasant; it was supposed to be ghastly and devastating. It was supposed to feel alive, and the prospect of mere comfort felt deadening. I wanted all of it, I wanted exceptional, even if it meant traveling to the very edges of sanity.

And this was the cycle. No matter how resolved I was to end my relationship with Rousseau—and there were more than a few occasions when I was—by the next morning the frost had always melted away. In the absence of consistent hurt, it was easy to forget these intermittent stings and remember only the way he touched me, the way he looked at me, all the ways he made me smile. Only remember that he tempered the pain, forgetting that he was part of the reason it was there in the first place. I felt a little insane some days, going from cold to hot in a span of hours. But those hours stretched out into minutes and seconds spent reliving our best moments. I lived months together with him in days, and he wasn't even there. My happiness and my anguish were bound together as if by string, seesawing back and forth in perfect proportion to one another. The deeper one burrowed into my heart, the more space there was for the other to fill.

27

GUS WAS ALREADY at the table with a plate full of scrambled eggs. I crossed the clubhouse lobby, put my sweater on a chair across from him and went to pick up a plate. A tourist's kid in knee socks was trying and failing to spoon up some tater tots—or whatever they called the French equivalent—from a big silver chafing dish.

"Do you need some help?" I asked him.

The kid looked at me quizzically, then picked up a tater tot with his thumb and forefinger and chucked it, hitting me squarely between the eyes.

"You're a dumpling!" he shouted and ran away.

"Little bastard," I mumbled, wiping the salt from my forehead. I spooned up a whole plate of tots and grabbed four croissants. Gus had witnessed the entire exchange and was still chuckling when I got back to the table.

"I see you're good with children," he said.

I ordered a cappuccino from the approaching waiter.

Gus scooped a spoonful of eggs. "Let's talk about Thomas Rousseau," he said, then shoveled the eggs into his mouth.

I picked up my water glass and took a big drink. "Okay."

"Have you heard from him lately?" He looked me right in the eye and I was sure he knew something. My eye started to twitch.

I paused to swallow another gulp of water. "No," I said.

"Really?"

"Why do you ask?"

"Just making sure everything is on track," he said. "You know, for the podium talks. Is everything set for my gala night entrance?"

I took a deep breath. "Yes, the entertainment coordinator is going to install the zip line."

"Great," he said.

"They want you to come over and do a few practice runs with a trainer the day before." I took a bite of croissant. Ah. The buttery layers crunched in my mouth. By now I'd eaten so much cheese that the thought of cheese made me feel a little sick. I'd moved on to croissants. Croissants were the source of all that was good and right in the world.

"Impossible," Gus said. "We'll be way too busy with the meeting. Besides, I don't need any practice."

"If you're sure," I said. I started on another croissant.

Gus took another bite of scrambled eggs.

"Have you decided what time to have the meeting with Clive on Friday," I asked, "to talk about the theme?"

"Oh, didn't I tell you? There won't be a meeting," Gus said. "Clive had to cancel."

"Oh," I said. "When do you think we'll be able to talk about the theme then?"

"Let Max handle it. He'll let us know when he's ready."

I scowled into my third croissant but didn't think it wise to protest.

Gus looked down at my plate. "That's a lot of croissants," he said with one raised eyebrow.

I stopped chewing. "It's not that many," I said.

He chuckled as his phone rang. "Excuse me," he said, getting up and walking toward the lobby. "*Ciao bella*," he whispered.

That night Darren elected to stay home with The Backpack, so it was just me, Max, Lauren, and the rest of Cannes. It would be the first and last time I ever went out with the two of them alone. I didn't know why they'd asked me in the first place. Maybe they thought they needed a buffer. Something bad had happened between them that filled the air around us with an angry fug. Max had become even more sadistic than usual, and Lauren vacillated between conspicuously chipper and conspicuously stricken. Tonight she was a little of both, depending on whom she was talking to.

"Did I ever tell you about the time I met 50 Cent?" she shouted over the din of music, hooking her arm through mine. She kept her eyes locked on Max, who was clearly conducting an inventory of the physical assets of every woman in the room.

"Yes," I said.

She took a sip of her vodka cranberry and pouted.

"Have you noticed the way Gus sneaks around talking on the phone sometimes?" I said.

Lauren perked up at the suggestion of scandal. "You mean the whole 'ciao bella' thing?" she said. "Yeah, Max and I have been trying to figure it out for months."

She turned. "Max," she shouted in his direction. He didn't hear her. "Hey, Max," she repeated, waving one arm.

Max had homed in on a doe-eyed brunette who stood

alone near the bar, apparently waiting for someone. He stood to go and talk to her.

Lauren took another gulp of her drink. A text message from Rousseau blinked on the screen of my phone.

"Where are you?" he said.

"At a club called Mixer with Max and Lauren," I replied, "which appears to have been a bad decision. Why?"

"Just wondering," he wrote. "Why was it a bad decision?"

"I don't know exactly what's going on, but there's some bad juju."

I put the phone back down. It was too loud to try to carry on a conversation with Lauren, so I sat back and looked around. This club was a place for forgetting yourself. People jostled and tripped through the black, strobe-lit halls. A man in tight leather leggings and thick black eyeliner tended bar.

"Let's do a shot," Lauren shouted, pulling me up with her.

She positioned herself at the bar near-but-not-too-near the spot where Max was speaking in broken French to the brunette. Every few seconds they laughed, and he flashed that mischievous, boyish smile that made him so irresistible.

"Two Jägerbombs," Lauren shouted, holding up two fingers. The bartender nodded and poured the drinks. I almost declined the one Lauren pushed toward me. After getting really sick on Jägerbombs one time in high school, the smell of Jägermeister made my stomach heave a little. But I rallied.

"To the Tantalus," Lauren said, clicking her shot glass against mine. She glanced at Max again, dropped the shot and chugged. "Two more!" she shouted at the bartender.

With every shot we took, the chatter, the drinks, the

music, the lights and walls and clothes and shoes and people became louder, floating. The louder the noise grew the more I withdrew into myself. People danced and kissed. Lights flashed. What was I doing here? It all felt forced and empty. And yet, there was some insane animal beauty in the possibility—always the possibility—that the night might abruptly and without warning turn magical.

I went upstairs to find a bathroom, hugging the wall for balance. Lauren followed me, and as soon as the door closed she sank to the dirty floor in tears.

"How can he treat me this way?" she cried.

"Who?" I asked stupidly, wishing she'd get up.

"Max!" she said, collapsing into her hands.

"Um, have you not noticed?" I said. "Max is a complete asshole."

"No, he wasn't like this," she slurred. I bent down over her as two stick-thin girls in sequined miniskirts pushed past us and entered toilet stalls. "You don't know him. He was really sweet."

"I'll bet," I chuckled. "You probably think Kim Jong-un is sweet too."

"Who?" she said.

"Never mind. Look, Max is a jerk. Seriously, don't waste your tears on him."

"No! You don't understand. He was sweet."

She proceeded to tell me about the day they got together. It was the day we moved into our condos. Max called her over to his place because he needed to steam one of his shirts and he couldn't figure out how to put water in the steamer. When she got there, he was holding a hand mixer without the beaters in it. He was so genuinely confused that his guard was down in a way Lauren had never seen before, and it made her feel like she had privileged access to some secret part of him. She was special. They laughed for a long time, and she immediately forgot all about her boyfriend back in California and fell into his arms.

"So what happened?" I asked. "You guys broke up?"

"I don't really know," she said, still teary. "He never *said* he wanted to break up, but we never talked about whether or not we were really 'together' either. He just seemed to be getting bored with me, and then after a while we didn't hang out as much. I tried talking to him, but he won't talk about it. He just won't talk. And now we're here and he's picking up other women! Did I do something, Halley? Do you think I did something?"

"No, I think he's an asshole."

A steady line of women shuffled past us, slammed stall doors. We heard the clicks of door locks, the swish of urination, the gorge of toilet flushes and sinks and hand dryers. Lauren laughed a drunk-person laugh, pushed herself off the floor, and wiped the mascara drips from under her eyes.

"You're nice, Halley," she said, staring at herself in the mirror across from us. Her face turned serious. "I'm sorry you had to make all those sandwiches for me. I'll make my own sandwiches at the Paris meeting, I promise."

"Oh," I said. That one caught me off guard.

"Tell me if you need help, okay? I mean, if I can help you. I always thought your job must be so much easier . . . you know, less responsibility . . . but after being here . . . it doesn't sound easy anymore."

"Thanks." I wondered if she would even remember saying it. I should have recorded it.

"I'm going to get a cab," she said. "Are you coming?"

"Yeah, I'll go tell Max we're leaving."

On the way to find Max I heard someone descend

the stairs behind me. I turned to look but it was so dark
I couldn't see. I could only make out his outline, tall and
slender. Then he said my name.

But it couldn't be.

"Thomas?" I slurred.

Was it really him? How did he get here? Maybe I was
imagining this. He came closer and I reached out and
touched the cotton of his sweater, his familiar hair, the
temple of his glasses.

"Stay with me," Rousseau said in my ear, and then he
kissed it.

Disbelief, maybe some shock, and then the over-
whelming safety of him. I pulled him around to a dark
place behind the stairs where nobody would see us. His hot
mouth on my shoulder. My hands pressed against the wall,
fingertips rubbing across the cold painted concrete. His
hands grasped, and his lips kissed. And then there we were,
walking through the door of a hotel room. There was a hard
kiss on the mouth. Then shoes off . . . hands searching . . .
knee bumping the bed . . . cursing and smiling . . . his sweet
breath on my face. A whole glorious night ahead of us. I
would have given anything to stay there with him forever,
despite the fact that I was slowly becoming an animal.

28

I woke up still fully clothed. When I opened my eyes, I recognized nothing. Not the white duvet or the blue-striped wallpaper, the dripping chandelier or the flat screen TV. I did recognize Rousseau, who'd fallen asleep on his side next to me, also fully clothed, holding my hand. I turned my head and was slammed with hangover nausea. There was a phone on the nightstand next to me and I reached for it.

A French voice answered, "*Allô.*"

"Yes, hello?" I croaked quietly, trying not to wake Rousseau. "Room service?"

"*Oui,*" the voice said.

"I need a bowl of soup and a bottle of Nurofen."

"Madame, it is 6:00 a.m. We do not serve soup until lunchtime."

"Look, I don't care how much I have to pay you. I don't care if you charge me a thousand dollars. I need a bowl of soup and a bottle of Nurofen."

"Madame . . ."

"I am begging you, sir. Soup. Nurofen."

"Please hold for a moment," he said. He came back a few seconds later. "Okay, Madame. Will there be anything else?"

"Water."

"*Oui, Madame.*"

"Thank you."

The knock woke us both up. Rousseau got up to open the door and sign the bill. The waiter rolled the linen-covered room service cart up right next to my face. A single pink carnation stood between my bowl of soup and my medicine. The waiter left silently, pulling the door shut behind him. My head throbbed.

"You're a mess," Rousseau said.

"I'll be okay as soon as I drink some water." He handed me the bottle, and as I drank, a thought occurred to me. "Hey, what happened to Lauren last night? She was waiting for me to get a cab with her."

"You don't remember?" Rousseau's eyebrows went up. "You must have been worse off than I thought. You went out and told her you were going to stay at the club."

I ran my fingers through my hair and pressed on my temples. "Great," I said. "She probably thinks I stayed with Max."

"You said that last night too, but at the time you thought it was funny." He smiled.

I looked around. "Where are we anyway?"

"A hotel a few blocks from the club. You kept saying we were going to get caught by Gus if we went back to your condo. Can I have some of your soup?" He grabbed the spoon. "I didn't have any dinner last night."

We finished the soup and drank half the liter of water, then went back to sleep again. I was restless as my body metabolized the remainder of the alcohol coursing through my veins. A couple hours later I woke up sweaty, but better. I drank some more water and got in the shower. A minute later Rousseau opened the shower door and stepped in behind me.

"Excuse me, sir, do I know you?"

"I must be lost," he said. "Have you seen my girlfriend?" And then he kissed me.

I wrapped a big white towel around myself and looked in the mirror, lips red from kisses. I wondered how long it would be, how many kisses I would need to store up, before the next time.

"Thomas," I called, walking out of the bathroom, "I keep meaning to ask you. Gus wants you to give one of our podium talks at DEVO. Are you going to do it?"

Rousseau stood in front of the closet door, buttoning his shirt. "Oh, yeah. He sent me a couple emails about that. Well, I've got a pretty packed schedule for that meeting, but I could make some time on the last day."

"Perfect," I said. "I'll email the conference organizer."

"I got you a copy of that journal you needed," he said. As I towel-dried my hair, he fished around inside his briefcase and produced a publication, set it on the desk.

"Sweet. Thanks," I said, picking it up and idly fingering through it. "Gus will be impressed I was able to find it." I smiled at him and we made eye contact for a few silent seconds, and there was that warmth in his eyes that I loved, the kind that made the lines appear at the corners. I registered the ease with which we coexisted. It could be like this, always. Why couldn't it?

"Do you think we're bad people?" I said, looking down

at the floor.

"No. What makes you say that?"

"You know. This."

Rousseau frowned. "It's not like we haven't done *this* before."

"I know," I sighed. "I just wish we didn't have to be so damned secretive all the time."

"Me too," he said.

He looked so good in his gray jacket, white Oxford shirt, and jeans. I felt a pang of ownership. I wanted the world to know that he was mine.

"Hey, can you do me a favor?" he asked.

"Sure."

"The company needs a new picture for the website. Tell me which of these you like."

I stood behind him while he pulled them up on the screen, from a photo shoot he'd done a few days before. Then I burst out laughing. Not only was he smiling the biggest high-beam smile humanly possible, but all four of the pictures looked exactly the same. Soon I started belly-laughing and couldn't stop. Maybe I was still a little drunk. My eyes began to water.

"You're a jerk," he said, but he started to laugh too. "What is so funny?"

"I'm sorry," I said. "I can't tell the difference." I could barely get the words out. Tears were streaming down my face.

"You could at least pretend I look hot."

I looked back at the pictures and doubled over again. "I think the third one is the best one," I said.

"I hate you," he said, smiling.

I wanted to stop time. It was such a stupid, inconsequential moment, and yet it was so perfectly lived that

I was simultaneously there and not there, watching us from outside myself and mourning the loss of everything we could have been, would have been, if things had been different. The days were always so short, and I would spend so much time remembering.

I looked away. "What should we do today?" I said.

His phone started to ring. We both knew it was her before he pulled it out of his pocket. He looked at me nervously and turned around to answer.

"*Allô*," he said tersely. "*Oui. Mmhmm. Oui* . . ."

My heart sank. I could hear her voice through the earpiece chattering away in French and I coveted the nonchalance with which she could talk to him, the certainty she must feel every day, knowing that he would always be there. Actually, it made me angry. She didn't know scarcity. She could gorge herself on him until she was sick, until she barely noticed him anymore. To be able to sit on the bed every morning and just watch him tie his tie . . . to laugh as he dorkily tucks his shirttails into his underwear . . . to have unimpeded oceans of time sprawling out in front of them, time to really talk, time to do everything together . . . I was dying of thirst and she stood in front of me with a cup of water, pouring it on the ground.

I felt cheap and trampy as I put my clothes back on.

"*D'accord*," he said and hung up.

He looked over at me, then at his feet. "She'll be here tonight," he said, pocketing his phone.

"What?"

"Chloe. My wife. She's on her way here now."

"Here to Cannes?"

"I'm sorry," he said.

"But . . . why would you bring her here? This is our place."

"When she saw my plane ticket she asked if she could come. I couldn't say no."

I stood. "Well, great. Have a good time," I said, not meaning it.

"I'm sure we won't," he said, "but thanks. I wish I was spending the night with you." He began rearranging things inside his briefcase.

"Liar."

He turned back toward me. "What?"

"I mean, you don't have to lie to me if you'd rather be here with her."

"Why would you think that?" he said.

"Oh, maybe because you invited her here?" I was on a roll now. The storm was building.

"Well, I'd much rather be with you," he said.

I crossed my arms over my chest. "Then why did you invite her?"

"I didn't—I told you, she invited herself."

I was thinking less about what he was saying than about how my words must sound to him. I could feel myself sliding into that sinkhole of unmitigated jealousy, looking for a way out and finding none, ready to unload a surplus of pent-up bile.

"And you couldn't have made some excuse for why she shouldn't come? Jesus. How often do I get to see you like this, Thomas? Once a month?" *Don't fuck it up, Halley,* I thought. *Don't fuck it up, Halley, don't fuck it up, Halley.*

Now he was getting angry too. "Oh, really? What excuse could I have made? Since you're the expert on my marriage."

"I'm sure you could've come up with something," I said. "This is bullshit—she gets to see you every goddamned day, and what do I get? Scraps."

He took a deep breath. "Look, she's not stupid. I can't just come up with random explanations out of the blue and expect her to believe them. It was hard enough getting her to wait twenty-four hours instead of coming over on the same flight as me. You and I almost didn't get to see each other AT ALL! Why can't you be glad about the night we just got to spend together?"

"Because we could've easily had more!"

"Well, if that's the way you choose to see it, fine. I'm sorry. I didn't invite her, I wanted to spend the time with you. It didn't work out this time. There will be other times."

"Fine," I said. I picked up my purse, turned, and left, letting the door slam closed behind me.

But the second the door closed I regretted all of it. *Give it back to me,* I thought. *Rewind the clock. I'll do it better, I promise.*

29

OCTOBER AND NOVEMBER were much the same. Rousseau and I had our up and down moments. He didn't have a chance to visit again, but we still talked almost every day. I tried to be satisfied, and became incrementally more jealous and disillusioned in the process. Part of me ached to go home to Ohio. I missed the orderliness of American life. The easy availability of tacos and peanut butter and my favorite brand of toothpaste. Fall had always been my favorite time of year. The silent macabre of nature winding down was a relief after the forced perkiness of summer. I could almost taste the apple cider frothy with spice, feel the crisp chill in the air and the crackle of acorn caps underfoot. The trees in the woods behind my parents' house would be all fiery oranges and reds. My dad would walk into the kitchen in his house slippers at dawn, sit at the table and drink his morning coffee to the oo-wah-hoo-hoo-hoo of mourning doves. When I was a kid I thought their coo was just the sound the earth made, like a great mournful sigh coming out of the ground.

But I also knew I didn't really want to go back, that being there would always pale in comparison to the memory of it. The truth of it was that the only place I ever seemed to want to be was somewhere else.

By December the urgency of our looming deadline pushed us to the brink of madness. Darren and I confined ourselves to our separate condos and worked and worked. Gus, Max, and Lauren traveled to important meetings. Only twice did Darren have to disrupt his work to hop on a plane and deliver something from The Backpack to Gus. I spent the days in a state of distracted tenacity, staring at phone and computer as if they were about to speak to me, as if I was going to miss something, the anxiety of one trying to wrap her arms around a noisy world and mistakenly believing it was possible to perceive it all at once. How much lovelier life must have been before phones and email. Before computers and electricity. Before humans decided it was necessary to fabricate a whole universe and then spend their lives maintaining the fabrication. Back when it was acceptable to spend eight hours a day foraging in the woods and contemplating infinity. Instead, I was slowly becoming my laptop. Soon I would sprout keyboard digits and power cord arms.

One particularly frosty evening I abandoned the proof-reading of banquet event orders to buy apples at the super-market and make a pie. The mindless tasks of peeling and slicing, grinding fresh cinnamon, rolling out buttery dough and crimping the edges, were cool water on the sauna stones in my head. My condo filled with sugary autumn smells. I listened in on two conference calls and then took the rest of the evening off. I cooked my favorite dinner—garlic green beans and mashed potatoes—and started watching a romantic comedy on my laptop. I had just finished eating a warm piece of pie with vanilla gelato when Rousseau called.

"Hey beautiful," he said easily. "How are you?"

"I made my favorite dinner," I said. "I feel really good."

"It makes me so happy when you're happy. It brightens my day."

I sucked in a breath. It annoyed me, his statement. Without skipping a beat it seemed to throw me back to the depths of my emptiness, because I didn't feel happy when he was happy without me, and clearly that made him a better person than I was. All I could feel about his happiness was envy and resentment and fire. His upbeat tone, as if everything in the world was grand, seemed to trivialize my suffering, make light of it as if it were nothing, as he giddily had his cake and ate it too. I wanted him to be as miserable without me as I was without him. I wanted him to be as hungry for me as I was for him. I wanted to hear "I can't live without you," not "La dee da, I've got it all." His happiness implied that I *should* be happy, despite everything. That it was my choice, it didn't have anything to do with him. See how easy it is for you to be happy, Halley?

When I opened my mouth, though, none of that came out. Instead I said, "I thought you were going to call me yesterday."

"I was planning on it, but I got busy," he said, still unaffected.

"Well, I waited all evening," I said.

He sighed. "Come on, Halley, I can't pay attention to you every minute."

Here we go again, I thought. "Do you know how many minutes you don't pay attention to me, Thomas? I'm not a robot, I have needs, you know."

"Can we please not do this tonight?" he asked. "We

were having a perfectly nice conversation just now."

My face flushed with anger. "Is there ever a good time to do this? I can't be perky and bright all the time."

"How about fifty percent of the time?" he snapped.

Ouch. "That's bullshit, and you know it."

"Jesus Christ, why are you being so difficult? Why do you have to ruin this?"

"Because this isn't how it's supposed to be!" I shouted. "When people like us find each other, we're supposed to find a way to work it out!"

The fear was there now, and the disbelief. How could I keep failing at this when I was trying so goddamned hard? And yet, the harder I ran, the faster Rousseau seemed to recede before me. Slowly but surely I was losing hold of the whole infallible world of my dreams. A world where hard work always led to success, where people who loved each other overcame all obstacles. A world that made sense.

"I don't understand how you can keep walking away from me," I said pleadingly. "How *can* you? Knowing that life will never be as good."

"I'm not walking away from you," he said placidly. "But I can't just uproot my whole life all of a sudden."

"All of a sudden? We've been doing this for months!"

"Yeah, and I've been married for fifteen years! I need time to think about it!"

"That's ridiculous! What is there to think about? What is more time going to change?"

"You said from the very beginning that you were going to be satisfied with this. Was that all just bullshit?"

"Oh, of course! I just said all of that to lure you in! All along, this has all been one big fucking trick. Surprise!"

I heard myself, the bitterness in my voice. I didn't want to be like this, I really didn't. I wanted to be on his side.

But I also wanted to stand up for myself and be heard, and there never seemed to be a correct way of being. I was supposed to be assertive, I was supposed to be submissive. I was supposed to be sweet, I was supposed to be sexy. Don't put up with any bullshit, do anything for love. Be ruthless, but be nice about it. Take a hint and bail, give it my best effort. Be myself, but follow others' advice. I wanted to say all the right things, but what were the right things? Rousseau and I understood the challenges of each other's lives, but there was no way for either of us to get what we wanted without someone getting hurt. And so we continued to find ourselves at this endless stalemate.

"Halley, I can't think about this right now," he said.

There was a hard coldness in his voice that I'd never heard before and could hardly believe. It frightened me more than anything he'd ever said to me before.

"I'm sorry," I replied quickly.

"You know, you think when you get older you'll have everything figured out, but it isn't like that. I'm just as clueless about all this as you are. I'm not the conqueror you think I am, moving through life always knowing what to do. I'm just taking things as they come." He paused, then sighed. "Sometimes I wish I could just go back to my old mediocre life again."

His voice was weary, as if he'd aged twenty years in the last twenty seconds.

"Look," he said, "I don't know why I insist on prolonging the status quo with Chloe. I think it's because, to tell you the truth, I'm too much of a coward to make a change. If you want to know what I really think, that's what I think. I'll probably never leave Chloe. And if I ever do, it'll be so far in the future that you and I will have already been to hell and back by then. If we do end up together, it'll be because you did the heavy lifting to get us there. And won't you be so bitter and fed up by then that we'll end up with some cancerous thing instead of the happiness you envision?"

The fear was now spraying my insides at full nozzle. "It doesn't have to be like that," I said. "We can have a great life."

"Maybe I don't need to have a great life," he said.

I wasn't sure what he meant by that, and I would spend a long time thinking about it. Maybe it was that he'd begun to believe life was supposed to be dissatisfying. And dissatisfaction was familiar. It was comfortable. In dissatisfaction, there was always the future to look forward to. In happiness, we had only to lose, but in unhappiness, we had only to gain.

Then again, maybe he was just tired.

"Okay," I said. "I can do the heavy lifting then, like you say. We'll just keep doing this until you're ready to change things. If that's the only way to preserve this, I'll do it. I'll do it."

"Look at us," he said. "We're tearing each other apart." He was silent for a few long seconds. "What if the only way to preserve this is to end it?"

My stomach lurched. "That doesn't make sense. What does that mean?"

He paused, as if someone had just entered the room. "I need to go."

"Okay," I said. I didn't know yet how worried I should be. Our lives had become so cloudy lately that I could no longer tell clouds from sky. I wanted to keep talking, to figure it all out and make things right, to feel the rush of relief when we both stepped back from the cliff edge. But there would be no figuring it out tonight.

"Good night," he said.

"Good night."

The silence after I hung up the phone was unbearable. I wanted to call him back, apologize a thousand times. I sat on the edge of my bed with the phone in my hands as if I could still turn it all around, still rewind the clock, as long as I didn't take one more step forward. I didn't move from that spot for hours.

30

THE NEXT MORNING, I awoke in a panic. The frustration fueling our fight the night before had, of course, disappeared entirely and been replaced with the fear that I'd destroyed everything. It was a physical fear, like waking up blood-covered to discover you've unconsciously murdered someone in your sleep.

I dialed Rousseau's mobile from bed. It rang until his voicemail picked up. I put my phone on the bedside table, took a deep breath, and stood up.

I should have eaten something, but eating food was about as desirable a prospect as eating mud. Instead, I took a shower. My legs shook, and black spots blinked in front of my eyes as I stepped back onto the bath-mat. I leaned against the wall for a second, then slid to the floor, waiting for the spots to go away. I held my hand up in front of my face. It trembled silently, as if it contained every fear and every desire I'd ever felt. I was a drug addict, consumed by plots to get my fix of him, refusing to believe in the possibility that it was over. It couldn't be over. With every inch that dream of him receded, my life seemed to lose a degree of importance.

I got in the car and drove to Cannes. I parked on the east end of the Croissette and walked. Everywhere I went reminded me of him, the places we'd been together all those months ago when everything was easy and bright. Everyone I saw looked happier than normal. The old men playing Pétanque. Kids screaming on the tinkling carousel. Dogs straining on their leashes to inspect passersby as their mistresses gossiped from those blue enamel chairs. The Francophilic tourists.

"Marcus, what if we just sell everything . . . we could afford a place here."

"God, Janice, can you imagine how perfect it would be to live here? Paradise."

"I don't think I could ever get tired of this view. We could eat croissants every day!"

I was so tired of croissants that the thought of eating a croissant made me feel a little sick. "No," I wanted to say, "take it from me, it won't last."

Dusk fell over Cannes and the glitterati emerged for their nocturnal recreations. I walked by the legendary hotels that loomed over me like giant white wedding cakes, the nightclubs loud with voices.

"*Tu ne devineras jamais.*"

"I am dying for a cigarette."

"*Où est Claude?*"

"Did you see her shoes?"

Cheek kisses. Anonymous fingers holding glasses of champagne. Strobe lights. Cars booming music. Bright lights from a gelato cart where people stood in line holding fistfuls of cash. Teenagers on the beach taking selfies. Everywhere, cameras flashing. Millions of selfies. The air full of text messages, their electromagnetic waves like a plague numbing everything that was vibrant in the world. The closer I was to it, the more vulgar it became. I was an alien in a sea of logo-covered couture, the masses here to see and be seen worshiping at the altar of capitalism. Abundance was supposed to have given us the space to do more, be more, make the world better. Instead it had given us this. I wished a bomb would drop on us, something to snap us out of this, shake us all awake. The excess and the noise was an assault on my whole body. I wanted to spontaneously disappear without a trace.

A bum sat on the sidewalk with a paper coffee cup in his hand, which contained change that he jangled when people walked by.

"*Tu es Americain*," he said to me as I passed.

I ignored him and kept walking.

Then he said in heavily accented English, "You should smile."

When I didn't reply, he laughed. It was that laugh that got to me—a laugh that said "You are nothing but a thing, here for my profit and amusement." That was when I lost my shit.

"Oh yeah?" I said to him, wheeling around. I had no idea what was about to come out of my mouth. "Who the fuck do you think you are? You think you can just sit here on your *stoop* all high and mighty . . . telling people how to look . . . and what to do?"

People on the other side of the street glanced in our direction, but kept walking. The bum blinked up at me. He may not have even understood what I was saying.

"You don't know anything about my life!" I shouted. "I could have said you need to get a job . . . or you need to take a shower! But I didn't! I minded my own business, because

I'm nice . . . I'm a nice person! Fuck you, I can frown if I want to!"

He laughed as I walked away.

I don't know how many hours I walked, but the tourists and pedestrians thinned out and eventually there was almost no one. Just me and the quiet streets, the dark shop windows and the smooth lapping of the sea. A ball of misery sat in my empty gut like a cancer. I had a strange compulsion to reach down my throat and rip it out.

"Dear Celeste," I wrote. "Please come to Paris next month. I need you. Please, I'll do anything. I'm sorry. I'm sorry. I'm sorry. Love, Halley."

Relationships like Rousseau's and mine don't begin and end neatly. Like sawing a leg off, the end came in ruthless hacks, one at a time and very slowly. Each morning the hope would build back up again, the possibility that everything might go back to the way it used to be. Hack. Every time I heard a sound I looked out the window, praying to see him at the door. But he never came. Hack. Hack.

Instead, Rousseau unloaded on me a relentless assault of silence. It was a message much louder than words. His silence had mass, a physical presence. It wasn't just the absence of something, it was stuffy and dark, a hot knife plunging through my chest daily until I didn't think I would ever breathe again. I lay awake every frigid winter night staring at the ceiling, violently lonely, confronting the meaninglessness of everything. And when morning finally came and I stepped outside again, the sunlight and the fact that civilization had survived intact seemed shocking and harsh. I feared those mornings more than anything. As much as I wanted to remain the person that he loved, in the cold light of morning the insult of Rousseau's silence made me boil over with a rage so strong I thought I might lose my mind. I felt a visceral disgust with him and with myself and with the world in general that overshadowed every good thing with spiritual emptiness. I rode through the days on a wave of sick, motivating fury.

One day after Christmas, Gus, Lauren, Darren, and I sat around Gus's dining room table watching Max, who stood next to his flip chart like the ringmaster at a circus. Gus seemed especially jovial, which Lauren pointed out in case the rest of us hadn't noticed.

"Why shouldn't I be?" Gus said.

Max smirked. "He's just happy because I killed the spy cat."

The rest of us stared.

"You killed a cat?" Lauren said.

"Yep."

"How?"

"Slit its throat," Max said casually.

I thought of Phil Collins, and my stomach began to hurt.

"Sick," Lauren said.

"You're overcivilized," Max said.

"Let's not forget the cat was a spy," Gus said. "He had it coming."

Lauren blinked at them, slack-jawed.

"Max," Gus said, "you're up."

"Okay," Max said, clearing his throat, "the moment we've all been waiting for. The Tantalus theme."

He flipped a page on the flip chart to reveal scrawled in black marker on the page beneath:

Countdown Clock

Around the words were various drawings and clippings of countdown clock concepts, which Max described to us with purposeless phrases like "target profile" and "vision statement" and "brand promise."

After Max was done, Gus said, "Great. Thanks, Max."

If a single additional thing had been wrong with my life, this would've been the moment Halley Faust went postal.

"Wait a minute," I said. "This is the theme we've been waiting *eight goddamned months* for? I proposed this idea at our very first meeting!"

There was a pause. Gus opened his mouth and then closed it again. Lauren and Darren both cracked a smile. Max studied me for a long few seconds, and then said, "Um, are you PMS-ing or something?"

"What?" I leaned in.

"Yeah, you heard me," Max said.

"Okay kids," Gus said, gesturing for us to take it down a notch. "The theme is fine. Max, I'll make sure you get the promotion we discussed. Now," his eyes focused on me, "we're all under a lot of pressure and there's still a lot to do, so let's get back to work. But first, I'd like to offer you all a cappuccino."

It caught us off guard, and we looked at each other for cues. Gus was going to make us *cappuccinos*? Max's gloating smirk said, *This is all thanks to me, motherfuckers.*

"Are you . . . sure?" Darren said.

Gus huffed. "Well, do you want one or not?"

"Yes!" Lauren said. The rest of us voiced our agreement.

"Darren," Gus said, "go get us some cups."

Darren skipped into the kitchen like a dancing sprite. He returned a few seconds later, all smiles.

One by one, Gus put the cups under the Jura nozzle, toggled, and pushed the button. As the espresso and foam spewed forth, the air around us filled with the burnt, nutty smell of it.

"Have you heard of kopi luwak?" Gus said.

We all shook our heads.

"It's the best coffee in the world. It comes from Sumatra and goes for about $300 a pound."

Gus paused to eyeball us, and then continued. "The civet, a type of cat, eats coffee cherries, which pass through its digestive system, and then the coffee producers collect the feces, remove the beans, and roast them. The digestive process takes all the bitterness out of the coffee."

"Wait," Lauren said, "so . . ."

Gus followed her train of thought and nodded. "Just try it. You'll like it."

Our smiles faded as we looked down at what we now realized were steaming cups of liquid cat shit. I swallowed a laugh. Why, oh, why did we have to have it all?

I walked back across the golf course as a cold wind blew through the evergreens, stirring the rusty needles beneath. A few determined golfers ambled by in their pastel sweaters and caps, but the course looked bleak. The wild rosemary and lavender were dried to spiky stalks.

My condo was warm. Too warm. I opened the sliding door to let some fresh air in. Now that I had the theme I could finally finish the graphics work orders. Which I did, and sent them off to Molly. She called me within minutes.

"Unfortunately, Halley," she said, "I don't think we have time to get these graphics done."

I almost screamed. "You know what we have riding on

this project!"

"Then you shouldn't have waited until the last minute."

"I *didn't* . . . it had nothing to do with me! I've been waiting months for Max to decide on the theme!"

"Well, maybe if you'd been a better manager—"

"Can we just cut the crap?" I said. "Why don't you stop pretending to be a nice person for once and just say what you really want to say to me."

The line was silent for a moment. "Fine," she said, with a change of tone so profound that I half expected her skin to fall away and reveal an imposter underneath.

"It was you, wasn't it?" I said.

"What was me?"

"You killed Phil Collins."

"Phil Collins, your goldfish?" she said. She sounded genuinely surprised.

"I know it was you."

"I didn't kill your stupid goldfish, Halley."

I didn't believe her.

"Don't try to make me feel sorry for you, like you're some kind of victim," she said. "I know what you've been doing over there."

"Jesus, is that what this is about? I'm sure you started that rumor too, so let me just set the record straight: there is nothing going on between me and Gus!"

"How about Thomas Rousseau?"

The sound of his name sent a grief spasm vibrating into my throat. I didn't say anything.

"Yeah," she said. I could hear her wicked smile through the phone. "Lauren told me all about it. She saw you with her own eyes. I can think of a few executives who would love to know what you've been doing on the company's dime, fornicating with our most important client like the

Whore of Babylon."

I shifted in my chair. "I don't know what you're talking about."

"I think you should quit," she said.

"Quit my job?" I sniffed arrogantly. "Why? Because you think they'll replace me with you?"

Molly cleared her throat. "That's none of your concern."

"I would love to see you try to do my job, Molly. I really would."

She must have sensed an angle, because her voice softened. "Just think about it, Halley," she said. "No more stress. You can finally get some rest. You can be free. If you walk away now, no one will ever find out what you've been doing. You'll leave on good terms. And with all the experience you have and the recommendation you'd get from Gus, I'm sure you'll have no trouble finding something better somewhere else."

It was like my conscience was taunting me. Those were my thoughts. I'd thought them over and over these past months. I could just quit. It would be so easy to quit, leave all of this behind. Go back home and sleep and sleep.

"Just quit, Halley," she said. "Give yourself a break."

But I couldn't. Rousseau, Paris, Level 3. It was all still out there, still reachable, if only . . . And I'd come too far, I wasn't giving up now. Now that I was almost there. Now that I was so close.

"What if I don't quit?" I said. "You'll go running to Gus?"

"Maybe," she said.

"And what makes you think he'll believe anything you say? You don't have any proof."

Molly inhaled loudly. "Oh, I'm sure there's plenty of proof out there, if I need to go that route."

It might have been true. Maybe she could find a way to dig up my emails, my text messages. Or maybe she was bluffing.

"I'm not quitting," I said.

She didn't respond for a few seconds. Then she let out a clipped, condescending bark of a laugh.

"You're going to wish you had," she said.

After we hung up, I wrapped myself in a blanket, walked out to the terrace and sat on a chaise, wondering if I'd just dug my own grave. My phone beeped with an email. Wearily, I looked down at the screen, fear and curiosity boiling in my blood. The name in the "From" line was one I hadn't seen in months, and it filled me with butterflies.

Halley, I'll be there.
Celeste

PART THREE

31

SOMETHING WAS WRONG. I went to find Alec, the towheaded lead booth builder, who was crouched in the storage closet with a power drill.

"Hey, can I talk to you for a minute?" I said.

He lowered the drill and looked at me with kind eyes. "I know what you're going to say." He sighed. "This is the final layout we were given by Molly."

I scanned the stark, blank wall in front of me. "There aren't any graphics."

"I was just as surprised as you are," he said.

"I mean . . . there aren't any graphics? This is the biggest launch Findlay has ever done, and she's actually going to fuck up the fucking graphics? Fuck!" I kicked an empty cardboard box, and it went flying across the booth footprint.

Alec stared at me silently.

I took a deep breath. "What did she say?"

"Something about getting the work orders too late." He cringed a little when he said it, as if I might really come unglued and clobber him.

I walked back to the entryway and looked at the booth in its entirety, wondering if maybe it would be okay.

Nope. Catastrophe. The managers might forgive a mistake like ordering too few dinner invitations or misspelling one of the reps' name badges, but they wouldn't overlook a blank booth. It would be the only thing about the launch that everyone would remember. "The biggest trade show booth fuckup in Findlay history" and oh how ironic that it was the result of the biggest and most expensive project the company had ever done, a project that had a dedicated Level 2 support staff person whose entire job it was to make sure things like this didn't happen.

I heard Molly's little squirrel laugh in my head. *You won't quit? You're going to wish you had.* She knew I'd be blamed. What had Gus said? *You're responsible for outcomes, so you're going to have to find a way to do what needs to be done.* And even if I could have blamed it all on Molly, she had the Rousseau story in her back pocket. She could call Gus up at any time and tell him. Goodbye, Level 3.

I looked at Alec. "What can we do?"

"Not much," he said. "I have some old graphics that I can sub in, but they're not going to be Tantalus-branded."

"Do it," I said. "Anything is better than this."

I didn't have time to discuss it because I had to go and meet Celeste. She waited for me at the entrance of the conference center—the famous Palais des Congrès—which was actually part conference center, part eerily vacant shopping mall. The building sat like a giant concrete island on the edge of the chaotic Place de la Porte Maillot roundabout. I crossed the all-white lobby, with its delicate blown glass chandeliers that looked like clusters of floating bubbles. Banks of automated conference registration machines lined the center, flanked by a perennially busy Starbucks.

I was nervous to see Celeste. I still didn't know why she'd finally agreed to come to Paris. Maybe she was hoping for a front row seat to my failure. Or maybe she'd worked out a deal of her own with Gus.

"Hi," I muttered as I opened the door. Wisps of cigarette smoke wafted over from the knots of smokers huddled outside.

Should I apologize again, try to break the ice? Or would it be better to act like everything was normal?

Celeste's expression was placid, but underneath that I could see a spark of my best friend, folded up and put away in a drawer somewhere deep in her heart. She was understandably still angry, or maybe seeing me made her angry all over again. She gave me a quick hug and then stepped aside.

Behind Celeste were two French service staffers—Level 1s—from Clive Villalobos's European office. Grace and Marion were their names, and they each gave me a double-cheek kiss and followed us inside. They were reserved and serious compared to Celeste who now seemed so confidently, ploddingly American. Grace had a button nose, hair almost as black as Celeste's, and a coquettish way of walking. She was the more talkative of the two. Marion had lithe, elegant features and long, wavy chestnut hair. She was quiet and almost-beautiful, the kind of woman that drives men mad. I couldn't help staring.

I gave them their name badges and the four of us crossed the airy lobby. Men in black suits stood on either side of the escalators leading up to the conference center. They scanned us through and we ascended, following the sounds of hammers and drills to the trade show hall and coming to rest at a table in one of the vacant cafés next to the side doors. The café would be full when DEVO started, but for now the dark bakery case held only cold steel trays and the promise of its imminent reanimation.

We got down to business. In my bag I had binders for each of us that contained the week's operating specifications, hotel rooming lists by arrival date and alphabet, the transportation manifest, a local area map, a conference center map, a list of important contact information, and a hard copy of each customer-facing event invitation. I handed out two-way radios with official-looking earpieces that I'd rented from a Parisian destination management company.

"When we're in the same building we'll communicate via radio," I said. They each unwrapped an earpiece from its plastic sleeve, inserted the metal tip. "Let's walk through the specs."

The three of them listened solemnly.

"Your binders are personalized. I've highlighted your specific tasks. Make sure you keep an eye on your individual responsibilities each day. When you're not doing anything specific I want you to float around and be available for random tasks.

"Starting with today, I've already checked on the booth setup and I'll tell you about that when we're done. We have a pre-conference meeting with hotel staff at two and another pre-con with Susanne from the destination management company at three. At four we're meeting the bell captain in the package room to organize. Susanne has arranged a trolley to transfer product and marketing materials from the hotel to the conference center. We'll get everything transferred and unpacked on the booth this afternoon so it's completely set tomorrow morning when the managers arrive."

Workmen and booth builders passed our table pushing

huge wooden crates on wheels. Hallway banners were released and fell from the ceiling in unnoticed fanfare.

"Okay," I said. "Tomorrow morning most of the managers arrive. Marion, you're responsible for checking on the cars that will pick them up at the airport. The managers and the transportation company have your mobile number."

"Should I be at the airport to greet them?" Marion asked.

"No, I need you with me at the hotel greeting them when they walk into the lobby. I've hired greeters with signs to wait at the airport and direct them to their cars. Please also make sure the VIP amenities are delivered to their rooms first thing in the morning, and remind them that Anthony is allergic to chocolate. I've already given the welcome cards to Lorraine at the hotel."

Marion made some notes in the margin.

"Celeste and Grace, you will be in the package room all day tomorrow. There are ten thousand flattened white boxes which need to have Tantalus stickers affixed to them. These are for the boxed lunches that will be served to all delegates on the second day of the conference. Once the stickers are done, I'll take the boxes to Monique, the conference organizer. After that I need you to stuff the welcome packets. All the materials are here, they just need to be put together. Then please be ready to help me set up the room for Wednesday's sales meeting. I'll be back and forth between the conference center and the hotel all day tomorrow and in meetings with the managers, but I'll be available by phone."

They nodded.

"Okay, let's look at the sales meeting specs."

We walked through the whole agenda. Room setups. Audiovisual requirements. Transportation duties. Catering orders. The sales meeting. The booth. The luncheon symposium. The podium talks. The booth announcement. The gala. The more we talked, the more the week sat hugely before us like a great elephant we had to eat. We could only digest it in small bits. When we got to the end of the agenda we packed up our binders and left the café. I walked them into the convention space to show them the graphic-less booth.

"Wow," Celeste said. "Did Molly do this on purpose?"

I looked at her meaningfully, and for a second it was just like it used to be, us against the world. God, I'd missed that. As if she could feel the air between us softening, Celeste's eyes went dark again, and the moment passed.

"Alec is going to put up some old graphics he has on hand," I said.

"The brand managers are going to flip out."

"There was literally nothing else I could do."

Celeste cracked a tiny, cruel smile.

It was noon and we had just enough time to grab a bite to eat before our next meeting. Across the Boulevard Gouvion-Saint-Cyr was a small bistro. The tables were lined with paper and reminded me of the pizza place where Rousseau and I had gone in Cannes. Where we'd sat in the sun, watching boats bobbing in the marina, talking about the brilliant future that was surely waiting for us just around the bend. The sunshine of the memory made me forget, for a second, where I was, as if Rousseau's ghost had just sat down at the table across from me. It had been weeks since our fight, since the night he said goodbye, and in some inexplicable way it simultaneously felt like years had passed since then, and also like it had only happened minutes ago. I'd found a way to push it all down deep, but in that quiet inner place I was still raw and heartbroken and furious. I wondered how he could have loved me if it was so easy for him to walk away. I still caught myself ruminating about what we could have done differently, about what he'd meant when he said, "what if the only way to preserve this is to end it," about what I would feel and say and do when I saw him again. For certain he would be here, would attend DEVO and our launch events—we still had him scheduled to give a podium talk on the last day—and I would see him. Any minute now, I might see him. The thought of it sucked the air out of me.

Celeste, Grace, Marion, and I filed over to a table next to the window, and a waiter handed us black leather menus.

"Do you have one in English?" Celeste asked.

"*Non*," he almost-shouted and walked away. I smiled at her, and she glared back at me. If it hadn't been for me, she would have been the one who could read a French menu and understand basic French phrases. By now she would have been accustomed to all the trappings of daily French life. She would be "cultured." To her outsider's eye, it must have looked like I was living the life she'd always wanted. She couldn't have known what difficulties and humiliations she would've gone through to get here. Like finding a beautiful canyon cut through rock, all she could see was the resulting vista, not the time and the destruction that had formed it.

I wanted to explain everything to her, to take her hand and talk the way we used to talk. But this wasn't the place for a conversation like that. It would have to wait.

32

Clive was the first of the managers to walk through the five-way revolving door, pointy-toed shoes clip-clopping across the hotel's vast lobby. He came toward me for the customary double-cheek kiss, but he went left and I went right and our lips touched in the middle for one brief and unbearably awkward millisecond. His eyes widened, then he turned around wordlessly and pulled his suitcase down the hallway to the reception desk.

"Sorry," I said to his back. I felt the memory of his aftershave sticking to my face, and wiped at it with my sleeve. Yuck.

Marion and I waited to greet the other early-arrivers, listening to voices in various accents echoing off the creamy granite hotel floor. Balding businessmen sat on light gray sofas and drank tiny cups of coffee. They spoke softly into phones, hunched close to one another in conversation, talking with their hands. I scrolled through my phone for emails, glancing up every few seconds to browse the faces for Rousseau. Everyone looked a little familiar, in that strange way they start to do when you've traveled enough to have seen every possible shape of human mouth and nose and eye. Each new face is just a rearrangement.

A limo deposited Max, Lauren, Darren, and Gus on the street out front. Gus looked pale and sick. He let the others go ahead toward the reception desk, escorted by Marion, while he pulled me aside to tell me the airline had lost his luggage.

"I'll get Marion to keep an eye on it," I said. "Were they able to tell you what flight they put it on?"

He wiped his hands against the sides of his pants. "No, you don't understand. The airline couldn't find it at all. It's a nightmare. Just a nightmare. What am I going to do without my stuff? Also, there's some medication in that bag I'm going to need tonight."

"What is it?"

"Prozac. I have to have it. You don't want me to be a dizzy wreck when I'm up there making the launch announcement in the booth. Can you call my doctor's office back in Dayton and get them to send an extra bottle? Darren has the phone number."

"Sure," I said. "But even if they send it right away, the earliest I think we could have it is the day after tomorrow."

He gave me a look.

"I'll make it happen," I said.

I walked him to the check-in desk and told the receptionist that one of our VIP guests had lost his luggage. The receptionist produced a bag of toiletries from under the desk, which Gus accepted glumly. Then she summoned a guest services manager to go out and buy Gus some clothes.

I pushed the talk button on my radio. "Celeste, come in."

"This is Celeste," she said.

"Who do we know coming to this meeting that might have Prozac?"

"Jamie takes Prozac," she said.

"Perfect," I replied. She would be on the company plane with Anthony.

"I understand, Halley," Jamie said, "but I brought the exact number of pills I need for this trip. So if I give you Sunday, then what am *I* supposed to take on Sunday?"

I'd forgotten how loud her normal speaking voice was. People seated in the lobby atrium craned their necks to look at us.

"I've already ordered another bottle to be sent from the States," I said. I tried compensating for her loudness by speaking extra quietly, but instead of taking the hint she squinted irritably and shouted, "What?"

"The new bottle of pills will be here tomorrow," I said. "So I can replenish you then."

She tapped her foot against her suitcase. "Are you sure? What if it gets lost in transit?"

"I'm tracking it. If it gets lost, there'll still be time to ship another bottle."

She reluctantly handed over the pill and watched it fall to the floor as it changed hands.

"Shit," I said, scrambling to pick it up as it rolled out of sight.

"I'm not giving you another one," she said, and walked away.

I dropped to my hands and knees and began to search.

"*Puis-je vous aider?*" the bellman said.

"I dropped a little green pill," I said. "We have to find it before someone steps on it."

The bellman dropped to his hands and knees too. We focused our eyes on the floor, which was not as clean up close as it appeared to be from a standing position.

"What are you doing?" a man said.

I looked up and into the eyes of the company president. Anthony looked down at me with the amused, good-natured expression of a person with whom no one ever disagrees.

"I dropped something," I said, annoyed at myself for not being ready for him. I stood quickly and switched back to greeter mode. "How was your flight?"

"Fine," he said. His wife Annabella strolled up behind him. She was tall with a boyish figure and brown hair that grazed the shoulders of her camel-colored cashmere coat. Her eyes radiated boredom. She scanned the lobby while Anthony spoke to me. "Everything still set for me to make the launch announcement in the booth? I heard there was some confusion."

"Oh," I said, swallowing my stomach. It was physically impossible to say no to this man, and I wasn't even going to try. Gus could duke it out with him later. "Yes, we're all set."

"Great," Anthony said with a twinkle. "Where do we go now?"

"This way." I walked them to the VIP check-in desk and introduced them to the receptionist. Then I went back to look for the pill again.

The bellman soon spotted it next to one of the charcoal gray rugs. I picked it up, blew the dust off of it, and carried it up to Gus's penthouse suite.

33

Gus emerged from the elevator wearing a gold shirt that reflected the light as he passed through the lobby. Apparently the hotel's guest services manager had unconventional taste.

"Look, King Midas is coming to dinner," Lauren said.

The others turned to look.

Max cracked up. "He looks like a go-go dancer at Studio 54. Now I feel underdressed."

Gus reached the group, and everyone went silent.

"What?" he said, scanning our faces.

I loaded them all into the van that would take them to a swanky Paris restaurant for dinner, and wondered, as it pulled away, when I would be the one in that van, a legitimate part of the group, going out for a nice evening while someone else stayed behind and attended to all the details. And, if I was a legitimate part of the group, would I know I was? Lauren and Max and Gus and Anthony all seemed surprisingly blasé about their status. When it was my turn, would I feel the thorough satisfaction of having conquered mediocrity, or would it all feel as bland to me as it seemed to feel to them?

A few minutes later, Celeste's voice spoke calmly through the earpiece of my phone. "We have a problem," she said.

"What is it?"

"I tripped on a puddle of water at the top of some stairs and twisted my ankle. I think it might be broken."

"Is this a joke?" I asked. "You don't sound like you have a broken ankle; you sound normal."

"Will you believe me if I start screaming? My fucking ankle is broken."

I gulped down a breath. "Shit, Celeste. Where are you?"

"I'm still at the bottom of the stairs in the conference hall. I crawled over to a chair. Can you take me to the hospital?"

"Um, okay let me think for a second."

I scanned the lobby for Darren, who was sitting at a table flipping through a binder and making notes. A few heads turned to watch as I sprinted in his direction.

"Can you help me with something?" I huffed, holding my hand over the phone's mouthpiece. "Celeste is hurt."

"Sure," Darren said, standing.

I nodded a thanks as he closed the binder and shoved it into The Backpack. "Hang on, Celeste. We'll be there in a minute."

Celeste had rolled her foot inward and the right side of her ankle was baseball-sized, rapidly accumulating a leeching purple bruise. It made me nauseous to look at it. Celeste's eyes were moist and she winced when we moved her, but otherwise she was her usual self. Like ducks on a pond we were, kicking and kicking below the surface, but perfectly composed on top. Darren and I got her into the back seat of a taxi. I hopped in the front seat, and Darren shuffled back across the street to our hotel.

The waiting room of the Hôpital du Perray was a circus sideshow of dislocated shoulders, uncontrollable vomiting, forehead gashes, fractured wrists turned inside out, old people turning blue on gurneys. I wondered at the bizarreness of being there, of going from a place full of people fighting to get the best hotel room rate, to a place full of people fighting for their lives. For a moment the launch and France and all that was important to me seemed absurdly trivial. I wanted my friend back.

"I'm so sorry, Celeste," I said, rubbing my eyes. "You were right about everything. So much has happened . . . it should have been you here instead of me. You would have done it better."

"I don't want to talk about it," she said.

"I just wanted to say—"

"Stop, Halley." She stared daggers at me. "Stop thinking about yourself for one minute. I'm in an emergency room in France with a broken ankle, and this is the moment you choose to unload your guilty conscience on me? I can't talk about this right now. I don't want to talk to anyone right now about anything."

"Okay," I said, running her words through my head. Would I ever be able to fix this? Was it really selfish of me to want to? I had so much to say, not because I wanted to unload my guilty conscience but because I wanted Celeste to know that I loved her. I needed her to know that, even if we could never go back to being friends again.

"Why don't you just leave?" she said.

I looked up. "What?"

The guy behind me laboriously dry-heaved, and I prayed to God he would stop.

"Go back to the hotel. I'd rather do this on my own."

"No way," I said, glancing over my shoulder.

"Seriously," Celeste said, grabbing her purse from my grasp and wincing from the movement. "I want you to go."

I snatched the purse back and held it on my lap. "I'm not leaving you here, Celeste," I said. If I couldn't apologize and I couldn't talk to her, at least I could sit beside her and hold her stuff.

We sat there for a long time without speaking, listening to the puker.

Eventually Celeste was wheeled through the double doors and back to a bed. They took X-rays and determined she had a fracture and a torn ligament, but it would heal without surgery. She was wheeled back out a few hours later with a blue cast on her leg, a prescription for crutches and pain medicine, and a bill for four hundred Euro, which I paid for out of my cash reserves. It was four o'clock in the morning when a taxi delivered us back to the hotel. I had just enough time to get Celeste up to her room and take a shower before I needed to be back downstairs to get ready for the sales meeting.

34

LAUREN WAS A nervous wreck, but she tried to hide it. Revealing her anxiety might tip everyone off to the fact that Darren had actually done most of her work for her, that she was taking credit for authoring the contents of a program about which she had only scant secondhand knowledge. She'd studied the plans and reviewed the materials, but Darren had written the curriculum. Darren had drafted the training booklets and sent them for translation. Darren had designed the activities and hands-on sessions. Darren had researched precisely the number of times to reinforce the Tantalus selling points to ensure maximum retention. Darren knew that program inside and out. I think we both secretly hoped Lauren would bomb it, at the same time that we hoped all our months of work would not be wasted on a shoddy performance.

Marion spent the morning handing out welcome packets at the hospitality desk while I stood in the back of the meeting room watching the sound check and talking the presenters through the agenda. We practiced the transitions between presentations and decided what times we would release everyone for breaks. And when I came back out to check on the hospitality desk, there was Celeste, doped up, trying to explain to Marion and Grace the difference between American crutches and French crutches.

"These crutches look like polio sticks," she said.

They stared at her blankly.

"Here, see, Halley will tell you. Halley, don't you think these crutches look like the ones Forrest Gump had?"

"Are you sure Forrest Gump had crutches?" I replied.

"Don't you remember that movie?" Celeste said.

"I think he had leg braces," I said. "But I know what you mean."

"I was telling Marion that the crutches we have in the States go under your arm pit."

Marion explained that the armpit kind are old-fashioned and made reference to the wooden one used by Tiny Tim.

"What are you even doing down here, Celeste?" I asked. "You should be in bed."

"I know, I was bored," she said. "I feel okay if I take enough pills. Give me something to do."

I studied her for signs of agitation, but she looked pretty relaxed.

"Okay," I said. "Anthony is getting ready to open the sales meeting and you know how he doesn't like it when people walk in and out of the room. You want to guard the door?"

"Yep." She pushed herself upright.

"If anyone comes out, just don't let them back in until Anthony's done. He's on the agenda for twenty minutes but you know how he is."

Celeste crutched her way over to the door and stood

like a linebacker on one foot, balanced on her polio sticks. If someone really wanted to get past her, all they'd have had to do was snatch one of the crutches and make a run for it and she'd have toppled right over. That reality didn't make Celeste any less menacing though.

We should have known that Lauren's presentation would be flawless. In the battle between image and substance, image would win a thousand times. Image was the thing we would protect at all costs. No one had any idea that Lauren hadn't been the architect of such a perfect performance. She had probably been practicing for days. After several minutes of applause, company executives could be heard murmuring about how pleased they were with her; how the training was the heart of the launch, how the curriculum, the training booklets, the activities and hands-on sessions, the reinforcement of the selling points, were all so ingeniously planned and executed, how Lauren was a superstar. No one, least of all Lauren herself, mentioned Darren's name as he sat in the back of the room, a spectator just like everyone else. The slate was wiped clean of him, and at the end of the meeting Lauren would be offered the management position of her choice.

DEVO started the following day. The conference hall was packed with people, branded name badges hanging on branded lanyards and branded DEVO bags full of branded product ads. You could tell the important people because they had "Guest Speaker" ribbons affixed to their badges; they nodded to one another as they rushed from one industry meeting to the next. The plebs made their way from booth to booth in search of free food.

First thing, Gus wanted to know what the hell had happened to the booth graphics.

"We brought you over here to manage these things, Halley," he said. "Where are the Tantalus graphics? Where is the theme that Max worked so hard on?"

"I'm sorry," I said. "I submitted the work orders . . ."

I trailed off. I was afraid to name Molly, afraid he would confront her and she would tell him my secret.

"Well?" he said. "What happened?"

"I don't know," I said. "Everything seemed to be on track. I'll look into it and get back to you."

"I'm very disappointed. I had hoped to offer you that Level 3 position after we were done here, but I'm going to have to rethink that decision now. This is a disaster."

The binder I was holding fell and hit the floor with a loud thud. I stooped down to pick it up, hands trembling, as Gus walked away. I felt the urge to sit in a quiet room for a while and think about what he'd said, what it meant for me and how I should react to it. He'd delivered the comment so casually, carelessly—to him this situation couldn't have been anything more than a passing annoyance—but what he'd said potentially affected the rest of my life. It was chilling, that one person's whole life was another person's passing annoyance.

There wasn't time to think too much about it though. Already there were a hundred other details that needed attending to. Without Celeste there to help, it was even more hectic than a normal meeting. We were fully booked for the gala, but some of the managers still had VIP clients they wanted to invite, so I sent Marion to figure out how to add more seats. Jamie had a headache and wanted us to find her some Tylenol. Nurofen was unacceptable—she didn't want any of that foreign stuff—it had to be Tylenol. I assigned Grace to the task. Gus's luggage was finally found and someone needed to wait in the hotel lobby for it to be delivered. Marion went. Everywhere I looked, I thought I saw Rousseau. Every gray suit. Every pair of glasses. Each one shot me full of fire. None of them turned out to be him.

At 11:30 a.m. it was time to start getting ready for the booth announcement—the big moment when we would officially launch the Tantalus. Both Gus and Anthony still thought they were announcing, and I looked forward to seeing who would crush whose spirit when the microphone came out. I pulled the boxes of Tantalus-branded champagne glasses out of the storage closet. The conference hall catering company started delivering bottles of champagne. Alec prepped the promotional video that Darren had scripted and produced. At 11:45 a.m. Grace and I started filling champagne glasses, which disappeared as quickly as we could fill them. Darren stepped in to help.

A crowd began to form. Waiters arrived with the hors d'oeuvres I'd ordered: smoked trout in Parmesan sesame cups, panzanella-stuffed mushrooms, goat cheese and fresh figs on leaves of endive, prosciutto wrapped prawns. They got lost in the swarm of grubby, grabbing fingers. Alec set up a small platform where our announcer (would it be Gus or would it be Anthony?) would stand. Darren and I continued to pour champagne. We got down to our last box of glasses.

Anthony and Gus approached.

"Ready for me, Halley?" Anthony said.

I looked at him, as Gus said, "Halley, I thought you told me I was making the announcement."

Anthony looked at Gus, then at me, then back at Gus. And in the brief moment when they locked eyes, something strange happened. Anthony appeared to grow physically taller at the same rate that Gus appeared to shrink. I'm sure I imagined it. But it was easy to guess who was going to win this battle. Gus glowered at nobody in particular, knowing he was out-ranked. "Of course, Anthony, if you want to make the announcement, be my guest," he said. He mumbled "wanker" under his breath as he walked over to stand in the crowd of onlookers, away from his stolen limelight.

I gave the last glass of champagne to Anthony as he stepped onto the platform. Alec handed him the live microphone. The crowd buzzed around, speaking to each other and eating hors d'oeuvres and drinking their champagne, ignoring him.

"Thank you, everyone," Anthony said, his voice completely drowned by chatter, "for coming to celebrate with us the launch of this revolutionary new device, the Tantalus." I heard Alec turn up the volume of the microphone from behind the wall, the brief hum-buzz rising and falling as he got the level right. "We are proud of the dedication and foresight of the hundreds of innovators who got us here today. This technology represents a huge step forward for the entire world."

Miscellaneous attendees came up while Anthony spoke and put their used glasses and dirty plates on the coffee counter next to him and walked away. Occasionally someone looked over at him as if he'd just randomly shown up to ruin their party. I glanced over at Gus, who watched this with an amused smirk on his face, and I felt unexpectedly embarrassed for Anthony. For all his dignity, in that moment he was just as disrespected as the rest of us. The chain of insult ran down our ranks: he took it from customers, Gus took it from him, and we took it from Gus.

Anthony went on to describe Findlay's mission, then he introduced our thirty second promotional video, which Alec played with perfect timing. The video's loud rock music filled the air.

"And now, ladies and gentlemen," Anthony said, "let us raise our glasses and toast the millions of lives that will be changed by this device. It gives me great pleasure to officially release the Tantalus for sale."

Glasses chinked. Conversations resumed, or, in some cases, continued uninterrupted. The whole thing was pretty anticlimactic. That's it, I thought to myself. All that work and anticipation, and the world moved on.

Gus pulled his phone out of his pocket and I heard him mutter a "Jesus" under his breath.

"Is something wrong?"

"Seven missed calls from Molly. Did she try getting you too? She probably wants to talk about the booth graphics."

I made a point of stacking dirty plates, averting my eyes. I knew what she wanted. Now that she had me at a disadvantage, she was going to tell him about Rousseau. The final nail in my coffin.

"Are you going to call her back?" I said.

He started dialing a number. "I don't have time right now. If you hear from her, tell her I'll call her later." He held the phone up to his ear and I heard him whisper "*ciao bella*" as he walked away.

I followed him. Waiters passed by collecting dirty glasses and plates. Gus paused to lean up against one of the booth's display tables and discretely finish his phone call. A waiter approached and I seized the opportunity to bump into him, causing him to spill his tray and its contents—

scraps of trout and panzanella and goat cheese mixed with splashes of champagne—all over the back of Gus's suit. Gus jumped aside in shock and dropped his phone on the floor, then turned around to see what was happening. The waiter apologized profusely and produced a small towel. While everyone's attention was on Gus and his soiled jacket and the mess on the floor, I nonchalantly kicked the cell phone into the storage closet and shut the door. Gus pulled his arms out of his jacket, held it up for examination and tsked. Clothing-wise, this was not his week. He rolled his eyes and held the jacket out to me.

"Halley, find someone who can clean this."

"Will do," I said. I moved toward the storage closet to collect my things. I could feel the cell phone glowing inside like a beacon. I prayed it wouldn't ring, and that no one would open the storage closet door before I could get to it. Already Gus was searching the floor where he'd dropped the phone. As my hand reached the door handle, Max walked up.

"Hey, can you get me a glass of champagne?" he asked. "I didn't get one when they were being passed around."

"Sorry, we ran out," I said, distracted.

Max's lips flattened into a look that said "You had *one* job." The annoying normality of his condescension focused me. I rolled Gus's suit jacket into a ball and put it on the floor in front of the closet door.

"Give me a minute," I said.

Keeping my eye on the closet, I went behind the counter where there were several empty glasses and a few partially empty glasses others had drunk from. I wiped off one of the empties with a napkin and poured remnants from the other glasses into it until I had a suitably full glass of miscellaneous backwashed champagne. The bubbles masked the tiny chewed up food particles. Max had walked across the aisle to talk to someone, and I ran over and put the glass in his hand. He didn't look up from his conversation. I watched him take a drink and I gagged a little.

I got back to the closet door and picked the jacket up off the floor just as Gus approached again.

"Have you seen my phone?" he said.

I pretended to look around. "Nope."

"Fuckety fuck fuck fuck," he groaned. "Someone is trying to give me a heart attack. We have to find it immediately."

"Probably one of the wait staff picked it up," I said. "I'll go talk to lost and found." I saw Alec walking toward us with his eye on the storage closet and estimated I had about five seconds to get in there and get the phone out before I was busted.

"No," Gus said, "I'll go."

As soon as his back was turned I dove into the closet to collect my prize.

35

I WAS IN the back of a taxi on my way to the casino where the gala would take place that night, when my phone rang. In the millisecond between the moment the chirp of my ringtone reached my ears and the moment my eyes locked on the caller ID of the device resting in my hand, I hoped with absurd, habitual optimism that the caller was Rousseau. But it was my dad.

"Are you in Paris yet?" he said.

"Yeah, the launch was this afternoon."

"How did it go?"

I hadn't talked to my parents since New Year's Day. Despite my mother's directive to never go home again after I missed Grandpa's funeral, they'd been angry that I hadn't visited for the holidays, and our last few conversations had been stilted and uncomfortable.

"Fine," I said. "Not too exciting."

"Oh, well I just called to say good luck."

"Thanks. That was really sweet of you."

Neither of us said anything for a few seconds. I watched

the traffic through the window. It was nice, just existing there in space for a while together.

I broke the silence. "What are you doing?"

"Oh, just watching TV," he said. "I'm supposed to stay off my feet for a day or two. I hurt my back taking our new mattress back to the store."

"What, why . . . Didn't you just take one back a couple months ago?"

"Yes, but it wasn't quite right."

"Hmm," I said, as the proper response gathered in my mind.

"I thought it was going to be a good one," he said, "when I tried it in the store. But I ended up not liking it."

As he spoke I pictured the Sam's Club parking lot, ringed with gray slush, shoppers traipsing to and from their cars carrying four-year-olds in thick white tights, their breath blowing in front of their faces in puffs. And my dad, struggling to carry the almost-but-not-quite right queen-sized mattress up to the sliding glass doors.

"The good news is, the new one seems perfect," he said.

I almost laughed, because that was the same thing he'd said about the last one. In my head the words "What do you think it is about you that causes you to be like this?" took shape, and then I realized those were my mother's words. Jesus fucking Christ. Rousseau was right. I couldn't avoid it. I was becoming just like them. In my judgment and my malaise, I was my mother. And in my perseverance, my refusal to accept anything less than perfection, and my idealistic belief that something better was out there waiting, I was just like my father. Like the Wheaten family, no matter how much I tried to avoid it, I would get hit by that train.

Findlay had given me hope that I could change, get

ahead, be a different person. A better person. With each new level, I would acquire a measure of dignity and status that would rearrange my cells into someone brighter and shinier. A movie star version of myself, new and improved. Only, it was all a farce. No amount of distance or workplace validation would turn me into that person, not in any meaningful way. No matter how successful I was, no matter what Findlay level I reached, I would always be Halley Faust.

"I had an idea the other day," my dad said.

"Oh yeah?"

"I want to start the family farm back up again. After your grandpa died, it got me thinking. I'm not getting any younger, and this is something I've been wanting to do for a long time. I guess I should just go for it."

"That's really great, Dad," I said.

"Would you want to help? Once we started making a profit, I could split it with you. Could be pretty good money if we can get it going."

I didn't say anything. Surely he knew what my answer would be.

"Hey, your mom just walked in," he said. I heard Guthrie barking in the background. "Want to talk to her?"

I hesitated. "Sure."

He whispered, "It's Halley," and I heard the phone change hands.

"Hi." My mother's voice was expressionless, our years of expectation and disappointment like extra layers of skin.

"Hi," I said, mirroring her tone.

"How's the product launch going?"

"It's fine. The sales meeting was yesterday, we had the booth announcement at noon today, and now I'm on my way to the casino to set up for the gala."

"Great . . ." she murmured.

That old familiar feeling rose in my throat. The anxiety and dissatisfaction brought about by our disconnect. "It's not that big of a deal," I said.

"If it's not a big deal then what are you doing there?"

"I didn't . . . I mean it is a big deal. You know, for the company. I just meant it's not as glamorous as it sounds."

"Hmm," she said.

I wanted to break through that barrier between us and live in some warm place with her, where I could tell her everything and she would accept me exactly as I was. Where I could be myself and be loved.

And yet, it occurred to me that I hadn't accepted her exactly as she was either. I could have changed the course of the conversation by saying "I love you" or "I miss you" or "you're doing a good job," but I didn't. I didn't want to. So, maybe this was just our way. Whoever said families are supposed to be happy anyway, or that parents are supposed to understand their children? Maybe it was all bogus, all the qualities parents *should* have. Maybe we were doing fine, exactly as we were.

My taxi stopped under the porte cochere of the casino and I stepped out onto the sidewalk. I handed the driver a twenty and waved for him to keep the change.

"Well . . . I should get back to work," I said.

"Yep," she said. "Good luck." Then she hung up, and I smiled.

36

THE RIGGING HAD been installed overhead. The circular bar, which was meant to look like it was made of ice, had been built in the center of the floor. On a normal day this space was used as the casino's dinner theatre, and a third of the room was dominated by black graduated balconies set with tables and chairs. Another third of the room was a stage. Between the stage and the balconies was the floor, which usually held more tables but had been cleared out for my gala. The room's walls and balconies were back-lit and covered in black cloth that was full of tiny holes, so that when the lights were turned up the holes glowed like thousands of stars.

Celeste arrived shortly after me. She crutched her way to the table where I was monitoring setup and sat beside me without saying anything. For now, our job was to watch and wait, like scientists at the table of an elaborate experiment. Would all of the elements come together as planned? Which parts would go wrong? Which parts would surprise us?

Entertainment had already begun to arrive and the bartender was stocking the ice bar with liquor and glasses. Electric white plastic cubes were positioned around the floor area to be used as pedestals for dancers. Gauzy white curtains were hung around the perimeter of the room. A giant red carpet was rolled out from the event space all the way through the casino lobby and outside where the buses would drop off. Near the entryway there was a column holding a crystal sphere with an etching of the Tantalus inside, lit up by a spotlight. When guests arrived, "bodyguards" with dark sunglasses would stand on either side of the crystal as if it was some kind of relic.

I phoned Lorraine at the hotel to make sure Gus, Anthony, and Clive had their tuxes. The tux shop was supposed to have delivered them to the hotel by noon and the concierge agreed to hang them in the men's closets.

Susanne from the DMC arrived with the bow ties and flowers I'd bought as party favors. We went over the agenda and timing one more time, and then Susanne went to find the catering manager to go over it with him.

Celeste started to doze off in her chair.

I nudged her with my elbow. "How many pills did you take today?"

"Enough that my fucking leg doesn't hurt," she said.

I backed up a couple inches. "Want me to call you a cab?"

"No," she said. "I'll just drink some coffee."

As I left to order her an espresso, I got a phone call from Anthony. "Halley," he said, somewhat exasperated, "my tux doesn't fit. It's too small."

Damn. "Okay," I said, "look at the tag. Are the measurements correct?"

He paused. "I'm looking at the tag. What are these,

centimeters?"

I sighed. "Hold on a second." I jogged back to the table where Celeste sat like a drunkard, and started rifling through my binder. "Okay, tell me what the tag says."

"It just says 52."

"Mmhmm, 52 . . . okay, that's not what I ordered for you. Let me make a phone call and I'll call you back."

I hung up, and my phone immediately rang again. Clive.

"Halleyamyesmokingdozenotfeet," he said.

"What?" I said.

"Eestoobeeg," he repeated.

"Oh good," I said. "You have Anthony's tux and he has yours. You guys need to switch."

Celeste tumbled into a laughing fit that made her face turn red. Her nose made snorting sounds.

Clive hung up, and I lowered my phone.

She continued to smile and I wondered if this meant I was forgiven. I didn't have the guts to bring it up.

I called Anthony back but Clive had already texted him about the mix-up. Celeste motioned to a passing banquet staffer and ordered the espresso I hadn't had a chance to get for her yet. In the nearly-setup event space, the entertainers practiced, then gathered on the floor for a group meeting with the entertainment coordinator. When I looked down at the army of people I'd hired, for a second I was amazed that I'd orchestrated something so huge. Occasionally they looked up at me or pointed me out, and I felt a little bit like the president of some small principality, pretending to be in control. I imagined most of the night's guests, back at the hotel by now, showering and blow drying and zipping and fixing cuff links. Soon they'd be trickling down to the hotel bar to listen to the live jazz, sip pre-gala drinks and munch on cheese straws, their temporary happiness hinging on me.

Susanne was in touch with the transportation company and announced that the buses were staged in front of the hotel. The police escort was there too—hired by Susanne to ride ahead of the buses and clear traffic. Without them the rush hour commute would have taken hours. She alerted me when the first bus departed. So far, we were running exactly on time.

As the minutes ticked by, I got more anxious. No, maybe anxious wasn't the right word. I was jumping out of my skin with anticipation. That magic moment was almost upon us, the moment when guests caught their first glimpse of the wonderland I'd designed especially for them. Entertainment was staged. The bartender started pouring our signature cocktail, a square rosé spritzer, into hundreds of Tantalus-branded glasses that were lined up on the bar. Tuxedoed waiters collected the drinks on trays and walked over to the room entrance where attendees could take a glass as they walked in. Celeste, Suzanne, and I put in our earpieces, and attached the two-way radios to our waistbands. Then we waited.

I walked out to the casino entrance to watch the police escort pull up. Although the sun shone, the air was cold, and I hugged my arms around myself. Soon the flashing blue lights of a white motorcycle pulsed into view. The first bus stopped at the end of the red carpet and the first guests descended. Smoking jackets. Lacy cocktail dresses. Red lips. Shoes buffed to a glossy shine. I'd hired a crew of fake paparazzi and cameramen to photograph and interview everyone on their way up the red carpet. The video cameras were hooked into a live feed inside the ballroom, so the people inside could watch others arrive. Random tourists started to gather in the lobby to see what was happening, see which celebrity they were about to encounter. I didn't want to tell them it was all fake. The tuxedos, the red carpet, the camera flashes—I'd constructed them to simulate a more profound, more beautiful reality, although I wondered now whether it wasn't the other way around. Whether it was the simulation which was constructing us. The tourists took pictures with their cameras.

At the end of the red carpet, two dapper casino staff members stood on either side of the entryway leading into the ballroom, opening and closing doors. Inside, contemplative underground lounge music circled and thudded. Waiters stood with trays of pink Tantalus cocktails for the taking, and more waiters approached with canapes: poached quail eggs with smoked salmon and caviar, sliced roast duck on discs of sweet potato, foie gras terrine with apple chutney. On the left side of the room, the Tantalus-spotlit crystal glowed. Guests photographed the two sober-faced bodyguards as if they were amusement park characters. On the right was a table with the giveaway bow ties, flowers, and a mirror. Straight ahead, the ice bar. In the foreground, scattered around the room, leather-clad men and women danced on white glowing cubes, as if under water. Aerial dancers hung from the ceiling, winding around long white silks that almost reached the floor. Two smooth, tan, almost-nude men performed a body art act on stage, muscles rippling. One of the men stood in a headstand while the other climbed up his body and held himself in a perfect T across his torso. At the back of the room, two models were being painted in six-foot watercolors by live artists, one standing and the other lying seductively on a lush white chaise. Projected onto a screen was a digital countdown on a black background, slowly making its way to zero. It was impossible to take all of it in at once. Standing in the middle of it, no matter where you looked, a hundred details passed you by.

I returned to my post at the dim corner table where Celeste still sat. We had a perfect bird's-eye view of everything from there. My eyes scanned the growing crowd for Rousseau. I wanted him to see what I'd done here, this world I'd imagined into being. It felt representative of me, as if he might understand me better by seeing it. And, somewhere in my heart, despite the confusion and the anger I felt about what he'd done, I still believed we could go back to the way we had once been.

But he wasn't here. I didn't know where he was. No one mentioned his absence, he simply ceased to exist, leaving in his wake only memories.

Soon it was time for Anthony to go onstage and deliver the welcome. When the countdown clock reached five minutes, I made sure his video was loaded, and then went to get him mic'd and ready. I found him standing in a cluster with some VIP customers, drinking a gin and tonic. When I signaled to him, he asked me to go to the bar and get him a Tantalus cocktail for the toast.

A French A/V technician clipped the black lav to Anthony's lapel and ran the thin wire under his tuxedo jacket, securing the battery pack on the belt at his back, as I approached with his pink drink. When he saw me, he turned and said, "This is nice, Halley. Good job."

It was the only time Anthony ever complimented me. Actually, it was the only time I ever heard him compliment anyone. All at once I felt the glamour of the moment raining down upon me in tiny, shimmery flecks of gold. And then, almost as soon as it came, it was gone. I looked around, struck with the desire to go back and do it all over again, to soak up that feeling until it penetrated me permanently. If I'd known how lovely it was going to be, I'd have paid more attention.

"Thanks," I mumbled, wishing I had a better word.

The muscled body art guys left the stage as the countdown clock reached ten seconds. The crowd began to shout. "EIGHT . . . SEVEN . . . SIX . . . FIVE . . . FOUR . . . THREE . . . TWO . . . ONE!"

BANG, a row of cold pyrotechnics shot off onstage, the lights in the room went out and the music went silent. The crowd cheered. The room was lit only by the ice bar and pedestals. The A/V tech started the video, a whirly music-pumped montage of product graphics and client testimonials that hyped the room into a united goosebumped fever. When the video ended, a spotlight followed Anthony onstage. For fifteen minutes he talked about Findlay, about the Tantalus and what it would mean to customers. He shared a few anecdotes about lives that had already been changed. There may have been a few tears shed in the audience. Then he held up his Tantalus cocktail and toasted our success.

"To the Tantalus," he said.

"The Tantalus!" they repeated, clinking and drinking.

Anthony gave the nod, and the DJ in the sound booth announced dinner. Jazz music came on the speaker system. As the group turned toward the balconies, where the tables were set, the lights were raised and the little white stars began to glow.

It was almost time for Gus's big entrance. I looked for the entertainment coordinator, but he was backstage taking advantage of the break to scarf down some food. All the performers were on a break except for the bodyguards, who still stood on either side of the Tantalus crystal with their crossed arms and their black sunglasses, forbidden to break character.

The main course was served. I started getting antsy. Attendees trickled out to smoke and go to the bathroom. Stuart Nadeau, of the Nashville Marriott biohazard incident, loitered on the main floor, obviously drunk. I wondered what mayhem he was going to cause tonight.

When the last waiter had served the last dessert, the balcony lighting began to dim. A spotlight trained in on two guys dressed like ninjas in black, "thieves" coming to steal the Tantalus crystal. They shimmied down some ropes on the right side of the stage. At the same time, three of our dancers walked by and "lured" the bodyguards away from their post. The crystal stood on its pedestal glowing and unprotected. One of the thieves grabbed it theatrically with his black-gloved hands and ran back toward the ropes. Another spotlight focused on a slick and tuxedoed Gus, as he emerged on a high platform near the ceiling, stage left. He took a deep breath, raised his arms above his head, grabbed the metal handles of the zip line and zoomed like lightning across the room, screaming all the way down. At the end of the line he crashed feet-first into Stuart Nadeau, who went flying into the starry wall and crumpled like a doll onto the floor. Gus tumbled next to him with a double roll and lay there for a few seconds, dazed. Then he stood up and walked toward the ninja crystal thief, who had started toward him to make sure he was okay. They engaged in a very mild version of the pre-choreographed fight scene that Gus had refused to practice, and Gus recovered the crystal in the end, holding it up and taking a bow. The audience cheered through their tarte tatins, delighting in the pleasure of our artifice.

But Stuart didn't move. I radioed Suzanne to call the med tech I'd requested, who was supposed to be waiting backstage to give Gus a once-over. She confirmed, and as the applause died down, two men discreetly carried Stuart out of the room, while Gus limped along behind them.

I returned to my corner table, where Celeste rested her lame foot on a chair. The DJ cranked the music. Lauren and Max were the first up to dance.

"Anthony said 'good job' to me," I said.

I should have been happy now, exhilarated. But I wasn't, really. Now that it was over, it all seemed like no big deal. All the triumphs and the glory in the world wouldn't stop time. And that was what we really wanted, wasn't it? To remain stuck in the golden moments forever.

"My leg is killing me," Celeste said.

"You should go. The first bus should be outside already."

"I think I'll take a cab. I don't want to climb the bus steps."

"I'll radio Susanne to call one for you."

I helped her up, grabbed her purse, and walked along-side as she crutched her way through the throng of dancers, up the steps, and down the red carpet to the casino entrance. She didn't look at me as she lowered into the taxi. I pushed her purse and crutches in after her and held the door open.

"Celeste, I've been wanting to say something."

She sighed exasperatedly. "What?"

"Even if we can't be friends again, I want you to know that I'm sorry and I love you. I would reverse it all if I could."

Celeste's face went gray with fury. Her hand shook as she reached for the open door, grabbed the handle and pulled it closed.

As I watched the taxi pull away, hugging my arms around myself, Suzanne's voice squawked through my earpiece.

"Halley?"

I took a deep breath and held the button down. "This is Halley."

"The man, Stuart," Suzanne said, "the one who got hit by the feet of Gus? He is dead."

37

I STOOD BACKSTAGE as the police questioned Gus, the casino manager, and the entertainment coordinator. The idea that Gus had premeditated an assassination by zip line would have been funny if the result hadn't been so dismal. Stuart's body was eventually taken away to be held for repatriation. The police assured us the death would be ruled an accident and said they'd get in touch with the local consulate.

On the other side of the curtain, the dance floor was full. Anthony was three sheets to the wind—something I'd never seen before—and decided it was a good idea to get up on stage with Lauren and do the "Thriller" dance. I guess even a guy like Anthony needed to lose himself every once in a while. His wife, Annabella, had disappeared. The videographer thought this was too good a spectacle not to project onto the big screen, and soon everyone else stopped what they were doing to watch.

"Halley! Halley!" Jamie shouted at me. She was out of breath and all in a frazzle. After all, any damage to Anthony's image was a blow to hers as well. I shifted backward to look her in the eye. "You . . . have to . . . get him . . . out of there! Look . . . people are taking videos . . . on their phones!"

"I'll get the videographer to take him off the big screen," I said.

I spoke a few words into my mouthpiece and Susanne passed the message on to the videographer. In a few seconds, the video switched to a floor shot.

"He's still dancing!" she shouted.

I looked at her.

"Well!" she said, "make him stop!"

"Look," I said, "it's going to embarrass him if I yank him offstage mid-'Thriller.'"

"Go tell him there's a phone call for him or something."

I looked around and then back at her again. "The song's almost over. Can we just let it go?"

"Do it, Halley," she said. "Do it now."

I studied her face. Her "Rachel" haircut. The stiff lines around her mouth and the threatening glint in her eyes. I thought about dead Stuart on his way to the morgue, evil Molly, Anthony's 'good job,' Celeste's silent rage, Phil Collins, Rousseau. Suddenly I felt very tired. Tired of everything.

"No," I said.

"What do you mean, no?"

"I mean no," I said. "If you want to get him off the stage, do it yourself."

She stared at me in semi-drunk, incredulous rage.

"You know who I'm meeting with tomorrow, don't you?" she said.

I looked at her and shrugged.

"Gus," she said with a smile.

Then she turned and walked back to her table.

I stepped out of the ballroom to get some air. Darren sat at the bar in the casino lobby, ashen-faced, chugging a glass of water.

"Hey," I said as I approached.

The bartender glanced at me and I pointed to Darren's glass. "I'll have what he's having."

"Vodka soda," Darren said.

"Oh," I said. "Even better."

His eyes glistened. "I quit my job."

"What?"

The bartender set a fresh drink on a little square napkin in front of me.

"Yep," he said. "I was talking to Gus right before he left. Asked him for a promotion. I figured I deserved it, since I've been the one doing most of the work around here. But he said no."

"No, now, or no never?"

"I don't know. Just no. He tried to tell me I was lucky to have had this opportunity, that the company cared about me, and I just lost it. Told him he has been exploiting me. Then I quit."

"What did he do?"

"He said he'd alert HR, then he took The Backpack, got in a taxi, and left."

"Look, he's had kind of a rough night," I said. "He zip lined a guy to death. He's not thinking clearly."

Darren's eyes widened. "Wait, Stuart *died*?"

I took a big swig. "Yep. Your prophecy has been realized."

"Wow." He stared at his hands. "I didn't think he'd actually die though. That's terrible."

"Anyway," I said, reaching out to touch his shoulder, "I'm sure you can go to Gus tomorrow, tell him you changed your mind."

"No," Darren hardened. "Fuck him. And fuck Findlay. There's no future for me here, except more of the same old shit." He sucked down the remainder of his drink and waved to the bartender for another one.

I sat there with him silently for a while, no idea what to say.

"Max did a half-assed autopsy on that cat he killed," Darren said. "You know what he found? Nothing. No cameras, no surveillance. It was just a regular cat. You know how many people have tried to steal The Backpack in all the time I've had it? Zero. I've never used that Taser once. Kathleen, Gus's wife he divorced because she was supposedly 'revealing trade secrets' to his enemies, swore up and down that she'd never spoken to Tim Cook or Jeff Bezos in her life. It's bullshit. It's all bullshit."

The bartender brought Darren's refill, and Darren took the lime wedge off and set it on a cocktail napkin. He took a big drink before he started talking again.

"Gus is just paranoid," he said, letting out a small hiccup. "He has accumulated all this stuff, and now his ego is so dependent on all of it that he spends every waking moment terrified of losing it. Actually, I think it feeds his ego, this fantasy that he's such a big shot and his projects are so important that Jeff Bezos and Tim Cook are desperate to steal them. That's the answer to our question, Halley. That's what's waiting for us after we've done our time. It never gets better, not even when you reach the top. It's just more of the same. It's a rat race. And I want out."

"So what are you going to do now?" I asked.

He looked solemn. "My uncle has an insurance agency down in Lexington. He said I could come work for him."

It sounded so dismal, and I wondered if he would end up regretting it. Maybe he just needed a break, some time to get back on his feet, and then he'd be back at it again. Or maybe not. Maybe we were shooting stars, meant to burn brightly and then burn out.

"I did get this though." Darren pulled a piece of paper out of his pocket, unfolded it, and held it up for me to see. The document said "Railer Design" at the top and contained a bunch of drawings and words I didn't understand.

"What is it?" I said.

"It's the engineering specs for the Tantalus. I've never been able to decipher it, but I know of a couple people who probably can."

"You wouldn't," I said, smiling.

He hiccuped again. "Let's see if Tim Cook and Jeff Bezos really are as interested in Gus's secrets as he thinks they are."

I left the casino on the last bus. It was 3:45 a.m. when I walked through the door of my hotel room. I put my bag and binder on the desk and poured myself a glass of water. I was washing the makeup off my face when the phone rang. Not my cell phone, the phone in my room.

"Hello?"

"Halley," he said.

"Gus?"

"I need you to come to my room right away. Don't ask any questions, just come."

"I don't think . . ."

"Halley, this is an emergency. Come to my room.

NOW." He hung up.

I thought about what to do. The middle of the night, your boss tells you to come to his hotel room, all kinds of things could happen. Had he found out about Rousseau? Was he going to fire me? Was he drunk, lonely . . .?

I reluctantly grabbed my room key and pulled the door closed behind me. I was still wearing my suit. The halls were quiet; the hotel slept. I took the elevator to the penthouse floor. I had to think for a second about whether Gus was in Penthouse A or Penthouse B, because Anthony was in the other one, and that would be an unfortunate mistake. Luckily, Gus had propped his door open by popping the lock out. I went inside.

The room was dim and messy. Clothes were strewn on the floor, on couches. An army of empty minibar liquor bottles stood uncapped on the coffee table, next to several haphazard little piles of white powder. I hardly noticed the baby grand piano, the beautiful floor-to-ceiling windows, the oriental carpets. Partly because of the oddness of the circumstance, and partly because my job had begun to inoculate me against a certain kind of hotel grandeur. For those who travel with the very rich, every new penthouse is a little shot of adrenaline; soon you build up a tolerance, and you must increase your dose to get the same high.

I followed the light coming from the bedroom. For a second I thought maybe I'd entered the wrong room, and I turned to leave. A person lay ass-up on the bed. A woman with the same face as Anthony's wife, Annabella, tossed there like a rag doll someone had grown tired of playing with. I looked closer and—oh, shit—it was Annabella. Then I saw Gus in a bathrobe, squatting in the corner of the room with his head down. He stood when he saw me. His eyes were red like he'd been crying. The pieces fell into place, Gus's secrecy, the phone calls. This was "*ciao bella*."

"I think she's dead," he said.

I stared at her. This could not be happening.

"You have to help me, Halley," he said nervously. "Normally I would call Darren for this sort of thing, but . . . I can no longer trust him to act in the company's best interests. I think she did too much coke."

He was really on a roll tonight, killing-wise. I walked over to get a closer look.

"If anyone finds her here," he said, "I'll be ruined. And if I'm ruined, Findlay will be ruined."

"Help me turn her over," I said.

We rolled the body over with one heave and I got to see Anthony's wife in all her naked glory. Gus had probably been screwing her just a few minutes ago. Ick. I wondered how long it had taken him to notice she'd gone pale and limp. I put my fingers to her neck and found a faint pulse. "Move," I said, pushing Gus out of the way. I climbed onto the bed, cupped my hands together and started chest compressions over her compact little breasts.

"Plug her nose and breathe into her mouth," I said. "Now!"

He bent over her face, smeared with crimson lipstick, and did as he was told.

I called it out. "One. Two. Three. Now breathe," I said. "Again."

We continued for five, maybe ten minutes. My arms started to hurt and I wondered if we were doing this right. I'd only practiced on plastic dummies. Gus let out a little squeal.

"I think she's breathing," he said.

I put my face next to her face that smelled like expensive perfume. "It's shallow. Gus, we have to get her to a hospital."

"How? If we call an ambulance they're going to come up here, people will find out." He spoke fast and his hand shook nervously. "I already killed one person today. This hotel room is covered with drugs. Anthony the Wanker is right next door. What if she dies? No, no. No."

"Well, she'll probably die if we don't get her out of here."

"Do what you have to do, Halley. Just take care of it, and don't let anyone find out." He turned around and walked out of the room.

"Are you fucking kidding me?" I said. "Get back here!"

Gus crossed the penthouse to the other bedroom, closed the door, and locked it behind him.

I sat on the edge of the bed next to Annabella and thought about what to do. There was a strong compulsion to leave, to quit, just like Darren had. This was insane! Insane. How had this become my responsibility? I should call an ambulance, that seemed like the right thing to do. To hell with Gus. But what if I was just overreacting, what if Annabella was going to be fine?

An idea came to me and I ran out of the room. I propped the penthouse door open with the swing bar and took the elevator to the lobby.

A lone bellman stood at the bell stand. "Do you have a wheelchair I can borrow?" I asked him.

He shook his head. "*Je ne parle pas Anglais.*"

I ran down the hall to the reception desk, my heels clicking loudly on the floor. "Do you have a wheelchair I can borrow?"

The man behind the desk nodded. I followed him back down the hall, past the coffee counter and the light gray couches, through the restaurant and bar, to a storage room near the back of the building. I held the door open while he went inside. In a few seconds, he wheeled the chair out for me.

"Call an ambulance," I told him.

"Sorry?" he replied.

"Emergency," I said. "Hospital. We need someone to drive a sick person to the hospital. I'll be back."

"*D'accord*," he said and made to follow me.

"No, you stay," I said, holding a hand up. "Call the ambulance. I'll come back with the sick person."

"Okay," he said.

I pushed the wheelchair to the elevator and back up to Gus's penthouse. When I got there, Gus was back in the room with Annabella again.

"Jesus, Halley, I thought you left," he said.

"Just to get this." I pushed the wheelchair toward the bed. "We have to put some clothes on her and get her into this thing. Reception is calling an ambulance. I'll wheel her downstairs and I'll tell them I found her like this. I found her in the hall, she was unresponsive, so I sent for an ambulance. The hotel will have cameras, but I'll make sure they get rid of the tapes."

"How are you going to do that?" Gus asked.

"How do you think?" I said. "Money."

We shimmied Annabella's black crepe dress back over her unconscious body. It took us three tries to hoist her onto the wheelchair. She kept falling forward, so I used Gus's belt to fasten her in. Her head drooped and rolled. I propped her feet on the foot rests, released the wheel brakes, and started down the hall, barely breathing. Gus closed the door quietly behind me.

I'd almost made it to the elevator when the door to Penthouse A opened. Anthony emerged, eyes searching.

"Halley?"

Every bone in my body wanted to run away. I could play dumb tomorrow, pretend I didn't know anything about it. What happened to Annabella? *Annabella who?* How did she get in a wheelchair? *Beats me.* Why were you pushing her down the hall? *Must've been somebody else.*

"Halley, what are you doing?" Anthony said.

It was hard to look at him, after seeing his awkward, dad-like "Thriller" moves. He was wearing a plaid bathrobe, pajama pants, and slippers, which was exactly the sort of thing I would've imagined him wearing to bed.

"Hotel security found Annabella downstairs. She must have had too much to drink," I said. I wondered if he could tell I was lying. To myself, it was obvious.

"I was bringing her back up to your room, but then I realized she's in pretty bad shape, so I thought maybe I should get her to a hospital instead."

"Oh," he said. He came over and prodded her a couple times, put a hand under her chin and tilted her head back, opened her eyes with his fingers.

"Whose belt is that?" he asked.

"I don't know," I answered quickly.

The air between us filled with awkwardness as he took note of his wife's smeared lipstick and recently-fucked hair. I was still just a Level 2, after all, and he was still the company president. The only way this situation could've gotten more personal was if I'd fucked Annabella myself.

"I'll come with you," Anthony said. "To the hospital. Just let me change clothes."

I waited with Anthony's still-unconscious wife in the hall. God, what a night. I said it to myself over and over again until Anthony came back out and I walked him and Annabella to the ambulance. What a night. What a night. What a night. What a night.

38

EVERYONE WAS A little worn out, a little hung over, still murmuring about the acrobats and dead Stuart and Anthony doing The Thriller. I left the conference center in the afternoon to freshen up before Rousseau's podium talk, the one event I knew for sure he would attend. The air was cold and damp, and traffic was heavy. A group of suited and name-tagged conference attendees waited to cross the street, and when there was no clear crossing, one of the guys walked out in front of a moving vehicle with his hand up. The car stopped and we passed safely to the other side like geese.

I walked through the hotel's revolving door, turned my eyes toward the elevators, and there he stood. It was really him. I was totally unprepared. I had assumed I would see him around the conference throughout the week, and I'd known I would see him giving his lecture up on stage in a few minutes. But this. The magnitude of him. Right here in front of me. I stopped breathing. He wore his gray suit and leaned against the coffee counter with his arms crossed, speaking with Eduardo Masio, another distributor, in Spanish. I'd imagined this moment for weeks, always in the most cinematic way possible. We would lock eyes, walk slowly toward each other and collide in an epic Hollywood kiss. But, as it happened, he didn't even see me.

I sidestepped a bellman and stood behind a tall potted plant for a few minutes like a stalker, watching him. The way he stood so still and confident. I wondered if he thought of me, if he remembered the things I remembered, the way I remembered them. I envied Eduardo, being able to talk so easily to him the way I once had, without any history or baggage. How was it that everyone in that lobby didn't fall in love with the laugh lines around his eyes when he smiled, and want to hear every thought he had about life?

I started multiple conversations with him in my head. "How have you been?" I might say. No, that was banal and awkward. How about: "How could you do this to me?" Nope, too accusatory. Maybe: "Sometimes I miss you so much I want to die." No, that was way too desperate. In the end I settled for "I think of you," and I hoped he would understand the rest.

When Eduardo walked away, I moved toward the place where he stood, ready with my arsenal of words. Rousseau turned his head in my direction, saw me and did a double-take. Our eyes met for several long seconds, frozen. For months, maybe years, I would try to dissect the look on his face in that moment. It defied description, that look. If there was a meaning behind it, it was one I could not comprehend. It was neither happy nor anguished. It wasn't placid or impassioned. He felt something, I knew he did. I just couldn't tell what.

I stood, steps away from him, and didn't speak. The

seconds pulsed loudly in my ears like heavy train wheels rumbling over steel tracks. Everything else—the hotel, the people, the potted plants—disappeared. We seemed to stand there for days inside the fusion reactor of our past, somewhere far away from Paris, all the words we'd said to each other bouncing and crashing into one another, all that we'd done swirling around us. Pizza. Night clubs. Hotel room kisses. Airport tears. Smart-assed banter. Crushing fights. *You're the thing I look forward to every day. What if the only way to preserve this is to end it?*

I had so many questions. I wanted to know what it was that had made us different, why that spark had existed between us if, in the end, we were destined to fade to nothing. We had always been possessed by the idea that what we'd experienced was not of this world. But was it? Or were we like prehistoric cavemen who attributed the existence of fire to God simply because they had no knowledge of combustion? Now, looking him in the eye, I wasn't so sure. He didn't run toward me and embrace me. He didn't even say hello. And what did that mean?

A cynical thought entered my mind, that maybe there had never been any cosmic connection between us. I didn't want to believe it, but as it began to take shape, I wondered. Maybe we'd felt so connected precisely because we knew we never really could be. If he walked toward me now and said, "I will go with you," if we left this place and moved into a house together and had the whole future ahead of us, if we could gorge ourselves on one another until we were sick, maybe we would have eventually ended up with exactly the same kind of life he had with Chloe. Maybe that was what he was really waiting all those months to figure out—whether time takes its toll on all relationships, no matter how predestined or cosmically perfect they seem in the beginning. Whether the mundane drudgeries of real life—the time-dulled feelings, the little hurts and resentments—affect everyone the same. He might have eventually strayed from me as easily as he'd strayed from her, endlessly searching for greener pastures. Because the truth was that what Rousseau and I really wanted was to want. To believe *it* existed. To set our horizons by it and run headlong toward it, and when we reached it, to hit the reset button and start all over again. The stagnation of life felt a little like death, and *it* was a doorway leading away from death. *It* was a return to youth, a return to all the wild possibilities of our future selves. Rousseau would never go through that door—of course he wouldn't—but he wanted it to be there, waiting on the horizon, just in case. And so did I.

Before I had a chance to second guess myself, I broke free of his gaze, turned, and walked away. I fought back tears, pressed buttons, and put my feet forward. I dropped my binder off in my room and changed into jeans. My phone rang, and I grabbed for it, believing it was him, ready to run to him, wherever he was, and take it all back a thousand times. But it was Anthony. I swallowed my grief and answered.

"Halley? I was hoping we could talk."

"Sure," I said, rubbing the wetness from my eyes with the back of my shirt sleeve.

"I wanted to say thanks for helping out last night, with Annabella. She's fine now. A little worse for wear, but we're back at the hotel."

"That's great. I'm so glad."

"She doesn't remember anything. I was hoping you could help fill in the blanks."

I thought about outing Gus. He deserved it. But I held back. If the worst happened, it might be useful to have this knowledge in my back pocket.

"I really don't know anything," I said. "What I told you last night is the whole story."

Anthony paused. He probably knew I knew more. He sighed.

"If you think of anything else, will you let me know?"

"Of course," I said.

I hung up the phone and lay back on the bed. My room felt saturated with silent ghosts. Thoughts, questions, histories, futures. So many things I'd always thought I'd have figured out by now. It was a cynical move, withholding information from Anthony so that I could use it against Gus. And the worst part was, I took pleasure in the cruelty of it. In the power it gave me over both of them. That's when I realized how much I'd changed.

I took a shower. The hotel soap smelled like pineapple. I wrapped myself in a big white towel and wrapped a second towel around my hair. The mirror had fogged over, and drops of water cut lines through the fog. I stood in front of the bureau and flipped through the room service menu. A salade nicoise, maybe. I was debating whether or not to order wine when my phone buzzed with an email. It was from Gus.

"We need to talk," it said. "Meet me at that oyster place a few blocks down the street at noon tomorrow."

Below that was an email that Celeste had forwarded to him.

from:	**Celeste L. Boudreaux** <celesteboudreaux@findlay.com>
sent:	January 16, 2017 15:11
to:	Gus D. Hanley <gushanley@findlay.com>
subject:	Something you should see

2016-06-24 20:30	+330140907846	+330475326541	Incoming	I wish I was there too.
2016-06-24 20:31	+330475326541	+330140907846	Outgoing	You know you could actually be here, right? Just a short plane ride away
2016-06-24 20:35	+330140907846	+330475326541	Incoming	You make it sound so easy.
2016-06-24 20:35	+330475326541	+330140907846	Outgoing	Do you think we could be happy together?
2016-06-24 20:44	+330140907846	+330475326541	Incoming	Without a doubt.
2016-06-24 20:45	+330475326541	+330140907846	Outgoing	Do you ever think about it? Do you think about how it could be?
2016-06-24 20:49	+330140907846	+330475326541	Incoming	Yes, I think about how it could be. I mean, I try to. I'm so used to my life the way it is, I have a hard time imagining it being different. Maybe I'm too literal-minded.
2016-06-24 20:50	+330475326541	+330140907846	Outgoing	How do you imagine me then?

I stopped reading, ran to the bathroom, and threw up in the sink.

39

CELESTE'S DOOR WAS propped open. I knocked anyway.

"Come in, Fredo!" she shouted brusquely from the bed.

"It's Halley," I mumbled. "Who the hell is Fredo?"

Celeste's bum foot was propped up on some pillows and there were more pillows between her back and the padded headboard. The room was a complete mess. Empty Pringles cans had begun to collect next to the bed and there was a pile of dirty towels partially covering Celeste's worn-out, tire-marked Tumi.

"Oh," she said. "Well since you're here would you mind filling up my water bottle?" She held it out toward me. "Also could you get me another pillow out of the closet? And that can of Pringles that's in the mini bar? Thanks."

"Anything else, your highness?"

"Oh yeah, I'm living in the lap of fucking luxury here. I'm sitting in a hotel room saving up a list of petty tasks for when the room service guy comes. Fredo. He had to help me off the bed so I could go to the bathroom this morning."

She flipped through the channels on the flat screen TV

and settled on BBC.

I opened the minibar cabinet that was under the TV, lifted the can of Pringles, and chucked it at her.

She ducked reflexively. The can hit the headboard and bounced onto the bed beside her. "What the fuck?" she shouted.

"My thoughts exactly."

Recognition crossed her face. "Gus doesn't waste any time." She cracked a gloating smile.

I stared at her, wide-eyed. "You are unbelievable."

She opened the can of Pringles and ate one. "Hurts, doesn't it?"

"You killed Phil Collins."

She leaned forward incredulously. "You ruined my life!"

"You killed Phil Collins!" I screamed. I took a step toward her and she recoiled. "How could you do that, Celeste? You *sick fuck*!"

That it had been Celeste and not some villain made Phil Collins's death seem more tragic than before. More avoidable. Who was this person? I'd known her practically all my life, and I'd never imagined she could do anything so terrible.

Celeste snorted a cynical laugh. "That's exactly how I felt. For months. Every day, sitting alone in a fucking cubicle, a Level 1, while you toured Europe, had affairs with married men, learned French, and moved up the ladder, all because you cheated me out of my big chance. It should have been me over here. And you fucked me over. Anything I've done to you pales in comparison to what you did to me."

I wasn't so sure about that. Stabbing a goldfish and hunting down my phone records to try to get me fired seemed a lot worse than the rash call I'd made to the transportation company in San Francisco. But that wasn't the point. The point was, this was Celeste we were talking about, and she wasn't capable of hurting me this way. She wasn't like this.

But, apparently, she was. We all were. All of us who dreamed of more, and were willing to sacrifice pieces of ourselves to get it.

We hadn't started out this way. I hadn't, and surely she hadn't either. Our darkness had been a journey. Each new crime became easier than the last. Easier to rationalize. Easier to justify. It was easier to sacrifice new parts of ourselves because of the parts we'd already sacrificed, the sunk cost. Our tolerance for it built up, like adjusting to a new drug, until we no longer recognized ourselves.

"You know what the real icing on the cake is?" she said. "You don't even appreciate what you have here. You keep saying you're 'sorry' and 'it's been so hard' and it should have been me here instead of you . . . So, not only did you steal my big chance, you wasted it."

I raised my arms in resignation and walked toward the door. "Well, you got me back, I guess," I said. "I hope you're happy now."

She sighed and stared at the bed for a few seconds. "Not really. I dreamed for months about what your face would look like when you got what was coming to you. But it doesn't feel as good as I thought it would feel."

"It never does," I replied, and left.

The morning sky was the color of dirty snow. I had some time before my meeting with Gus, so I took a walk. I passed the Gare du Neuilly-Porte Maillot and the row of motorcycles in front like a picket line. Mist turned into rain and back to mist again. Shuttered storefronts and endless clouds of cigarette smoke mirrored my own alienation back to me. Paris was both beautiful and brash, and had none of the aura I'd expected it to have, the aura I'd always believed I would somehow absorb into my character by simply being here. It was just another place. A place like any other place, made of the sum of its parts, simultaneously indifferent and gross and lovely. The sidewalks were polluted with trash and I nearly stepped in a pile of dog shit. There were tourists everywhere. I walked by a shop selling dusty phonographs, and a bookstore with a sleeping cat in the window. The smell of dead fish wafted over from the market across the street, mixing with the smell of baking pastries. Wrought iron balconies swirled overhead.

When I eventually entered the restaurant, Gus was already parked at a table by the window. I bypassed the maître d' and sat down. A waiter brought me a menu. "*Un verre de vin blanc, s'il vous plaît*," I told him.

I bent over, reached into my bag, pulled Gus's "lost" cell phone out and handed it to him.

"You found it!" he said.

"Lost and found," I muttered, glancing up at the returning waiter, who set an empty glass in front of me and poured into it a stream of cold white wine from a green bottle. I took a big slug and braced myself for whatever was about to happen.

"Let's talk about Halley Faust," Gus said, extracting a stack of papers from The Backpack and handing it to me. I was a little bit startled to hear myself referred to in the third person like that; this must be serious. I looked at the document I'd been given. At the top in big block letters it said "TANTALUS REPORT: HALLEY M. FAUST." Below that was an executive summary, followed by a section titled

"CONSUMPTION SCORES."

Gus watched me for several long seconds as waiters passed back and forth and cars zoomed by outside the window.

"What is this?" I said.

"I know we've been rather opaque about the mechanics of the Tantalus, so I thought I'd tell you a little bit about it today."

He adjusted in his seat and sipped his wine as I continued scanning the document nervously.

"The Tantalus is a large-scale data collection tool," Gus began. "It analyzes everything from browser histories and emails, to spending habits and public records, then uses complex algorithms and predictive analytics to assign a series of consumer scores that will very accurately predict your preferences, your future purchases, and your likelihood to act in a variety of ways."

"Revolutionizing consumerism," I said, repeating one of our talking points.

"Right. Businesses can use these scores to create products that suit the needs of consumers, and better market the products they have already created to precisely the people who want them. That means no more junk mail. No more spam emails. Every communication you receive every day will be exactly what you want. There are plenty of companies collecting 'big data,' but none of them have algorithms as sophisticated as ours, and none of them have a collection mechanism on par with the Tantalus."

There was a twinkle in his eye now, so I knew this next part must be the kicker. "If our projections are correct and our supply chain partnerships hold up, a Tantalus device will be imbedded in every cell phone in the United States by the year 2020. More people today have cell phones than toilets—that's a fact—so the prospect for this product is huge."

I sat back in my chair and thought about this. They put this thing in cell phones? Oh. *Oh no.*

"Now, this device has implications beyond just consumer goods," Gus continued. "We can also use it to monitor and motivate employee behavior as well. And that's precisely what we've been doing. Everyone on the launch team, except me, of course, had a Tantalus inserted into their cell phones. I've been analyzing the data in order to tailor my management style to best suit your needs."

"Wait a minute," I said. "You've been *spying* on me?"

Gus cleared his throat. "Not exactly spying, no. Data collection."

I raked a hand through my hair. "But you knew everything I was doing. Who I was talking to. . ." I trailed off. And then it dawned on me. "You didn't even need that email from Celeste, you already knew about Rousseau."

"Yes, I already knew about Rousseau," he said.

"What else do you know?"

"It's not as bad as you think. I know what I need to know. For example, I know you sabotaged Celeste in San Francisco last year. That was why I hired you for this position. I needed someone on this team who would do whatever it took to succeed, at any cost. Someone relentless, a bulldog. This launch was going to be tough, and I needed to know you could take the heat, that you wouldn't buckle under pressure."

"Do you know about Molly?"

"You mean about the booth graphics?"

"Jesus, Gus! You knew about that too? I was a nervous wreck about that! And you let me think I was getting fired."

"Would you have performed as well if I'd just said, 'oh

don't worry, it's fine'? The data says no."

I looked at the document again. There I was, the essence of me mapped out on a piece of paper.

Subject is part of most highly desirable consumer group: "Insatiables." Insatiables are idealists, dreamers. They prefer imagined lives over real lives. They love the chase. As soon as they get something they want, they get tired of it and want something else, so they must be rewarded slowly and sparingly. Many insatiables feel an acute sense of inferiority among their peers, and they use advancement to give themselves a false sense of superiority. They often derive validation from work, and so work becomes the center of their life . . .

I stopped reading. Was that really me?

Gus interrupted my thoughts. "I'm creating the new position I told you about last year. The Level 3. Halley, I want you to take it."

The waiter delivered a tray of raw oysters that Gus must have ordered before I arrived. Gus squeezed a lemon wedge over one of them and drank it dry, setting the pearly, calcified shell back in its place on the bed of ice.

"There are great things in store for you, Halley. In fact, you remind me a little of myself when I was your age."

I looked back down at the report again.

"Now," Gus said, "you can relocate to Europe permanently and work from here, if you want. It'll be a field-based position. Since you'll be traveling so much, you can live anywhere. Your pay and benefits will stay the same . . ."

I interrupted. "Give it to Celeste," I said.

Gus stared at me, another oyster poised in hand.

"The job. Give it to Celeste," I repeated.

"I heard you the first time. I just think you're confused.

You need some time to think."

I shook my head.

His expression was serene. "Look," he said, "maybe I haven't explained this clearly enough. Everything I'm saying—these are all good things. You have succeeded here. This is your moment, it's what you've been dreaming about."

What I'd been dreaming about. What I'd been dreaming about . . . But what if that was the problem? It was dreaming that had gotten me into this mess. Gus had practically spelled it out for me just now, the way he'd been using my dreams to control me. My dreams had become commodities, opportunities to be leveraged. It was dreams—of the person I might become, the things I might do, the way I might feel—that pushed me to consume, to perform. And fulfilling them was never as good as it was supposed to be. For any of us. We got the things we thought we wanted, but then we got sick, or somebody was mean to us, or our rental car wouldn't go in reverse. Our guests complained—because nothing lived up to their expectations either. Our families were dysfunctional, despite all of our efforts to shape them into the people we wanted them to be. The joyous moments were too short and too far apart.

As if he could read my thoughts, Gus said, "Our society depends on dreamers, Halley. On ambition. Business is the bedrock of civilization as we know it. Everything we have, cars and airplanes, the clothes you're wearing and the phone in your pocket, is because of someone with a dream willing to give 100 percent to see it realized. Innovation. People willing to increase efficiency, to grow."

Gus took another oyster and offered me one. I watched the way he squeezed the lemon, the way the shell barely touched his lips as he tossed the oyster and the juice down his throat. I took one from the tray. He wiped his mouth with the edge of his hand.

"You don't have to decide now," he said. "Just think about it. This is an incredible opportunity for you. Truth be told, I'm envious. I wish I could go back to where you are, do it all over again. You've got it all ahead of you. And if you don't do this, what are you going to do? The data says it all: you'll be bored out of your skull without a new challenge. You are the right person for this job. I believe in you. I am giving you everything you want. You're in the big leagues now. Step up to the plate."

"I'll think about it," I said, although I knew what I was going to do. Still, the potential, the big, wide-open road waiting there in front of me, filled the hollows of my heart. For right now, in this moment, *it* was within my grasp. I squeezed a lemon wedge over the oyster and raised it to my mouth, feeling the gritty, stony shell touch my bottom lip. When I tilted it back, the cold brackish liquid ran over my tongue, then the meat, which tasted fresh and coppery, and for a moment I was happy. Happy perched there between two worlds, luxuriating in a future ripe with possibilities.

EPILOGUE

My FATHER HOISTS himself into the driver's seat and turns the key in the ignition. He looks over at me.

"Scribbling away again," he says. He puts the truck in gear and heads toward the hay field.

I take my tanned feet off the dashboard. "I told you. If I don't get it all on paper now I'm going to forget it."

He chuckles. "You used to say you wanted to forget."

"Not anymore."

It's been five years now. Five years since I left Findlay, five years since I gave Celeste my job. Five years since I crossed the clean and brightly lit terminal of the Cincinnati airport, past the same Starbucks and McDonald's and atrium full of flags I'd seen so many times, and discovered how much I'd truly missed Ohio. Magazines and newspapers and CNN on the terminal televisions were all in English. The illumination of mindless comprehension made me feel like a genius: I was wealthy with words. The exquisite freshness of the place, the familiarity and the smiles and the ability to buy anything I needed without incident . . . I was finally safe again. I knew all the rules. It was all so easy and bright, and I saw how much I'd always taken that part of it for granted.

When I saw my parents waiting for me outside the security checkpoint that day, my body relaxed and my eyes watered as if I'd just returned from war. My mother pulled me into a hug, and the smell of her perfume conjured thousands of unconscious memories, school plays and green bean casserole and trips to the pumpkin patch. For a few minutes I wanted never to leave Ohio or her arms again.

Of course, it still isn't perfect between us. We haven't miraculously stopped seeing the distance between what our relationship is and what we've always wished it was. But over time I've come to accept that theirs is a door that my key will never quite fit. And, paradoxically, the more I accept that, the better we are.

After I got back I lost touch with everyone on the launch team, and with Rousseau. Celeste sends me updates from time to time, although I don't talk to her very often either. Too much was damaged between us, and that kind of damage can never be completely undone. Still, she keeps me updated, which is nice. After Darren anonymously sent a copy of the Railer document to Findlay's competitors, the company got hit with several lawsuits, on the basis of the Electronic Communications Privacy Act. The lawsuits were all eventually dropped because of some legal loopholes, but Anthony decided that the bad press was damaging enough to Findlay's brand that the Tantalus should be taken off the market. Shortly after that, he fired Gus. The official reason was because Gus violated security protocol by revealing trade secrets via the Railer document. But the real reason, according to Celeste, was that Anthony finally found out about Gus's affair with Annabella. Sometimes I still think about Gus, clinging to his cappuccino machine as he fades to obscurity, and I wonder, if he'd known how it was all going to end, would he have done anything differently?

As for the others, Lauren became Findlay's North American Sales Manager. But since she hates Dayton and refuses to buy a house here, she has to fly in from LA every Monday and back every Friday, which amounts to a pretty harried life.

Max took Gus's place as Vice President, much to everyone's dissatisfaction. With him at the helm, Findlay has begun to decline. As a new leader, Max's first inclination was to make his mark by doing the opposite of everything Gus had done. He decided that the division had gotten too loose with money and, although he, himself, had enjoyed the lifestyle that that money afforded—in fact, it had been one of his biggest reasons for coming to Findlay in the first place—he embarked upon a massive division-wide belt-tightening.

He and Lauren designed a series of systems that would make things more efficient and create more oversight where there previously was none, consisting of a bunch of re-orgs, shared databases, and elaborate approvals processes. The effect of these changes was, in essence, to create a little fiefdom where management had absolute power and control, and to effectively pull the ladder up behind them. Their biggest mistake was they failed to realize the necessity of the dream. Without the dream, that mad relentless do-anything sprint toward achievement that Gus inspired in people began to die. One by one, the achievers dropped out and were replaced with people who merely show up, do the minimum required to get their paychecks, and go home. As much as the dreams corrupt us, as disappointed as we ultimately are when they don't deliver, without them we are nothing. And now, as the organization descends into mediocrity, our year in France has become a heyday of sorts in Findlay's history.

But these days I'm living a different sort of heyday. You could call it a "hay-day," as a matter of fact. I am helping my dad revive the hay farm. It's not what I want to do for the rest of my life, but it beats the rat race. At least, that's what I tell myself. I don't know. Those sweltering late-summer days when I'm out baling, sweaty and exhausted, the memories of summertime in Cannes seem as far off as a fairy tale. Which is why I need to remember now. Every day, Findlay's conniving plots, the sleepless nights, the insufferable grasping and incompetence and sabotage all grow smaller in my memory. And soon my insatiable fool's mind will only recall with wild joy how goddamned marvelous it all was and wish to be back there again.

Acknowledgments

I owe an enormous debt of gratitude to the following people, who have each made this book better. My deepest heartfelt thanks to:

Cassandra Farrin and Jenny Miller, for your crackerjack editing, funny notes, and patient counsel in the midst of all my panic attacks and countless emails.

Kayla Church and Dayna Anderson, for having faith in me and giving this weird little book a chance.

David Williams, Susan Williams, and Kelly Kish, whose encouragement and flexibility gave me the time and energy to keep writing.

Bryon Quartermous, Barbara Rogan, Angela Tharp, Jennifer Piurek, Marc Beugelink, Tim Waters, Rafael Macia, Derek DiMatteo, Tiffany Kretler, Dave Weaver, and Pam Weaver, for reading and editing my first drafts and being early advocates of Halley's despite her many glaring flaws.

Germano Melissano, for dispensing the best writing advice I've ever received—"Aim for progress, not perfection"—and to Will Saroian, for your unfailing friendship and support.

Joshua Ferris and my cohort at the Tin House Writers Workshop—Nicole Miller, Jon Durbin, Jessica Mooney, Michele Nereim, Jeff Boyd, Spencer Ruchti, Abigail Shrier, Rowena Singer, Cab Tran, Susie Yang, and Barrett—whose invaluable mentorship, feedback, and guidance came at exactly the right moment. I wish we could all hang out in Portland forever.

Karen Joy Fowler and my cohort at the Kentucky Women Writers Conference—Tara Badstubner, Cynthia Beal, Cynthia Ellingsen, Judy Goldsmith, Marvis Hartman, Leatha Kendrick, Hayley Lynch, Dierdra McAfee, Sarah Moore, Catherine Pond, Michele Ruby, Natalie Sypolt, and Nancy Tafel—for whipping my first chapter into shape and taking me seriously as a writer when I had no idea what I was doing.

To my family and friends, I continue to be humbled by your unwavering love and enthusiasm. You give me the courage to fail big and keep trying again. Special thanks to my mom, Lisa Wisely: I never would have started this project if you hadn't laughed at all my silly stories.

And to Christi Olson, the sender of epic text messages, the host of many late night back porch beer binges, who laughed with me and cried with me and read every draft. I could not have done this without you. Thank you.

About the Author

Brittany Terwilliger grew up in the Midwest and, after graduating from Indiana University, spent several years living and working in France and Ireland. This is her first novel.